THE GOOD BODY MAN

THE GOOD BODY MAN

A James Buckner Novel

Christopher C. Gibbs

Copyright © 2003 by Christopher C. Gibbs.

Cover photo: American Automobile Association; Author photo: Jean Buckner Gibbs

Library of Congress Number   2003090178
ISBN: Hardcover   1-4010-9145-8
              Softcover   1-4010-9144-X

All rights reserved. No part of this book may be reproduced or transmitted in any form or by any means, electronic or mechanical, including photocopying, recording, or by any information storage and retrieval system, without permission in writing from the copyright owner.

This is a work of fiction. Names, characters, places and incidents either are the product of the author's imagination or are used fictitiously, and any resemblance to any actual persons, living or dead, events, or locales is entirely coincidental.

This book was printed in the United States of America.

To order additional copies of this book, contact:
Xlibris Corporation
1-888-795-4274
www.Xlibris.com
Orders@Xlibris.com

17679

CONTENTS

Friday, October 22 7
Saturday, October 23 9
Sunday, October 24 38
Monday, October 25 70
Tuesday, October 26 93
Wednesday, October 27 135
Thursday, October 28 155
Friday, October 29 162
Friday, October 29 192
Saturday, October 30 207
Sunday, October 31 221

For Janet Beckmann

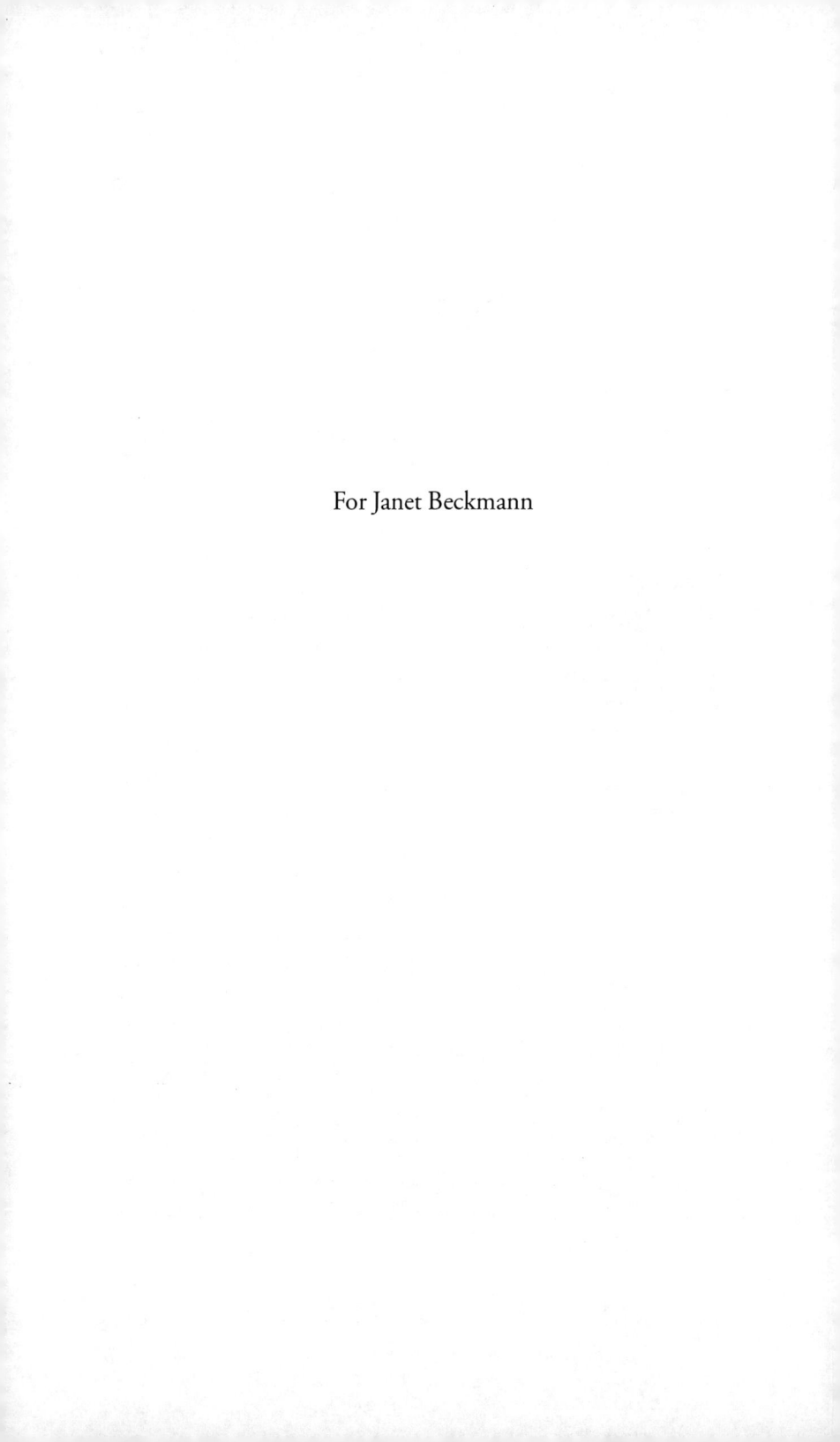

FRIDAY, OCTOBER 22

AT SIX THIRTY on a morning in late October, 1920, Louis Boyer swung his feet onto the bare wood floor, sat on the edge of the bed, and tried to rub the sleep out of his eyes with blunt, dirty fingers. He seldom got up this early, but he was expecting company today, and he wanted to be ready. He pulled denim trousers over his long johns and put on a red and black checked flannel shirt that had holes in both elbows. He opened his door and stepped out into the early autumn morning. The air was sharp but not cold, with a bright clarity that illuminated the pale blue sky over the Ozark Mountains, which lay across the southern horizon. Louis Boyer had other concerns. He could see the outhouse, not twenty feet away at the edge of the cornfield, but he unbuttoned where he was and urinated into the pile of trash by the stoop. He blew his nose in the same direction, holding first one nostril, then the other, with his thumb. Then he went back inside and slid his bare feet into a pair of battered brown boots that he did not bother to tie. There was water left in the basin, and he splashed some on his face. The icy shock of it made his skin tingle. A piece of mirror hung on the wall and he looked into it while he combed back his hair with his fingers. I may be getting old, he thought, but I still have all my hair.

He smiled at the image in the mirror, then immediately closed his mouth. Better not do that; didn't want to scare anybody away. He thought about shaving, but decided against it. He turned to the food shelf, but the idea of eating in the morning made his stomach churn. He could use a chew, though, and reached into his pocket for his plug. He bit off a piece and put the rest back in his pocket. For a moment, he just held the wad of tobacco in the back of his mouth, between his teeth and his cheek, and savored the first sweet surge of the drug.

That was better. A quart jar sat on a table by the stove, and he picked it up and drank off the last few drops in the bottom before putting the lid on and setting it carefully with the others. He opened the drawer in the table and stared at the pistol that was lying there. No, he wasn't going to need that, he thought. He never had in the past, that was for sure, and he wasn't going to need it now.

Was that a sound?

He went outside and around to the front. There was nobody in sight, so he pulled open the door that had "Louis Boyer Body Shop" painted on it and went in to wait.

An hour or so later, Louis Boyer would, briefly, think about the pistol in the drawer, and regret that he had not stuck it in his pocket.

It was the last thought he would ever have.

SATURDAY, OCTOBER 23

SOME TWENTY-FIVE HOURS later, and six miles away, Highland County Deputy Sheriff James Buckner stood in front of a telephone pole and tried to find a place to put up the handbill he was holding.

It wasn't easy; from knee-high to ten feet up, handbills covered the wood. It seemed as though everyone who wasn't in jail (and some who were) was running for office. Governor Cox from Ohio was the standard-bearer of the Democracy, and his running mate was somebody named Roosevelt, though not the Rough Rider Roosevelt, who had died the year before. Senator Harding, another Ohioan, was the Republican Party candidate for president, with Calvin Coolidge, a famous Massachusetts strikebreaker, as his running mate. (Buckner wondered briefly how former Boston policemen, fired by Coolidge, would vote.) The Socialist Labor Party had also nominated someone named Cox. Buckner didn't think it was the same as the Democratic Cox, but wasn't sure. Eugene Debs, still in prison for opposition to the war, headed the Socialist ticket. The Farm-Labor Party had a presidential candidate; so did the Prohibition Party, which Buckner did not understand at all, since the manufacture and sale of booze was now unconstitutional as well as illegal.

He finally spotted a handbill for Stillson Foote, the Republican candidate for Highland County Sheriff. Foote was a courthouse lawyer from Jackson with no police experience, but he was blaming the incumbent, Elmer Aubuchon, for all the excesses of the Democratic party reaching back before the Civil War to the Buchanan Administration.

Buckner tacked his handbill for Aubuchon directly over the serious, honest face of Stillson Foote.

At least Aubuchon was not pinning his seventh reelection bid on party loyalty. "Vote Aubuchon for Sheriff" read the handbill Buckner had just posted. "He has the weight of experience." It only grudgingly acknowledged, in tiny black print toward the bottom, the sheriff's life-long association with the Democratic Party. Below that, in letters even smaller, was a reference to Cox and Roosevelt. Clearly, it implied, if those two hacks ever got to the White House, it would only be on Elmer Aubuchon's coattails. As Elmer Aubuchon had held office for almost three decades, since the second Cleveland Administration, James Buckner was inclined agree.

He gathered up the reins of the bay gelding he had ridden out earlier that morning and walked to the next telephone pole. He avoided looking down the road. The line of poles that paralleled the macadam ribbon followed the gentle contours of the rolling countryside until they seemed to stretch all the way to Kansas. "Get every single one of them, clear to the county line," Aubuchon had told him when he delivered the box of freshly printed handbills.

"Yes, sir," Buckner had said. He almost saluted. All his years of military discipline made the response virtually automatic. Just as he reached the next pole, the sound of an engine made him turn. A truck was coming towards him. He led the bay over to the barbed wire fence that ran along the edge of the cornfield to give the truck plenty of room. The bay was not afraid of automobiles, but Buckner didn't want to take any chances.

To his surprise, the truck stopped and the driver got out.

"Found Louis Boyer out at his shop," said the driver abruptly.

His name was Jim Ates, and he had a blacksmith shop north of town. "Somebody stove his head in."

Louis Boyer had never been much good to anybody. Everybody who lived down in the south end of Highland County agreed on that. The first time Buckner had seen him was shortly after becoming deputy sheriff. Two Corinth policemen had dragged him in and were booking him for drunk and disorderly. He had picked a fight with a couple of Italians from the lead mines up in Taylor, and was getting the worst of it. The policemen stepped in, mostly to save Boyer's life, but he began swinging on them. They had calmed him down with their nightsticks and now he hung between them, suspended by their arms under his, blood pouring from several gashes on his head and face, clothing filthy and stinking, gap-toothed mouth mumbling vile curses on Italians and policemen alike. They let him sleep it off in one of the cells, and he had departed the next morning, his curses even more violent now that he was approximately sober.

Buckner had run into Louis Boyer only occasionally after that. Usually it involved some petty offense that seemed to bring more harm to Boyer than to his victims. Now, if Buckner thought about him at all, it was as a man bent on self-destruction.

But self-destruction was one thing. Murder was something else. So he listened closely to the blacksmith's story.

"I had that little two-year-old roan mare of Lester Staple's for shoeing over to my place and she's a little rough yet, so when my granddaughter dropped her dolly in the mud and started to bawlin', she kicked in the off-side door of my brand-new truck. Thursday afternoon this was. Sprung it so it wouldn't open. You can see it, right there." He pointed. The door was badly dented. Buckner suddenly had an image of a little girl kicking in the side of a truck, but he was sure that couldn't be right, so he kept listening. Ates talked on without stopping. "So I went over to see Louis on account of he ain't on the telephone and he said to come on in first thing this morning. So I taken it over to his place to have him fix it. I'd pound out the dent myself, but I only just got it, the truck, I mean, this past August and I kind of wanted to keep it looking nice, since it's going to get pretty beat-up looking before too long as it is."

"Good looking truck, Jim." Buckner slid his compliment in edgewise.

"Anyway, when I got over there, I parked in the yard in front of his shop and hollered, but didn't nobody holler back, and I couldn't see nobody around, so I went on in."

"Was the door open?" Buckner asked.

"Yeah." Ates had a deep, gravelly voice, and he mumbled so badly that any listener practically had to know in advance what he was going to say and then just nod while he said it.

"When was this?"

"About nine, half past. I had chores," Ates said. "Didn't want to get there too early. You know sometimes old Louis sleeps late on account of drinking a little too much the night before, but he knew I was coming and I seen the shop door open and figured he was up and around. I hadn't gone two steps inside when I seen the body. Thought he'd passed out 'til I seen the blood. Big mess of it, all around his head, though most of it had soaked in. Real shame, too. Louis could be an SOB when he wanted to, but he was the best body man in this end of the county. Anyway, I come right on down to tell you, but the fellers at the police station said you was out here campaigning for reelection."

"You didn't go check to make sure he was dead?"

Ates just snorted at that. He was in his fifties, of medium height, with a huge upper body. His shoulders and arms were powerful, his hands thick and scarred. He had an incongruous belly the size of a basketball that stretched the buttons of his checked flannel work shirt. Even the baggy denim trousers he wore could not conceal his thighs, grown massive from years of working in the half-crouch that horseshoeing required.

"Knew a feller once," he said, "got kicked in the head by a Belgian he was shoeing, killed him stone dead. He didn't say nothin', just fell right over, didn't have a mark on him, except for a kind of a horseshoe-shaped dent in the side of his head, but no blood at all. Old Louis's head was spread all over the floor."

"Touch anything?"
"Nope."
"All right," Buckner said. He stuffed the remaining handbills and his hammer and roofing nails into his saddlebag and mounted. "You go on home, and I'll head back up there. And thanks."
"You know, you ought to get yourself an automobile, Buck. Save you time getting around."
"I like riding when I can," Buckner answered. "Besides, what'll you do for work if everybody takes to driving automobiles?"
"Oh, hell, that'll never happen." Ates cranked his new truck to life and climbed in.

Buckner waited until Ates had turned around and driven off, then pointed the bay in the same direction. Smelling the barn, the big horse moved into a slow canter that he kept up half way to town. Buckner eased him into a trot, then a walk, and by the time he got to the barn the horse had cooled down completely. Buckner unsaddled him, rubbed him down with a burlap feed sack, and left him for Walter, the stable hand, to feed with the others.

Buckner went to the Corinth town hall and down to the police department in the basement. He stopped at the booking desk. Randall Givens, the desk sergeant, was alone.

"What'd Jim Ates want?" Givens asked.

"He said he found Louis Boyer dead on the floor of his shop this morning."

"Sure he wasn't just passed out?"

"Said he was lying in a pool of blood."

"Hm." Givens shrugged. "Good riddance. Getting drunk and getting in fights was all he was good for, seems like. Though I expect now the county'll have to pay to bury him."

"I expect so," Buckner agreed. His office was at the end of a long corridor that ran along one side of the building. It had originally been the Jim Crow jail cell, for black prisoners only, but the town decided it could not afford the luxury of segregating its prisoners by race, and donated the room to the county sheriff in the spirit of police cooperation. At least they had replaced the bars with a real door.

He left his saddlebag and coat on his desk, and headed back out again. The county's old wood-bodied Ford Model-T sat in the lot around back. Buckner cranked it up and drove Corinth's dusty back streets and alleys until he stopped behind Coy's Drug Store. He left the Ford running and climbed the stairs that angled up across the back of the building, then knocked at the door at the top. There was no answer. He tried the door, but it was locked. Buck knocked again.

"Peck! You in there?"

After more silence, he went back down the stairs. He walked along the alley and into the town square. The day was beginning to warm up, but even now, at the peak of Indian Summer, Buckner would keep his sweater on. A few shoppers passed him, nodding greetings, walking on. He went into Murtaugh's Funeral Parlor. Abel Murtaugh was tall, robust, smiling. He wore his thinning hair arranged carefully over a large, pale bald spot and fixed in place with heavy hair cream. Murtaugh always stood with his hands clasped before him, as though he were praying, or about to pray, or had just finished praying and was waiting to make sure he had not left anything out.

"Good morning, Deputy. How can I help you?"

Buckner could not help feeling as though the man regarded him, indeed everyone, as a potential customer, his eyes unconsciously measuring them for a coffin, his mind storing the information away for future use.

"I need you to send a wagon up to Louis Boyer's place on the Jackson Road to pick up his body."

"So he finally drank himself to death," said Murtaugh. "I can't say I'm surprised. A shame, in a way, though. He was a good man with a dented fender."

Buckner said only "You have any idea where I can find Jeff Peck? Nobody answered when I knocked on his door."

Murtaugh's chuckle was as rich and sweet as overripe fruit. "Try the back room at the Dew Drop Inn."

Buckner thanked the undertaker. "Don't forget to send somebody to pick up the body," he said. "I'll want Peck to do an autopsy. Then just hold it here until we see about burying it. Send your bill to the county coroner's office and send me a copy for my files."

"Certainly, Deputy. Always a pleasure working with the county. And speaking of the county, I hope you haven't forgotten the Commercial Club luncheon today. We're expecting a good talk from you. We have to make sure folks around here don't forget the party's rock-solid record on crime. Law and order, Deputy, that's what's going to decide this election."

"I haven't forgotten," Buckner said. He left Murtaugh smiling expectantly and returned to the Ford.

He still had no idea what he was going to tell the town's leading businessmen. They wanted reassurances that he could not give them. They complained constantly of the "criminal element" that threatened life and safety, and profits, in Corinth. Every black who didn't bow and scrape, every unemployed man passing through looking for work, anybody new and different and poor sent them rushing to the police. They saw anarcho-syndicalists, Black Handers, rapists, and murderers in every unfamiliar face. Buckner wondered how the city police handled the problem. He knew he only irritated people when he pointed out that most crime in Corinth was committed by local, established, white residents of the community. Still, Murtaugh was probably right. A strong law and order speech could mean a lot of votes on election day.

The Dew Drop Inn was on Washington Street, a stretch of dirt road near the edge of town. Buckner parked outside and went in. The place had once been a private home, but a few years before the war, a St. Louis businessman had moved in and converted it to a restaurant. The ground floor was taken up largely with a lunch counter, a dining area with three or four tables, and a kitchen. A door off the kitchen led to a small back room. The traffic in liquor that went on in that back room, in defiance of the Eighteenth Amendment and the Volstead Act, was an open secret. Even Buckner knew about it.

As a rule, Buckner tried to avoid knowing who was violating

Prohibition. He found the whole exercise pointless, and he was reluctant to make criminals of those of his neighbors who took an occasional drink. Fundamentally, he realized, he could not accept the premise that underlay the new law: that most of society's ills could be resolved by doing away with booze. Buckner had been born and raised a Calvinist—what a friend once called a Bible-burning Presbyterian. So he believed in Evil, and that the damned human race preferred sin to righteousness. Outlawing liquor would not change that. It just made his life more difficult.

The tables were laid for the noontime rush. Vincent Marolis, the St. Louis businessman, was big and heavyset, wearing a clean white apron over a clean white shirt and black string tie, black trousers, and gleaming black shoes with narrow toes. He stood at the far end of the lunch counter, chatting with a stocky, balding man in a brown overcoat and a brown fedora pulled down low over his eyes. An envelope lay on the counter between them, and as the two men looked over at Buckner, Marolis quickly scooped it up and put it in his pocket. A pretty waitress in a short dress with an apron over it teetered in Buckner's direction on high-heeled shoes.

"One for lunch, Deputy?" she said with a toothy smile. She had a high, almost childlike voice. Her lips were painted bright red and her eyes were darkly lined in the style of movie vamps.

"I need to see Jeff Peck," Buckner said. "Is he back there?"

"Back where?" the girl asked, flapping her long, dark, artificial lashes at him. Young Theda Bara, thought Buckner.

He walked around her and headed for the kitchen.

"Vince!" the girl called in alarm.

Marolis left his place at the end of the counter and came to stand before Buckner. He folded his thick arms across his chest and glowered.

"Is there a problem here, Deputy?" Marolis demanded.

"I'm looking for Doctor Peck. Is he back there?"

"Back where? The kitchen?" The man at the end of the counter laughed.

Buckner sighed. "Back there where you serve the drinks."

"We don't serve no drinks. That's against the law now. Or didn't you know that, Deputy?"

Buckner looked at Marolis for a moment, then glanced down at the man at the end of the counter, who was now giving the menu his close attention. "This is not a raid, Vince," he said softly. "I don't care about what you've got going here. This isn't my jurisdiction. But I need to see Doctor Peck on business, and I don't have time to play games with you. Stand aside, please."

"I don't think so," Marolis rumbled. "I think you're leaving."

Marolis reached out for Buckner's shirtfront with one hand, drawing back the other in a fist that looked as big as the end of a tree stump. Buckner stepped back. As Marolis extended his reach for the shirtfront, leaning forward slightly, Buckner grabbed his wrist with both hands and pulled. Marolis lurched into the dining room, scattering chairs and tables. Buckner stepped aside and kicked his feet from under him, sending him sprawling to the floor.

Buckner turned to face the stocky man at the end of the counter, who had half risen from his stool, one hand reaching under his overcoat for his hip pocket.

"Go ahead, Harris." Buckner said. He held his hands away from his sides to show he was unarmed.

The man stopped, frozen halfway between sitting and rising, his hand still reaching, hesitation in his eyes.

Buckner watched the man intently. The man glared at Buckner for a moment, then sat down carefully, resting both hands open on the counter.

Buckner nodded and glanced at Marolis, who had staggered to his feet and was heading his way, thick hands groping. Buckner stepped forward and drove his left fist into the man's thick midsection. Marolis folded double with a whoosh of air and sat down heavily on the floor. "There's going to be hell to pay, Deputy," said the man at the end of the counter.

"There usually is," Buckner answered. He turned and headed into the kitchen and through the door into the back room.

Three men sat drinking, each one pretending he was alone in

a dingy, windowless, eight-foot-square room. Two looked up, surprise and consternation on their faces. Buckner knew them vaguely. The third, a man about Buckner's age, with a smooth, unlined face, and startling, dead white hair and hollow, empty eyes, merely frowned slightly in annoyance.

"Don't worry, boys," he said to the other two. He got to his feet. "It's me he wants." He looked up at Buckner. "I thought you were out campaigning to make sure your boss gets reelected next week."

"I was. Now I've got something else to do, and I need your help."

Peck looked at the tumbler that sat, half-full of dark liquid, at his place at the table. He picked it up and held it out to Buckner. "I'm going to need this, aren't I, Deputy?" and drank it off without waiting for an answer. He set the tumbler carefully on the table. "Let's go view the remains." He headed for the kitchen.

"Not that way," said Buckner, catching him by the elbow and turning him toward the rear exit. The two remaining drinkers sighed and freshened their glasses.

"Are we avoiding someone?" the Doctor asked as they walked around the building to the waiting Ford.

"I walked in on Vince Marolis and City Detective Harris exchanging an envelope, and they acted like I caught them fencing the 'Mona Lisa.' I don't want to have to deal with them again," Buckner said. He backed the vehicle carefully into the street.

"I thought I heard the sound of something heavy falling," Peck seemed pleased. "Was it Detective Harris?"

"No. Vince Marolis."

"Oh." The doctor looked downcast. "There's got to be someplace else in town where you can drink before noon."

"There are several," said Peck. "I imagine you'll be hearing about all this from Chief Bushyhead."

"Why's that?" Buckner asked. "I didn't hit Harris."

"Maybe not," said Peck. "But you'll be hearing from him anyway."

Buckner drove on. After he had turned onto the Jackson road heading north, he asked, "How are you feeling?"

"You mean, am I too drunk to look at another corpse for you?" Peck snapped.

"Yes," Buckner answered pleasantly. "That's what I mean."

"I'll manage just fine. Looking at dead bodies doesn't take a lot of skill; or sobriety."

"I heard somewhere you were trying to quit."

"And I heard somewhere that your leg is all healed up good as new and all that scar tissue has completely vanished." The Doctor's voice was bitter. Buckner still limped from a wound he received while serving with the Canadian army on the Western Front.

He did not respond to Peck's challenge.

After a while, Peck asked, "Where the hell are we going, anyway? And whose corpse am I examining for the county?"

"Louis Boyer. Jim Ates found him dead on the floor of his shop this morning."

"Oh," said Peck. He did not sound surprised.

The two drove the rest of the way in silence.

Louis Boyer's shop was two miles north of town on the road to the county seat. Boyer had been apprenticed as a child to Jules Boyer, a relative who was a wheelwright in his hometown of Potosi, over in Washington County. He had in time become a journeyman, moved to Corinth, and set up shop. For years, he repaired wagons and carriages, then trucks and automobiles, when they became more common. But he was a drunk, and a mean one, and he could never make a real success of his work.

Sometime in the early nineties Boyer took his two children and his wife and moved into the shop on the Jackson Road. For the past twenty-five years, the wife and children long gone now, Louis Boyer survived, barely. He seldom came to town, had few friends, and spent what little money he made on liquor provided by a local moonshiner.

Buckner pulled into the yard and shut off the engine. Boyer's shop was a large, one-story, clapboard building sitting in a niche in a cornfield just off the road. The building was divided into a work area in front and living quarters in back, with a wall between. The entrance to the shop was a large sliding door set on rusted metal wheels. Between the road and the entrance lay an open, graveled area, littered with scraps of wood and leather, broken tools, broken wagons, and empty bottles. A pre-war Pierce-Arrow presided over all this, sitting wheel-less and engine-less, its seats gone, on four upended elm logs. Its once elegant, bright yellow shell had faded to gray. Someone had smashed out all the windows, and the empty sockets of its headlamps stared blindly toward the cornfield across the Jackson Road. There was no sign, nor any other indication of what went on inside the shop.

Buckner just sat for a minute or two, looking at the littered yard, the building, and the corn that surrounded it on three sides. The corn was six feet high and more than ready to harvest. "I'm in no hurry," the Doctor said after several minutes. "And I expect old Louis isn't going anywhere. But shouldn't we get out and have a look?"

"Sitting here like this, nobody can see us unless they pass right by," Buckner said, glancing over his shoulder at the two dozen yards of road not hidden by corn.

"Yes," Peck agreed. "And we'd look like just another auto waiting to be repaired. Also, there aren't any houses for a mile in either direction."

Buckner nodded. This was the real reason he brought Peck along: another pair of eyes to see, another brain to think. He stepped down from the Model-T and walked toward the shop. The Doctor followed. The door to the shop faced west, and the interior was gloomy. The windows in the north and south walls were caked with grime, but they let in enough of the slanting afternoon light to see by. Buckner could make out tables lining the walls of the work area. They were laden with tools and wood. Sheets of wood and metal stood stacked in a corner. The floor was packed dirt saturated with oil and covered with sawdust and wood chips and little curls of metal shavings. In the middle of the floor lay the body of a man, face down, arms and legs spread.

A dark stain surrounded the head. The still air of the shop smelled of oil and excrement and putrification, and the body had begun to swell.

Peck walked over, knelt down, and wiggled a foot. It moved easily.

"Dead twenty-four hours at a minimum," he said with finality. He rose and sniffed the air. "Good thing it was cold last night, or he'd be pretty ripe by now."

Buckner took a small notebook and a pencil from his shirt pocket and began taking notes. Elmer Aubuchon had originally suggested this method of supplementing his memory, and now Buckner did it automatically. He used the kind of notebook sold to students each fall, filling them up and storing them, dated, in his filing cabinet.

He went over and stood next to Peck and they looked down at Louis Boyer's earthly remains.

Buckner pointed. "Head bashed in," he said.

"More than bashed in," Peck agreed. "With that, I imagine." He nodded toward a two-foot long length of one-inch galvanized pipe. He knelt again, this time near the head, and waved his hand over it. A mass of flies buzzed angrily into flight, and then settled again. "Whole back half of the head's mashed to a pulp."

Buckner ignored the length of pipe and instead began to prowl the shop. He started with the floor near the corpse and spiraled outward, his eyes searching, his pencil scribbling. When he reached the tool benches, he examined things one by one, carefully, touching little, but peering closely. He went from one table to the next until he had done them all, then he returned to the piece of pipe. He bent and picked it up.

Peck had gotten to his feet during Buckner's search and had simply stood and watched. Now he joined him.

"Blood, hair, and probably brains as well," he said, indicating the smeared, matted material at one end of the pipe.

"Yes," Buckner agreed. "But no chance of finger prints. No finger prints worth the bother, anyway. I expect this came from that pile of pipe on that bench over there." He aimed a thumb over his shoulder. "Somebody just walked in here, grabbed this, and killed him with it."

"Somebody he knew, maybe?" suggested Peck.

"Maybe. Why?"

"Well, anyway, somebody he felt comfortable turning his back on. All the blows, and it looks like there were several, are on the back of the head."

"Maybe he was running away," Buckner offered. "He went down with his head toward the door."

"Whoever did it left with blood on his hand, and probably on his sleeve as well." Peck pointed to the body. "There's blood and brains splattered on the back of his collar."

"He's probably washed his hands by now, don't you think?"

"Yes," Peck answered. "But it's hard to wash blood out of clothes, as I recall—" He stopped abruptly, as though he had forgotten what he planned to say next, and stood there silently, a look of utter horror twisting his face. He, too, had been in France, though later than Buckner. The memories of the smashed bodies that streamed endlessly through his aid station just behind the front still brought him bolt upright out of a sound sleep. There was not enough booze in the world to drown those images, no matter how much of it Peck consumed.

"Yes," Buckner interjected. After a moment, he said, "One thing's certain, though. Boyer had not been working much lately. A lot of those tools are covered with dust and the cutting edges are rusted over."

"Are we finished here?" Peck asked suddenly.

"I want to look at where he lived. Around back. You can go on into town with the body if you like. You might even do an autopsy," Buckner suggested gently.

"You think he died some other way than multiple blows to the back of the head with a blunt instrument? Maybe he was shot full of poisoned darts fired by an Asian pygmy. Why do you always bring me along on these little expeditions of yours, anyway? I got a bellyful of dead bodies in France and I'd have thought you did, too."

"I bring you along because you have more experience with bodies dead by violence than all the other doctors in this county combined." Buckner's voice was cold. "This is only the second time in over two years that I've asked for your help. I'll take help wherever I can get it. And I want an autopsy to try to get a time of death. Can you do that?"

Peck shrugged, resigned. "It might help if I knew when he ate last, but I don't. I guess I can use body temperature, lividity, things like that. But I won't be able to pin it down the way you want me to."

"Get as close as you can," Buckner said. "Let's go outside. There should be a truck from Murtaugh's along pretty soon."

They went out. Buckner heard a sound from the south and looked up. A flatbed REO pulled into the yard and stopped next to the Ford.

Buckner waved the truck over. The driver, a young man with a bad complexion, a greasy wool cap, and a ready-made cigarette dangling with careful casualness from the corner of his thin mouth, rolled down the window.

"Almost drove right past," he said. "Where's the stiff?" One eye squinted against the cigarette smoke.

"In there," Buckner said. He didn't know this one, but he recognized a type that was becoming increasingly common around town. With jobs scarce, boys like this one gathered in pool halls and on street corners, smoking and leaning against walls with their hands pushed into their pockets. They made rude remarks to passersby and spat on the ground, and Buckner knew that Chief Bushyhead had given orders to his officers to move these young men along, but they simply regathered once the blue uniform had gone away. This was part of that criminal element people were always telling him was so dangerous, but all Buckner saw was boys with lots of energy and nothing to do. Maybe he'd been lucky. When he was that age, he was in the cavalry, learning the fine art of manhunting from Apache scouts out of Fort Huachuca.

The young man peered into the now gloomy shop, nodded

once, and cranked the wheel of his truck. With a few deft moves, he had turned the truck around and backed it almost into the shop. He applied the brake and jumped out, leaving the truck idling in neutral. Then he went around to the back and pulled out a stretcher. He went to the body, opened the stretcher, and set it on the ground. He stood, waiting, looking at the two men.

"I can do this all by myself," he said. "But I usually appreciate a little help."

Buckner nodded and went over. Peck didn't move.

"Sorry," Buckner said. "I haven't done this sort of thing much lately."

"Nothing to it," the young man answered. "I've handled them sometimes when they was so rotten, they'd come to pieces in your hands when you tried to pick them up."

"Uh huh," said Buckner. He knew about rotting bodies. On the Western Front, today's bombardment could throw up corpses from last year's battle. Even the living began to decompose. Standing in water for hours on end caused flesh to fall off the feet in chunks; men who had been gassed coughed up pieces of their lungs. Lice and other minute scavengers nibbled constantly at scalp and skin.

They placed Louis Boyer's body face down on the stretcher, then lifted and carried it to the truck. As they were sliding it onto the bed, one of Boyer's hands fell from the stretcher and hit the wood, scraping the knuckles. The young man reached over and flipped it back onto the stretcher. When the stretcher was in place, the young man covered it with a blanket, then strapped it down securely with wide leather belts bolted to the bed. Then he got back into his truck.

"Wait a minute," Buckner called. He turned to Peck who had been watching the shadow of the corn spread across the gravel yard. "You going back to town?"

"You need me anymore?"

"Not here I don't. But when you get back, stop by the Commercial Club luncheon at the Elk's Lodge and tell them I won't be able to make it. I'm supposed to give them a law and order speech so they'll vote for Elmer. Don't tell them about Louis; just say it was county business."

Peck took out a watch and glanced at it. "I think it's a little late for that," he said, and put the watch back in his pocket.

Buckner just nodded, relieved, his mind on the murder he now had to deal with.

Peck climbed into the truck next to the young man, who raced the engine, waved jauntily, and roared out of the driveway in a cloud of dust and flying gravel.

Buckner watched them go, waiting until he could not hear the truck anymore. The air was still. A calf bawled somewhere; a high, circling hawk searched the ground below. Although the sun was well up and the air was still warm, Buckner shivered and wished he had brought a coat.

He went around to the back of Boyer's shop. An outhouse and a chicken coop stood at the edge of the cornfield. Their wooden sides had weathered to a silvery gray, and the roof of the chicken coop had collapsed in the middle. A cistern with a rust-streaked pump stood to one side of the door. The door, in the center of the back wall of the building, was flanked by two small windows and guarded by an odiferous mound of trash. Two fieldstone steps led up. The back of the building showed signs of having been painted white once, many years ago. The door and windows had been painted green, but everything was faded now, and blending into the same pale gray.

Two quart glass jars filled with pale milky liquid sat on the stone step by the door. Buckner picked one up and twisted off the lid. The sharp smell of moonshine stung his nostrils. He replaced the lid and put the jar back on the step.

Buckner tried the door. The cracked enamel knob spun loosely, and the door swung open at a push. In the shadowed interior, he found a brakeman's coal-oil lamp. He shook it and heard liquid sloshing in the bottom. He levered up the sooty glass, took a match from his pocket, and lit the lantern, then lowered the wick and replaced the chimney.

The light from the lantern was yellow and weak, but there

was little to see. Boyer had lived in one large room some ten feet deep and fifteen wide. A pot-bellied stove in the middle of the room provided heat for warmth and, judging by the coffee pot and saucepan sitting on top, cooking as well. Buckner put a hand on the stove. It was stone cold. He opened the door. A large clinker lay in the bottom. The scuttle next to the stove was full, as was a box of kindling.

Where did Boyer get his coal? Buckner wondered. Or his booze? Or his food, for that matter, since he had to eat sometimes. There were a few cans of stew and beans on a shelf; and whatever was congealing in the pan had probably been edible once, before it started to grow green fur. How did he get around? Buckner remembered seeing Boyer in town only a few times in the past year, and always on foot. Did he walk everywhere?

He pushed aside the tow sack curtains that covered the window to let in the afternoon light. Then he searched the room carefully.

A metal cot with a thin mattress covered with an olive-drab army blanket and a ratty quilt stood between the stove and the left-hand wall. Along the right hand wall, clothing hung from a row of nails, including a wool hat, wool-lined denim jacket, a pair of overalls, two wool shirts, and one khaki shirt. A heavy pair of boots with worn-down heels sat on the floor under the overalls.

A small table and chair stood against the back wall. A half-dozen empty Ball jars with lids clustered in the center of it. There was nothing else on it, but it had a drawer. Buckner picked up one of the jars and sniffed it. Moonshine again. He put the jar down and opened the drawer. In it he saw a Smith & Wesson revolver, a cleaning kit, and a half-empty box of .38 cartridges. The pistol was fully loaded and smelled of gun oil. Buckner opened it and looked down the barrel. Even in the dim light, he could see the light sheen of oil.

At least the old bastard kept his weapon clean, Buckner thought as he put the pistol back and closed the drawer.

But he hadn't been carrying it when he met his murderer.

Buckner pulled the chair out next to the stove and sat down. The pistol had to be the only clean thing in the place. Unlike the shop, this part of the building had a wooden floor. But the pine planks were worn and dirty, littered with empty cans, torn and filthy items of clothing, mouse droppings, a knife handle. Buckner got up and went to the bed. He picked up and shook out the quilt and blanket. They yielded only dust. He threw them in a corner. The mattress was spotted with dark stains. Buckner flipped it onto the floor, revealing a small envelope. He opened it and took out a pack of illustrated playing cards. He'd seen others like it in Paris and wondered how Boyer had come by this one. He fanned the deck and noticed again that, no matter how much they smiled, the women on the cards always had dead and empty eyes. He tossed the cards onto the bed.

Removing the mattress had revealed a small trunk under the bed. Buckner got down on his knees and dragged it out. It was locked shut, but he pulled hard and the rivets holding the hasp in place tore through the cheap cardboard. He opened the lid.

Inside the trunk, Buckner saw a young girl's clothes: little dresses, stockings, underwear. The material was cheap and thin, and the print on the dresses had faded. Everything had been carefully folded and laid away as though packed for a journey, or awaiting the wearer's imminent return.

Buckner took the pieces out one by one and unfolded them on the floor. There were at least three complete outfits in different sizes. He held up a faded cotton dress with daisies on it and a matching belt. He guessed it might have fit a twelve-year-old. It was the biggest item in the collection. He looked at the clothes for a long time, then folded everything carefully and put it back. He shut the lid and slid the trunk back under the bed.

Buckner stood for a long time in the very center of the room and tried to see it as Boyer had. It oppressed him. It was barren and squalid, and he could feel the loneliness of it like a weight. With nothing to do and no work, or very little, to occupy his hands and his mind, Boyer must have spent much of his time here drinking and staring into space. Buckner began to realize that if he lived here like that, he would drink, too.

He extinguished the lantern and walked out. To his surprise, the sun was just over the tops of the corn tassels. He checked his watch: four-thirty. The outhouse was empty except for a stack of magazines and a bucket of lime. The broken down chicken coop was empty, too, without even the smell of its former occupants. Buckner pushed his toe through the pile of trash by the door, but spotted nothing that invited a more thorough search. He blew out the lantern and set it beside the two moonshine jars on the steps.

The evening sky was clear, a dark, metallic blue, and a few stars were visible to the east. Buckner stood for a long time in the growing darkness. A light breeze came up and set the corn to rustling. The sounds made him shudder briefly, bringing up memories. Once, when he was five or six, and visiting some relatives who owned an enormous farm up in Pike County, he had wandered into the cornfield and immediately become lost amongst the towering stalks. After a few minutes of panicky tears, he had spotted his father coming toward him, striding down the row, taller than the corn. They held hands and walked out together and he was safe, but for years, the rustle of corn had frightened him. Now he found, to his surprise, that it was a comforting sound. Perhaps because, since then, he had heard sounds that were so much more terrifying. He stood without moving in Louis Boyer's back yard until it was full dark, thinking, letting the night close in around him, then went back to the front of the shop and pulled the door closed. The rusty wheel shrieked in protest, and there was no lock. He cranked up the Ford, got in, and drove back to town. The Ford's headlights projected cones of light before him on the road, and he met no other traffic along the way.

He drove the Ford down a dark, tree-shaded street, and parked it in front of a small, two-story frame house. He went through the gate in the picket fence, up the flagstone walk and through the front door. His mother was clearing the dinner dishes from the dining room table.

"We missed you at dinner," she said pointedly.

"Stew?" he asked.

"Yes." She carried dishes to the kitchen. He picked up the rest and followed.

"Any left?"

"Yes. For your father's lunch tomorrow."

"All right."

"You know when we dine. If you wish to join us, you are welcome, but I won't be serving dinner at all hours of the day or night."

"I understand." He went to the pantry and got a chocolate bar and some crackers. He poured a glass of milk from the pitcher in the icebox and sat at the kitchen table.

His father was gone, probably upstairs already. Buckner's father had been a successful physician in the county seat of Jackson. A stroke ended his medical practice and Buckner's college career. Buckner joined the cavalry and spent the next several years patrolling the Mexican Border, sending most of every paycheck home. When the war came, he joined the Canadian army. He served with the First Canadian Division, surviving the first use of poison gas in Germany's attack on the Ypres salient, only to be badly wounded a few months later in a routine trench raid. After he recovered from his wound, in 1917, he moved his family from the big house in Jackson that they could no longer afford, to the small town of Corinth. There he took up the job of deputy sheriff.

His father's condition did not improve. He remained bitter and withdrawn, and refused to care for himself, even though the stroke had only slightly impaired his physical abilities. The situation had finally driven away Buckner's sister, Martha Jane, who had cared for her father while her brother was away. Lately, after over a decade of passive, unmoving anger, the old man had begun to work at his own recovery with the same determination that had carried him through four years with Sterling Price's dismounted cavalry during the Civil War. He had marched twenty miles a day back then, through the rocky, rugged terrain along the Arkansas-Missouri border, dodging Yankees and living on chicory and green corn, barefoot much of the time. But he had been a boy then, just twenty when word came of Lee's surrender at Appomattox, and then Johnston's in North Carolina. Finally, the tattered remnants in Missouri had taken a vote to see whether they would join Jo Shelby and head for Mexico, or go back home and try to find ways to live normal lives again in a world without marching and fighting and dying. Most voted to end it and went home. Some joined Shelby, while others drifted away to become bushwhackers and road agents and train robbers, hunted men brought to bay finally by the law and their own nightmares.

Buckner's father found work in iron foundries and as a riverboat deckhand and saved his money. He went to college, then medical school in St. Louis, before moving back to his home town of Jackson to set up his practice and marry the daughter of one of the county's leading citizens. That big, strong man had rescued a frightened little boy from the corn. Now it took all the strength this bent old man possessed to shuffle his slippered feet around the house. His father was nearing eighty, Buckner acknowledged, and had lived a hard life for many years, and could not reasonably be expected to live much longer.

Buckner shook his head. He was not ready to think about that, not just yet.

But the house was more spacious now. After Martha Jane had moved to St. Louis and his father began getting around on his own more, Buckner was able to persuade his mother to get rid of the enormous, dark, heavy table, with its twelve chairs, that they had brought with them from the big house in Jackson. That table, even with none of its four leaves in place, had filled the little dining room in the house in Corinth. Now, however, a plain round oak table that comfortably seated four took its place. Six fit with the one leaf in it, though they had never used it.

Having guests in for dinner had slipped out of their lives. The old table and chairs had gone to the African Methodist Episcopal Church on Fourth Street, where they were the object of numerous comments involving the Last Supper.

Buckner ate slowly while his mother stood at the sink filling a tub with steaming water from the teakettle.

"I'm sorry I was late," he explained. "Someone murdered Louis Boyer, and Jeff Peck and I went out to view the body."

"Hmph," responded his mother. "Those two were cut from the same cloth."

"Jeff Peck and Louis Boyer? I'll admit Jeff's got a problem with the bottle." He remembered the room Boyer had inhabited in life. "But he isn't near as bad as Louis Boyer."

"Perhaps not," his mother admitted. "He's never had a family to drive away, has he?"

"No, I believe with Jeff it was the other way around: they drove him away. Anyway, he was supposed to take over his father's society practice in St. Louis. He told me once it drove him crazy, coming back after the war and having to prescribe pills for rich old ladies with make-believe problems. He didn't last six months. Said he came down here to get away from all that. But I didn't know Louis Boyer drove his family away."

"So I've heard," his mother said. "Wife and two children, I recall. But that was years ago. Before the turn of the century. And he drove them away with his drinking and . . . other beastly behavior."

Buckner smiled. "What beastly behavior, Mother?"

"The drunken old goat used to chase women. Back before drink rendered that a pointless activity." Blushing slightly, his mother took a damp rag and went out to the dining room.

Buckner finished his supper and went to the sink. He dipped his hands cautiously into the hot water, and began washing dishes. He scrubbed with a brush before rinsing them in clear water, then placing them in the wooden rack to dry.

He hated washing dishes. He had done his share of kitchen police in the army, and had vowed never again. But after his sister left, his mother demanded some measure of help from him, and he agreed. He prepared many of his own meals, which was no hardship after years of cooking over army fires, and took his laundry to the Chinaman who had a shop on the square.

By the time his mother returned from wiping the table and running the carpet sweeper over the floor, Buckner had finished with the dishes.

"Would you like some coffee?" he asked as he poured himself a cup from the pot on the back of the stove.

"Lord, no," his mother answered. "I'll be up all night."

Buckner sat at the kitchen table and sipped the hot, bitter liquid. Every cavalry post he had ever served on had an enormous, blackened pot of coffee simmering on top of every pot-bellied stove. He remembered old first sergeants who seemed to have a coffee cup in hand at all times, often even at formation. He soon fell into step, and found that coffee did not disturb his sleep at night, yet helped to wake him up in the morning.

"How is he?" Buckner asked.

His mother put a few finishing touches on the kitchen, then opened the bread box and took out a plate holding a small square of chocolate cake, and sat opposite him.

"Surprisingly well, considering his condition this time last year." She began to eat the cake slowly, carving off minute shreds with her fork and chewing them slowly. It was a small luxury, and she savored every bite of it. "He walked down to the post office to get the mail this morning. I offered to go along, but he insisted on going alone."

Buckner was surprised, and pleased. "He hasn't done that since, when, ought-seven."

"Yes. Since the stroke."

"I was home from school the Christmas before, studying for finals."

"Going to parties, you mean."

Buckner laughed.

"Yes," he said. "I joined the cavalry that September. By that Christmas I was at Fort Bliss."

In the next seven years, he served at almost every post along the Border, from Bliss, near El Paso, to Yuma, in far western Arizona. The Indian wars were over by then, and cavalry life meant routine patrolling. The land was unforgiving, dry and sun-blasted, and everything living there seemed equipped with horns or thorns or fangs. Sometimes there were sharp, short fights with reservation-jumping Apaches, Yaquis raiding over the line from Mexico, or the numerous smugglers and gunrunners who plied their hazardous trade across the harsh, barren desert. But mostly he spent endless hours at drill, or garrison duty, or in the saddle, fighting deadly boredom and the brutal weather. Buckner had spent the time well, though, and in time, he had become a better than average tracker and scout, skilled in ambush, hit-and-run fighting, sneak attacks. In 1914, bored with the routine of Border patrol, he enlisted in the Canadian army and went to France because that was where he thought the real fighting was. He quickly got more than his fill. A blinding flash of scarlet light in the snow lifted him up into the air and slammed him down into darkness, ending his military career.

The next thing Buckner remembered was being jolted into a pain-filled consciousness in the back of an ambulance. The Tonkinese driver jabbered alternately in gutter French and in his own tongue, smoked cigarettes that never left the corner of his mouth, and seemed determined to drive through every shell hole between the front and the aid station. He passed out and woke up some time later, warm and dry for the first time in months, in a hospital in Rouen. By now, he had not seen the desert in five years, and he never saw the Western Front again.

"James?" his mother asked kindly, laying a hand on his arm.

Buckner smiled at her. "Was I wandering again?"

"You certainly were. Here I was, going on about your father's health, in response to your question, and you're not even listening."

"I'm sorry."

"I'm glad he's doing better," his mother admitted. "It makes things much easier around here."

Buckner looked at his mother. She was just over fifty, almost thirty years younger than her husband, and a commanding presence. Strong-featured and strong-willed as well, she continued to wear her iron-gray hair piled high on top of her head, in the fashion of the nineties. She held herself ramrod straight, was tall for a woman, and found it easy to impose her will on others. Buckner secretly believed she had set her cap for his father because he was the only man she had ever met that she could look up to, literally as well as figuratively. In any case, both she and her daughter had grown up tall and strong-featured, with dominating personalities. Buckner had come to terms with the rougher edges of his nature in the army. His sister continued to struggle with hers, since it seemed to frighten away most eligible men.

"Have you heard from Marthy lately?" he asked.

"Just that letter last week that I showed you."

"I wonder what she's going to do now."

"Well," his mother said dryly, "I don't think she's going to move back home and marry some local boy and settle down, if that's what you mean."

"No," Buckner agreed. "It would take more than her boss dying to send her home."

When Martha Jane Buckner left home the year before, during the summer of 1919, she went to St. Louis and took a job working as a feature writer for *Reedy's Mirror*, a magazine famous for its editor/owner's progressive opinions. But William M. Reedy had recently died, and with him, his magazine.

"She seems to think she'll be able to find another job quickly enough."

"Yes," said Buckner. "That's the way she was raised."

"What do you mean by that?"

"I mean if she is independent-minded and determined to make her own way in the world, then it's because that's the way she was raised."

"Perhaps," said his mother, unwilling to concede the point. "Still, I wish she'd give some thought to starting a family of her own. By the time I was her age . . ."

"You had two children. I know. But Marthy's got plenty of

time to find a husband, and probably a better chance in the city than down here."

Buckner's mother had finished her piece of cake and was scraping together the last crumbs, picking them up by pressing the fork down on them, finishing every morsel of her dessert.

"I'll be much easier in my mind when she's chasing children instead of a job. You might give some thought to getting married yourself, James."

Buckner met his mother's steady gaze with a grin. "Plenty of time for that. You and Father didn't get married until he was near fifty. Besides, I don't meet a lot of nice girls in my line of work."

"That's not true. What about that young woman you met last year, up in Taylor?"

"Mrs. Garrett," Buckner said. "She left town." His tone of voice ended discussion of that topic.

"Well," said his mother. "I just don't want you to wait as long as your father did. You get stubborn and set in your ways and you won't have much room for other people."

"I need to ask you something about Louis Boyer."

"You just want to change the subject."

"Yes," he admitted. "But I need information, too."

"I'm not sure I can help you. I did not know the man. I know absolutely nothing about him, other than the barest outlines of his wretched reputation."

"You said something about him having a family and driving them away. Do you know anything about that?"

"Very little," his mother admitted. "I have heard that he was married at one time, but that his wife left him, ran off someplace, leaving her children behind."

"Why did the wife leave?" Buckner thought of the trunk filled with little girl clothes. "What happened to the children?"

"I believe he sent the children off to live with relatives. As for the wife, nobody ever heard from her again."

"He must have treated her very badly," Buckner said.

"The way the story goes," said his mother, warming to the subject, "he would get drunk and beat her something awful. But that wasn't very often, because he spent most of his time with his fancy woman that he kept here in town."

"Who was that?"

"Oh, I don't know. I'm just telling you what I heard."

"Who would know?" Buckner persisted. "Who told you all this?"

"Well, several people, I suppose. But I believe the person who could tell you the most is Antonia Clay. She knows where every skeleton in Corinth is buried."

Mrs. Buckner got to her feet. "If that's all, I'm going to bed," she said. She put her plate and fork in the sink, kissed her son on the cheek, and went upstairs.

Buckner sat alone in the kitchen, finished his cold coffee, and thought about his own childhood. Vague images were all that remained, like the incident in the cornfield, but they dissolved like smoke when he tried to grasp them. Newer, starker images intervened, vivid and detailed: smells of human waste, wet canvas, smokeless powder, and fear; sounds of moaning, shrieking; and the terror-laced boredom. He knew he'd had a happy childhood; he could see it. He just couldn't reach it anymore. The war kept getting in the way.

Finally, he got up. He rinsed his cup and his mother's plate and fork and left them to dry. The wash water went down the drain, and the pots were upended on the edge of the counter. Buckner turned off the kitchen light and walked down the hall to his room. The small bulb in the ceiling cast its pale light over the room's simplicity and brought him back to his present.

This room was his little piece of the house, and he kept it to suit himself. The floor and walls were bare and spotless. He enjoyed the stark military precision of the furniture: the chifforobe, its drawers filled with neatly rolled socks, carefully folded underwear and khaki shirts and trousers; the plain wooden desk and chair; the metal-frame cot. He undressed and stuffed his clothes into the laundry bag that he had tied to the foot of the bed in the maddeningly precise military manner. Why was the army so obsessed with unbuttoned pockets, dangling pieces of rope or string or leather? he wondered.

As he padded around the room, the floor cold against his bare feet, he tried to imagine Boyer's family living in that shed. Had it been neater, cleaner with a wife to tidy up? Where had the children slept? He thought of Mexican huts along the Border, Apache wickiups, farmhouses in the French countryside, dark tenements in London and Paris and New York. Most people in the world lived in conditions as bad, or worse, than those of the Boyer family.

How did that shape them? Was Louis Boyer bad because of bad conditions, or were the conditions bad because Louis Boyer was bad? He didn't know. He was paid to arrest people who broke the law, to gather evidence to ensure their conviction and punishment. Did he care how they came to break the law? He wasn't sure.

As the sun had gone down, October's chill returned, and the evening's light breeze had risen, so that gusts now rattled the panes of the room's single window, whipping the dogwood tree in the side yard against the wall of the house. Goose bumps rose on Buckner's skin as he unfolded the second blanket and got into bed. There was a small reading lamp on the table, and a worn copy of Xenophon's *Anabasis* open beside it. Instead of resuming the Greek general's long trek home, Buckner switched off the light. He turned on his side and pulled up the blankets. There, in the dark, naked under the covers, he let his right hand slip down his bare thigh until his fingertips brushed lightly against the thick mass of scar tissue at the back of his leg, and he thought about the jolting ambulance and its jabbering Tonkinese driver until he fell asleep.

SUNDAY, OCTOBER 24

IN THE MORNING, Buckner drove the Ford to the town hall and left it in the lot behind the building. He walked around to the front, up the stairs and through the big double doors. Givens, on the desk, was devoting full attention to a Sears-Roebuck catalogue and only nodded briefly. Buckner nodded back. There was no one else around. He poured a cup of coffee and walked back to his office. The building's furnace was working overtime, and the radiator in the corner behind his desk clanked and hissed angrily. Opening the window let in some fresh air. Buckner took off his hat and sweater and tossed them on top of his filing cabinet.

He went to his desk and took two Report of Crime forms and a piece of carbon paper from a drawer. Aligning them carefully, he rolled them into his new Remington typewriter. It had taken two years of nagging, but the county had finally sent him one. He wasn't very proficient in its use, but it was still faster, and neater, than his handwriting.

For the next hour, he tapped laboriously through the form, detailing the nature of the crime, the name of the victim, plus a wealth of other information that would be referred to throughout the life of the case, by himself, any other investigators, Sheriff

Aubuchon, and any lawyers that might get involved if the thing ever got that far. He included an overhead sketch of Boyer's shop and the grounds around it, and a drawing of the interior, including the disposition of the corpse, represented by a stick figure.

He finished his coffee and put the original report and the sketch into a large envelope. As soon as he had an official cause-of-death report from Jeff Peck, he would add that and send the whole thing off to the Sheriff's Office in Jackson.

He took out his watch and glanced down at it. Not yet nine o'clock. Too early to go knocking on Peck's door.

He got out his city directory and looked up Antonia Clay's address. She lived in a boarding house just off the square. Probably a shade early for calling on her, too; or she might be at church.

Buckner put a stamp on his envelope, put on his sweater and hat, and left.

The town had come to life, and the square was busy with people on their way to worship. Automobiles and a few trucks sat parked on the edges of the square or clattered along the street. People in their best clothes greeted each other on the sidewalks. The morning had warmed considerably as the lingering days displayed their dazzling colors. The high temperatures had attracted a few hardy souls to the wrought-iron benches that ringed the square. But, unlike August, when the sitters remained motionless for hours, today they would move as the sun moved, avoiding shadows, and they would all be gone by late afternoon.

Buckner went down the steps, angled across the square to Coy's, and entered. Men lined the lunch counter, each one hunched over a thick white china mug of steaming coffee, several with their faces in the newspaper. A few greeted him with brief nods or mumbled "good mornings." Mrs. Coy, behind the counter, already had his cup filled as he swung his left leg over the stool and sat down next to a man in gray wool shirt and trousers, a striped brakeman's hat pushed back on his bald head.

"Mornin', Buck," said the old railroader.

"Mornin', Benny." Buckner sipped carefully at the scalding liquid.

Fred Linderman, down the line, leaned forward and called, "I hear somebody did for old Louis Boyer." Like everyone else in town, he pronounced the name "Louie Booyer." The first Europeans to settle the area had been French, and traces lingered, even after two centuries.

"Somebody's husband finally caught up with him," came a voice from the far end. Nobody bothered to laugh.

"You figure out who done it yet, Buck?" asked Benny, his eyes twinkling.

Buckner shook his head and drank his coffee.

"You will, though, pretty soon," someone said.

"Seems like a waste of time, somehow. Old Louis wasn't worth the powder and ball it would take to shoot him, much less the county money to find out who done it."

"Good body man, though. He fixed up the front end of my Chevrolet that time it run into that telegraph pole up on the Taylor Road. He made it look like new."

"Yeah, but he used to get pretty mean when he got drunk."

The conversation ranged up and down the counter for several minutes, quiet, matter-of-fact observations and opinions, as the coffee-drinkers discussed the many defects and scant few merits of the deceased. Then, as Buckner showed no inclination to participate, the talk shifted gradually to the high school football team's chances this year, quickly tapering off into silence once more. The team's chances apparently were not promising.

Buckner was well into his second cup of coffee when the door opened slowly and Jeff Peck entered. Moving with exquisite care, as though sudden movement or abrupt contact with anything solid would shatter the thin shell that kept him intact, Peck took a seat at the end of the counter and ordered coffee in a rasping whisper.

Buckner picked up his envelope and coffee cup and joined him. He signaled Mrs. Coy for a refill, and waited for her to move back down the line.

"Do you have a cause-of-death form on Boyer?" He tapped the envelope on the counter. "I want to send this report up to Jackson."

"I thought you would be out papering the town with handbills this morning." Peck's face was nearly as white as his hair, and his skin had a rough, grainy look. He was unshaven, and wore a gray overcoat buttoned up to his chin. The cuffs of the once-elegant coat were frayed; the fur on its collar was worn away in spots. Peck's thin body seemed lost in its heavy woolen folds and barely strong enough to keep it from collapsing to the floor.

Buckner grinned. "That would be dereliction of duty, what with this murder to investigate."

"You're not much of a politician," Peck observed. "Not that it matters much."

"What do you mean?"

"Harding's going to win," he muttered. "Cox doesn't stand a chance. If Wilson backs him one hundred percent, he gets tarred with that brush: you know, the war, the draft, the League of Nations. And if Wilson doesn't back him, it looks like the party leadership doesn't support its own candidate. Like I said, Cox doesn't stand a chance."

"Maybe, at the national level," Buckner said. "But this county hasn't gone Republican since Reconstruction."

"I've heard that." Peck let out a dry wheeze that might have been a laugh. "But it's going to this time. You watch."

"Folks around here are still pretty mad about the war," Buckner acknowledged.

"It's a kind of a symbol," Peck said. "A bunch of other things get hooked up to it. Hard times, conscription, the food and coal shortages, hell, even the flu epidemic." He ticked them off his fingers. Some ten million people had died in the Great War, and another twenty million in the Spanish influenza pandemic that raced around the world in the months after the Armistice.

"People around here really hated all that," Peck continued. And it all kind of gets rolled up into a ball and laid at the feet of the Democratic Party. It doesn't make sense, from a rational point of view, but it might just cost you your job."

"But the women are voting now," Buckner pointed out. "That could change things."

"Horse manure," Peck observed without animation. "They won't be any smarter or any more principled than men have been for a hundred and fifty years. Anybody counting on women to rescue us from our own greed and stupidity is doomed to disappointment."

"Do you have the cause-of-death form?" Buckner prodded. He always felt outclassed whenever he discussed politics with Peck. Besides, he had business to attend to.

As though every motion pained him, Peck reached cautiously into the inside pocket of his coat and took out several pieces of paper. He examined each one carefully, unfolding it with precise, delicate motions and looking at it, then refolding it and selecting another. Finally, he found the one he wanted, and handed it to Buckner. Buckner glanced quickly at it. Peck's findings were written with a shaking hand, but they were legible. Louis Boyer died as a result of "multiple blows to the head with a piece of pipe found near the body with decedent's hair and blood on it." The space for time of death indicated sometime between midnight and noon Friday, the twenty-second.

"How do you figure the time of death?"

Peck shrugged cautiously. "I combined careful evaluations of air temperature at the site, body temperature taken rectally in my office yesterday, post-mortem lividity, rigor. Then I put them all together and guessed."

"Science," sneered Buckner.

"Art," the doctor corrected, almost in a whisper.

Buckner nodded and folded up the form and slid it into his envelope. He licked the flap and sealed it shut, then slid off his stool. As he reached into his pocket for a dime, he looked at Peck.

"Want to walk this over to the post office with me?"

Peck said nothing, but eased off his stool and followed Buckner out the door.

The post office was in the block behind the town hall. Neither man spoke during the short walk. Buckner pushed his envelope through the "Out of Town" slot in the door.

"Where are you going now?" Buckner asked when they had returned to the street.

"About time for my morning bracer," answered Peck. To prove his point, he took out a watch, opened it, closed it, and returned it to his pocket without looking at it.

Buckner nodded. "I've got to pay a call on a lady in the matter of Louis Boyer's past. You want to join me?"

"Who's the lady."

"Antonia Clay."

"Not young."

"No," Buckner shook his head. "Not young."

They walked in silence as Peck considered Buckner's offer.

"I guess so," said Peck.

"Too late to change your mind," Buckner answered, stopping at a quiet corner. "We're there." He pointed to a large, two-story, rambling house. Every inch of paint seemed to peel and flake, as though the surface were diseased. One corner of the porch sagged into an untrimmed yard littered with leaves from a large maple near the sidewalk. Several windows lacked panes, and squares of cardboard, cut to fit, took their places.

Peck followed Buckner onto the porch. Buckner knocked and a hard-faced, round woman in her forties opened the door.

"Ya?" She pulled her lips back in a smile, showing bad teeth. Her eyes gleamed flatly, like the sun off rolled steel. Her hair hung in two long braids almost to her waist. She wore a checked housecoat and slippers over a body shaped like a sugar hogshead.

"I'm Deputy Sheriff Buckner, this is Doctor Peck. We'd like to speak with Antonia Clay."

The woman peered closely at the two men for a minute, then said, "This way," she said, her German accent thick and heavy. She showed them into the front parlor. "Please make yourselves comfortable. I'll get Miss Clay."

The room was dark, with rose-patterned wallpaper and a blood red carpet, thin as a sheet, covering the center of the floor. The only light came from a large window that looked into the side yard. A long sofa upholstered in mud brown stood against one wall, with two dark wooden chairs nearby. There was no other furniture, and the room looked bare and forbidding. The stone fireplace contained only dust.

"Like an ice box in here," said Peck.

Buckner nodded.

In a few minutes, a woman appeared in the doorway.

"Good day, gentlemen. I am Antonia Clay. How may I help you?" She had a high, melodious voice that seemed to come from a much younger woman, though Buckner guessed her age to be between fifty and sixty. She wore an old, shiny, black wool dress that brushed the toes of her buttoned shoes. Over the dress, she wore a heavy black cardigan that was out at the elbows and frayed at the cuffs. She wore woolen gloves with the ends of the fingers cut off. She either wore a wig or dyed her hair, because it was coal black and fell in startling, perfect Mary Pickford ringlets to her shoulders. Her face was layered with white powder, her eyes darkly outlined in black, and bright rouge spotted her lips and cheeks.

She sat at one end of the sofa and thrust her hands into the pockets of her sweater. Buckner introduced himself and Peck, and then pulled up one of the chairs to sit opposite her. Peck remained standing by the window, as though seeking light and warmth.

"I would like to ask you some questions about Louis Boyer, Miss Clay," Buckner began.

She frowned slightly at the name but said nothing. Buckner thought he detected a tinge of real color under the powder.

"First, Miss Clay, I should tell you that Mister Boyer is dead. Doctor Peck and I found his body on the floor of his shop yesterday."

Antonia Clay's bright red mouth compressed into a hard, thin line, and it was a long time before she spoke. Finally, she shook her head, once, with finality.

"Drank himself to death at last," she said. "Well, I can't say I'm surprised."

"Somebody caved in his skull with a piece of pipe," Peck said evenly. He seemed to be feeling better, Buckner noticed.

The woman's eyes rounded with surprise. "Murdered?" She did not seem to think it the unlikeliest fate in the world for Louis Boyer.

"Yes," said Buckner. "I'm afraid so."

"Who did it?"

"That's what we're working on, Miss Clay. I understand you once knew him and his family, and I was hoping you might tell me something about him."

"That was a long time ago," she said, and then fell silent.

"When, exactly?" prompted Buckner.

"I had just gone to work as a switchboard operator for the telephone company." She straightened up and withdrew her hands from her pockets. In one, she held a package of cigarettes. She shook one out, put the end in her mouth, and lighted it with the lighter in her other hand. She inhaled deeply and exhaled with a satisfied sigh. "I used to roll my own," she said in response to Buckner's look of surprise. He had known some very daring French girls who smoked, but few women in America; certainly none his mother's age.

"I met Louis Boyer at a dance at the Grange Hall," she continued. "My sister made me go, Lucille this was, she died of the flu last year. I didn't want to go, but she dragged me along. I knew almost everyone there, of course, especially the young men. Had known them all my life. That's why I didn't want to go, I guess. But that's what made Louis Boyer so damned attractive. He was new, you see. He was also the best dancer in the place. But more than anything else, he was the handsomest man I have ever seen in my life, right down to this very day. Not pretty handsome, you understand, but wild handsome, like a stud horse in springtime. He had a dangerous spark in his eyes and a go-to-hell smile. When he walked into that room, God knows from where, he seemed to take it, us, all in, with a look that said he'd seen better, but we'd do for now. I swear you could hear every girl on the dance floor let out a sigh."

She laughed. "And the boys grind their teeth. They never stood a chance against Louis. None of us did. The boys were mostly just too familiar. Louis was older, and he was the mysterious stranger. They were trying to be the kind of young men our mothers approved of, at least when our mothers were around. Louis was the kind our mothers warned us about. That made him all the more attractive."

She shook her head and laughed again and puffed at her cigarette. The ashes fell ignored onto her lap.

"And he picked you," Buckner said.

"Yes. I was the first. I suppose there's something in that." She thought a moment, then added, "The first in Corinth, anyway."

"Did he ever say where he was from?"

"Sort of. He mentioned Washington County, I believe. It didn't really matter. After a while, his wife showed up with a couple of kids and set up housekeeping, first above a shop he rented in town, later, when that failed, in the back of that shop he bought up on the Jackson Road. Not that they slowed him down any. He seemed to do whatever he damn well pleased, and, if she objected, it never changed him. The only effect his family had, as near as I could tell, is that it made him extremely careful, you know, with his outside activities."

"Why?"

"He didn't want any more children, Deputy. Not at all. No, sir. Said he had plenty. So he always 'took precautions,' as they say."

Buckner, embarrassed, looked down at the floor.

"Condoms?" asked Peck in a clinical tone, ignoring Buckner's modesty.

"Yes," she said casually, exhaling a cloud of smoke that she brushed away with a gloved hand.

"You said you thought you were the first," Buckner went on. "Do you, ah, know who came later?"

"Some of them, yes. One or two of them quite well."

"Would you tell me their names?"

"No."

"I assure you, Mrs. Clay . . ."

"Miss."

"Miss Clay, that I will keep the names in strictest confidence." She shook her head.

"Miss Clay, this is not just curiosity on my part. The man was killed. My job is to find out who killed him."

Antonia Clay shrugged and tossed her cigarette into the empty fireplace. At once, she took out another and lighted it. "I really don't care about that, Deputy. You see, as much fun as Louis was, and that was a good deal, he really was a bad man, just as our mothers had told us. He thought of women as property. He'd enjoy one for a while, a few weeks or months, then cast her aside, and after that it was as though she did not exist. If he met her again, or if she spoke to him or wrote him long, pleading letters in which she made a complete fool of herself, he simply did not respond. He had no regard at all for . . . for the feelings of anyone but himself. And I'm not sure he liked himself very much, either. He seemed to need to mistreat people to make himself feel better. So, as the years went by, he just mistreated more and more people. He drove his wife away, and his children. When there was no one left to mistreat, he turned on himself until he, too, was ruined. And now you want to go talk to a bunch of old ladies like me, dredge up what I feel sure are painful memories for them, just to find out who put Louis Boyer out of his misery. There's really no point to that, Deputy."

"He seems to have enjoyed considerable success for so unpleasant a man," said Peck.

"Yes," she answered, thinking. "But, as I said, he was so very attractive. And he could be charming if it got him what he wanted. He fooled a lot of people, some for a long time, others only briefly. But, eventually, the charm began to wear off."

"But whoever killed him . . ."

"Did him a favor by hastening what must have been a long, agonizing process for a man who didn't have the moral courage to put a bullet in his brain."

"What about his children?" Peck asked from his spot by the window. "You said he drove them away."

"I don't really know what happened to any of them, just rumors. The family broke up, that's for sure, but it was after my time."

"Why would a man like that bother with a family anyway?" Buckner asked. "Wouldn't they just get in his way."

"Oh, a man like that wants to have his cake and eat it, too, Deputy. He can have a place in the community, someone to keep house, children to pass on his name, and he can have his good times as well. Something a woman can't do, you see." Her voice was bitter. "Once a woman is tarred with that brush, once she has fallen, it becomes almost impossible to find a decent man who will even give her a second look. All they want is one thing."

"His wife left him eventually," Buckner said.

"Victoria, yes. Some time in ninety-five or six, I believe. She went to live with her family in Jefferson City. I suppose I can't blame her. And then, Louis and his son, Albert, didn't get along any too well. It got worse as the boy got older. Finally, Louis sent him off to live with his brother over in Cape Girardeau. The girl left not too long after that, Charlotte, her name was, but I don't remember where. She just ran off, like her ma."

"You weren't seeing Louis anymore by that time?"

"No," she answered firmly.

"How did you happen to keep track of his family?"

"I didn't keep track of them, Deputy. I just heard, over the years."

"A telephone operator must hear a lot," Peck said. "About a lot of people."

"That's right, Doctor. Even when you'd rather not. People go on and on, say the most awful things about other people, about themselves, too. They never think that somebody might be listening. But people used to tell me things, too, on purpose. It was like they didn't want to seem to be gossiping, so they'd tell me. I guess it was like the Catholics when they confess—you know, talk to somebody through a screen, somebody they can't see. The telephone was like that. Anyway, I heard more things about more people in this town than you can ever imagine. But I keep it to myself, I can promise you that."

"Do you know if the son is still in Cape Girardeau?"

"I never heard different."

"You sure you won't tell us the names of any of the other women Louis Boyer kept company with?"

"Yes, I am." She smiled. "If that's all, I have to get ready for church." She added, "Baptist, by the way; in case you were wondering. Hard Shell."

"Presbyterian," said Buckner. "Southern church."

"Doubter," muttered Peck. "Unorganized."

From the look she gave the two of them, Buckner could not tell which of them she regarded as the greater sinner.

"Well, then," Buckner said, getting up. "I guess that's all. We won't trouble you any more. Thank you for your help."

He and Peck left Antonia Clay standing in the cold, dark room with her hands jammed hard down into the pockets of her cardigan, a freshly lighted cigarette sticking out of the corner of her scarlet mouth. The smoke, curling up in a thin, blue ribbon, made her squint one black-rimmed eye, so that she looked as though she were winking at them. Maybe she was, Buckner thought, as they walked down the front steps and into the sunlight.

"I'll bet she spent most of her time listening to folks' conversations," said Peck. "And without being asked."

"Maybe," Buckner said. "You know," he went on, "this is the damndest town."

"What do you mean?" Peck seemed truly curious.

"When I was growing up, we all thought Jackson was a big city; St. Louis, Chicago, places like that, well, they were beyond big. But Corinth, hell, we just thought Corinth was nothing more than a wide spot in the road that and full of hillbillies to boot."

"Maybe it was, back then." Peck fell in step with Buckner, and the two headed back to the center of town.

"Maybe. But, what do you figure the population is now, three thousand?"

"About that, with another thousand in surrounding farms and places like Pekin; add a thousand for all the miners and their families up in Taylor." Peck had treated patients all across the southern end of the county.

"Yeah, that's about what I figure, too. Five thousand people. Still not a lot, really, but in the three years I've been here, I've found out there's more going on here than you might think. Every kind of crime, for instance, robbery, extortion, obviously murder. And now it's beginning to look like the local chief of police could teach Boss Tweed a thing or two about corruption."

"What are you talking about? Chief Bushyhead? Corinth's sainted police chief?" Peck's sarcasm had a bitter edge to it.

"Oh, just some rumors I keep hearing, stories about the city police riding shotgun on bootleggers' trucks coming down from St. Louis, collecting protection money."

"Does any of that surprise you?" Peck asked with a light sneer in his voice. "What the hell did you expect? You think people are going to be paragons of virtue just because they live in a small town?"

"I'm not really sure." Buckner hoped to avoid the doctor's cynicism.

"I am. I think you spent too much time in the army. Living like that cuts you off from normal society; you get strange notions about it."

"Oh, bullshit," Buckner responded sharply. Peck had hit a tender spot. His sister had often berated him for "running out on the family," in her words, when they needed him the most. His protests that he had sent the bulk of his pay home did not deflect Martha Jane's anger.

"I'm serious. About half the professional military men I met during my brief stay with them thought civilians were ignorant clods barely worth defending, at best, and at worst, dangerous anti-military pacifists and Red revolutionaries. The other half were like you. They had half-baked notions of Jeffersonian yeomen farmers and democratic virtues that it was their job to protect. But their ideas were all based on ignorance."

"You got a point to make?" Buckner demanded, feeling himself grow angry. "Or are you just going to keep on bullyragging the military?"

"I do indeed have a point. You need to start thinking like a civilian again. If you don't, you aren't going to be able to see these people as they really are. And if you can't do that, you aren't going to be able to do your job properly."

"I've done all right so far." His voice was hard now.

"That's because so far you haven't come up against anything really tough." The doctor paused. "Until now. What're you going to do about this killing?"

"I don't know. Go to Cape and try to find the son, I guess."

"Why? Why start there?"

"Where should I start? Who should I talk to? The son, Albert, is the only solid lead I've got."

"There's the wife," Peck reminded him. "Antonia Clay said she left for Jefferson City."

"If I don't get anywhere with the son, I'll try her next."

"Keeping it in the family, so to speak."

"That's where these things usually are," Buckner said, remembering the living quarters behind Boyer's shop. "After you left yesterday, I stayed around for a while, hung around back in that shed where they all must have lived, right on top of each other."

"Not for long, it seems," said Peck.

"Long enough, I think." They had reached the town hall and stopped there. "It was like an animal's den. It had a bad smell to it, and I think it had smelled that way for a long time." He changed the subject. "You want to drive down to Cape Girardeau with me?"

Peck looked at him. "You planning on discovering any dead bodies down there?"

"No. Why?" The clock above their heads struck noon.

"Because I have some drinking to do. Despite your best efforts to save me."

"I'm not interested in saving you," Buckner protested.

"Whatever you say, Deputy. Good day."

Buckner went into the building and down to the police department, stopping at the booking desk. Sergeant Givens sat at the desk absorbed in the Sunday funny papers. One index finger traced the dialogue between Maggie and Jiggs.

The county had yet to determine that the Corinth substation of the sheriff's office needed its own telephone, so Buckner had to make do with the phone belonging to the city police department. He kept a record of his calls and paid for them out of his own pocket, receiving reimbursement from the county later. He tried to keep them to a minimum, not only to save money, but because the telephone sat right on the counter at the booking desk, and anything he said over it became public knowledge.

Buckner took the earpiece from its hook, turned the crank, and told the operator to connect him with the sheriff's office in Jackson. Although Givens continued apparently to be absorbed in the funnies, Buckner could practically feel him listening, so intense was his concentration. After half a minute of clunking and chiming, someone answered.

"This is Buck, in Corinth," he shouted down the line. "Let me talk to the Sheriff." He felt sure the impending election would have brought Sheriff Aubuchon to the office on a Sunday.

"Hi, Buck," came a voice. "Sheriff ain't here. He's out having lunch with the American Legion, trying to convince them they ought to endorse him."

"All right. Let me talk to Jack Rogers."

Rogers was the Undersheriff, Aubuchon's second in command.

"Can't, Buck. He's having lunch with the . . . wait a minute . . . the Associated Women Voters Club of Highland County."

"What!" Buckner's impatience with politics was making him short tempered.

"The Associated Women Voters . . ."

"Okay, I heard you! Who the hell's in charge up there?"

"Well, I guess I am. Sorry, Buck. Election's coming up next

week, you know. You ought to be out doing some campaigning yourself."

"I've got a murder down here!" Buckner shouted angrily. "What am I supposed to do with that?"

Sam Givens kept his eyes glued to the funny papers.

"Take it easy, Buck. No need to holler."

Buckner stood looking at the floor, breathing heavily down his nose, the earpiece in his hand. He put his lips to the mouthpiece.

"All right. Sorry. I'm not yelling at you . . . . Who is this, anyway?"

"Pete. Pete Dickman." Buckner vaguely remembered an impossibly young face with a peach-fuzz moustache and traces of adolescent acne. He began to feel guilty for yelling at the department's newest, least experienced deputy.

"I'm sorry, Pete. Just tell the Sheriff when you see him that I've sent him a report on the killing. He should get it in a couple of days. And tell him I've got to go down to Cape to interview a relative of the deceased. Tell him to call the sheriff over there and let him know I'm coming."

"Right, Buck. Report on the way; call Cape. Anything else? Need anymore handbills?"

"No. Not just yet. Thanks."

He hung up.

Givens looked up from the papers, his finger marking his place, and smiled.

"Working hard on that murder, Sarge?" Every man on the Corinth police department knew Buckner had been in the army, and it amused several of them to use his former rank to try to needle him. Buckner understood fully what they were doing and ignored it.

"Yes," Buckner snapped. He started for his office.

"One thing, Sarge?"

"What's that?"

"Chief wants to see you. Sarge." Givens lingered over the last word, savoring it.

"All right." Buckner, wondering what could have brought Chief Bushyhead to the office on a Sunday, headed down the hall to a door marked "Chief of Police. Knock First." He opened it without knocking and walked in.

The white-haired old man behind the big oak desk glanced up sharply, his look of irritation changing into a beaming smile. City Detective Gerard Harris sat in a chair to the right of the desk. He looked like a man about to get his fondest wish, but he said nothing.

"Howdy, son," said the Chief, his voice rich with cordiality. "Good to see you. Thanks for stopping by."

"Givens said you wanted to see me, Chief." Buckner entered and shut the door.

"Yes. I've spoken to Vincent Marolis, over at the Dew Drop Inn, and he says you barged into his place with hardly a howdy-do and started throwing him around. Detective Harris here was a witness." The Chief managed to sound both saddened and shocked at what he had learned.

Detective Harris frowned sadly and nodded, recalling the unfortunate incident.

"He sure was," Buckner said. "Did Marolis come crying to you?"

"He reported the incident, yes. You know you have no jurisdiction within city limits, son," said Bushyhead, a kindly grandfather forced to rebuke a wayward young favorite. "You're just a regular citizen here in town."

"I was pursuing an investigation, Chief. Marolis got in my way, then he tried to hit me and he missed and fell down, that's all."

"Vincent Marolis is a respected member of the business community here in Corinth, Buck. He was on the verge of swearing out a complaint against you for simple assault." Bushyhead's tone was soft and placating, almost a whine. It set Buckner's teeth on edge. "I managed to talk him out of that, but he's not happy, no sir, not a bit. We're going to overlook the whole thing this time, son. Try not to let it happen again, though, all right? If towns like Corinth are going to survive, we're going to need investment and leadership from the cities." He chuckled. "Won't do our future any good if you go beating up the kind of men we're trying to attract. Now, I've known Sheriff Aubuchon a long time and I've always got along real good with his people down here. Things have gone real smooth. I believe Elmer would like to keep it that way, especially when he's running for reelection."

Buckner began to feel his neck get hot.

"Look, Chief," he said, his voice tight as he fought to control it. "I don't know what arrangements you've got with the Dew Drop Inn, and I don't particularly care. But you tell Vincent Marolis that I am not on the payroll, do you understand? I go where my work takes me, and if that takes me through him, or Tubby, here," he gestured toward Harris, "or you too, if it comes to that, then so be it."

The Chief smiled. A bland, placid kindliness spread across his face. His soft, white hair encircled his head like a fluffy halo, revealing the yellowing, spotted skin beneath.

"Now, son," he soothed. "You don't have to get in an uproar over this. It was just a misunderstanding, that's all. But you do need to be careful what you say and where you step around here. You'd have a pretty hard time doing your job without help from my department."

"Your officers, Chief, have never helped me worth a nickel."

"Oh, it's not what they do that matters, Buck; it's what they don't do." Bushyhead was still smiling. "Some of those boys are pretty high-spirited, and would like nothing better than take you out behind the barn for a good talking-to. But more important is what I let you do." His hollow, self-satisfied smile broadened and his tone softened even more, while his eyes glittered with malice. "Just take care where you go throwing your weight around is all I'm saying. You don't want to run up against my bad side, son, because if you do, then you'll think you stumbled into a hornet's nest, and even Elmer Aubuchon won't be able to help you."

Buckner focused intently on Bushyhead. The white-haired old man's smiling face infuriated him. "Chief," he said, his voice quivering, "I've been threatened by professionals, and to be honest, you just don't carry the weight."

Detective Harris laughed. Chief Bushyhead, all forgiveness and understanding, just smiled and made no response at all. Buckner turned and walked out.

Well done, he thought as he went down the hall. On the eve of an important election, in the middle of a serious investigation, you've just made an enemy of a very powerful man.

He shook his head in self-disgust. Still, he couldn't let that deter him. The people of the county paid him to, among other things, solve crimes, and so he would solve this one. He had seen political rivalries in the army and knew the crippling effect they could have on unit effectiveness. That experience made him even more inclined to concentrate on his mission above all else. He would try to stay off sensitive toes if he could, but if not, then he would deal with the consequences later. He walked on.

* * *

Cape Girardeau, Missouri, lies near the apex of a vast delta that spreads south to the Gulf Coast plain. San Antonio, New Orleans, and Mobile lie along the base of this expanse of rich alluvial soil, and Cape Girardeau has more in common with them, and the towns in between, than with up-country places like Corinth, barely one hundred miles to the north and west. With all its French and Spanish ancestry, Cape Girardeau was a southern place, with a population made up largely of people as black as the soil they worked but seldom owned. The cotton they planted and cultivated, picked and baled, was owned by companies with offices in St. Louis, New Orleans, and New York, with stockholders as far away as England. The Delta made many people wealthy, but all of them were white, and few of them lived there.

Buckner left straight from town hall. He drove through Flat River and Farmington and Fredericktown, where church bells were still ringing. He drove for three hours, with stops to fill the radiator from the five-gallon can in the boot. The sun rose high and the day grew warmer. The road twisted through dense forests and past spare, hill country farms, but led always lower and lower, until it broke through the last stand of trees and emerged onto the open bottomland. A few minutes later, he was driving through the outskirts of the town.

The first place Buckner went was the county courthouse high on a hill on Broadway near Spanish Street, overlooking the vast expanse of the Mississippi. It was closed. People were leaving church now. One of them paused long enough to direct him around back of the courthouse, to the sheriff's office. This was a squat building of gray limestone blocks and narrow, barred windows. The windows reminded Buckner of firing slits, and the place looked like a defensive strongpoint between the ornate columned court house and the balconied Merchant's and Planter's Hotel down the street, looking as though it had been transplanted from New Orleans. Since the incumbent was also running for reelection, the Sheriff's Office was open for business. A deputy at the booking desk sent Buckner to a door on the right marked "Ralph W. Polk, Sheriff." He knocked and entered.

A gray-haired man with a square jaw and a trim, Black Jack Pershing moustache sat at a wide, gleaming mahogany desk. The desk held only a telephone and an open file that the man was reading as Buckner entered.

"With you in a minute," the man said pleasantly without looking up. He waved Buckner toward a chair.

Buckner sat. A row of file cabinets lined one entire wall. On the opposite wall hung a large painting of black men, naked to the waist, loading bales of cotton onto a stern-wheeler.

At least I have a window, Buckner thought as he looked at the man's neat gray suit and vest, carefully knotted red tie and gleaming white shirt and collar. Gold cufflinks winked at his thin, almost hairless wrists as he closed the file, pushed it to one side, and smiled at Buckner with thin lips and cold gray eyes.

"Elmer Aubuchon called a while ago and told me you'd be coming down to pay us a visit. Nice of you to stop by."

"Always check in with the commanding officer first," said Buckner, returning the smile.

The man nodded. "Elmer said you're ex-cavalry. I spent some time in the Rough Riders, myself. Course, we were just volunteers. And we fought the war on foot anyway." He chuckled.

"So did I, in France."

"Yes. I think we've seen the end of the cavalry. Machine guns make it sort of impractical, don't you think?"

"That, plus barbed wire and trenches. And armored vehicles." Buckner did not like talking about the war and wanted very much to get off this topic.

"Yes, tanks. Did you get the chance to see any in action?"

"Not up close," Buckner admitted. He was home recovering from his wound by the time tanks began operating on the Western Front. "But you're right. There won't be any cavalry in the next war."

"Too bad, in a way. All that heavy machinery makes the whole thing more inhuman, somehow."

Buckner nodded but said nothing. What was it before, he wondered, a church picnic?

"So what can I do for you? Elmer said you've got a murder you're looking into."

"Yes. Man named Louis Boyer. I understand his son, Albert, lives here."

Sheriff Polk opened a drawer and pulled out a city directory. He turned pages and traced down a column of names with a long forefinger.

"Right," he said. "I know him. Albert Boyer. Owns an automobile body shop on River Street." He read the address to Buckner.

Buckner thanked the man and stood. Polk also got up and held out his hand. As they shook, he asked, "You going right over there? He lives over the shop, so he's probably open today."

"Thought I would. I want to talk to him and get back tonight if I can."

"You want me to send somebody along with you?"

"No, thanks. I'm just here to talk."

"Albert's not easy to talk to." He looked Buckner up and down and smiled. "But you look big enough to take care of yourself."

"Is he going to give me trouble?" Buckner asked.

The man shrugged. "Depends on how drunk he got last night."

Buckner nodded. "Thanks for the warning."

The sheriff waved it away. "Give Elmer my regards next time you see him."

"I will."

"He campaigning hard for re-election?"

"I guess so. He's never in the office, anyway."

"Tell him not to worry. The Republicans haven't taken Highland County since Reconstruction. He hasn't got a thing to worry about."

"I'll tell him," Buckner promised. "But I don't think it'll do any good. He campaigns like his life depends on it." He put his hat on and left.

River Street, as Buckner suspected, paralleled the Mississippi just west of the levee that protected the town from all but the worst floods. Those happened often enough, he knew, and were prominent features of the town's folklore. Local residents boasted of the worst ones, proud of disasters confronted and survived. Several buildings had small signs, each with a date, placed at the different high-water marks. Some were well above the first floor.

Buckner drove south, past the edge of town, where homes and businesses thinned out, to be replaced by rail sidings, warehouses, shacks, and junk-infested lots. Albert Boyer's shop was the bottom half of a two-story clapboard with a pronounced list toward the river. It sat surrounded by trucks and automobiles, some badly battered, rusted out, smashed, others looking fresh and shiny as new ten-cent pieces. Evidently, Albert was doing much better than his father had been doing, at least at the end.

Buckner pulled into the yard in front of the big, open double doors and stopped. As he pulled back on the hand brake, a young man with midnight black skin came out wiping his hands on a red rag. He glanced at Buckner, but his attention was on the Ford, assessing it judiciously, experience in his eyes. He ambled over, still looking at the Ford, his expression becoming puzzled.

"You want a paint job?" he asked.

"No," Buckner answered. "Can you . . . ?"

"You got a dent back there where I can't see it?"

"No." Buckner stepped down from the car. "Can you tell me where I can find Albert Boyer?"

"Maybe. Who wants to know?" The young man now stared at Buckner with narrowed eyes. He stuck the rag in the hip pocket of his overalls and let his hands hang loose at his sides, his hands curving into casual fists.

"I do," Buckner said. "I'm the Deputy Sheriff from over in Highland County." He smiled slightly at the young man, standing calmly, waiting for an answer.

The young man frowned and dropped his gaze, glancing toward the interior of the shop. The rag was suddenly in his hands again.

"Inside," he muttered. He turned abruptly and entered the shop.

Buckner thanked his retreating back and followed him. The shop was well lighted. The walls were lined with workbenches, but if there was clutter, Buckner recognized it as the clutter of a busy place. The tools were clean, the metal bright along the working surfaces. The floor was cement, and held only the day's accumulation of dirt. A Hudson roadster sat in the middle of the floor. One fender, badly crumpled, lay on the floor next to its fresh, unpainted replacement. Next to the Hudson, by the wall, another vehicle sat swathed in tarpaulin. Buckner could see only tires.

The young man was alone in the shop. In a corner was a door marked "Office." Buckner went through it. A man sat at a desk, rubbing his eyes with soiled fingertips.

"I told you to knock," he snapped without looking up.

The man was in his mid-thirties, powerfully built and darkly handsome, with a square, cleft chin, and crisp, curly, dark brown hair that spilled in ringlets over a broad, pale forehead. His liquid brown eyes were blood-shot, but thick, dark lashes gave them an almost feminine beauty. His bold, thin nose already showed burst veins. He needed a shave. Buckner could smell the alcohol in his sweat.

"Albert Boyer?" Buckner asked.

"Yeah. What?" The man seemed distracted, lost in contemplation of some unseen world.

Buckner closed the office door. As he did so, he saw the young man with the red rag lifting the new fender onto the roadster. Buckner turned and sat in a chair opposite Boyer.

The office was small and over-heated. Like the shop, everything was carefully ordered and clean. A small trophy on the desk read: "Fourth of July 100 Mile Race," and "Second Place, Albert Boyer."

"I'm Deputy Sheriff Jim Buckner, from over in Corinth," he said. "I'm sorry to have to tell you this, but your father, Louis Boyer, is dead."

Albert Boyer just looked at him, blinking his dark eyes, his distracted expression changed only by a slight lifting of his heavy brows.

"That's it?" he said. "Well, thanks for letting me know." He nodded toward the door. "I'll be seeing you."

"I'm afraid it's not that easy, Mister Boyer. You see, your father was murdered."

Boyer turned in his chair and looked straight at Buckner. The distractedness in his face had not diminished at the question; in fact, it seemed to have increased.

"Murdered?" he said listlessly. "Who'd bother?"

"I don't know," Buckner admitted. "I was hoping you might be able to help me out on that."

"Well, I guess I can. I didn't kill him."

"Thank you. But I was also hoping you might be able to tell me about him, kind of fill in the picture for me. I didn't know your father . . ."

"You're lucky there, Deputy." Albert Boyer gave a grim smile. "I did. Not lately, though. Nor for the past twenty-five years or so. But before that, I knew him as well as I wanted to, and more."

Buckner nodded. "You came here to live with your uncle, didn't you?"

"I didn't come here. My father sent me."

"Did you have any contact with him after that?"

"Some. He sent Henry, my uncle, money for a while; you know, for my keep."

"Did he visit you?"

"Once or twice."

"You ever visit him?"

Boyer shook his head.

"Write him?"

"No," Boyer answered impatiently. "I'm not much on writing letters. And he was too busy with his fancy women."

"Women?"

"Yeah. He had a whole string of them."

"Do you remember any in particular?"

"Just the one he had that year. The year everything went to hell." Boyer seemed almost to be speaking to himself.

Buckner watched him and said nothing.

"He was mostly living with her full-time by the time he sent me away. He'd come home every now and then to catch up on his work, though he didn't have a lot of that by then. Just enough to keep us in food and him in booze, and to support her.

"Not enough to buy a decent house for us to live in, or some new clothes so we didn't have to go to school looking so shabby. But after a few days, he'd go off again. Not that having him around was so wonderful. He worked during the day, then at night he'd get drunk and knock us around. My mother, too, even when she was pregnant. How could she have stood him enough to . . ." He shook his head as if to dislodge the thought.

"Who was she?" Buckner asked softly. "The woman?"

"I followed him once, on my bike." Boyer laughed bitterly at that. "Just a dumb kid on his stupid bicycle, tagging along after his dad while the old man goes to get his ashes hauled." He was quiet for a minute, then spoke again. "I followed him right into town to the boarding house where she lived. I stopped outside and just waited there. I don't know why. But he must have seen me through the window. Anyway, he came out and told me to go on back home. I asked him to come home, too, but he just backhanded me upside the head and laughed and told me to stay the hell away from him. So I left. But I went back plenty of other times. Sometimes I just rode past and went home without stopping. Sometimes I stayed. I hid so he wouldn't see me. I watched them go out to have dinner in town, then come back. I watched 'til I saw the lights go out."

Boyer's voice was lower now, and Buckner realized that he had nearly stopped breathing in order to hear.

"What was her name?" he finally asked.

"Angelina Robideaux. That time. I heard later, after he dropped her, she married that old Jew that owned the grain elevator out in Pekin. He had others, though, after her. And before, too, I guess. It's what finally drove my mother away."

"When did your mother leave?"

"After the baby was born, she just never got her strength back. The way we lived, it started to make her, I don't know, kind of crazy. We all lived in that one room, you see. For a while, it wasn't so bad, when it was the four of us. But then the baby came, and she was colicky, I remember, and cried that whole summer long. I remember thinking for a while that my father stayed away just to get some sleep. Anyway, I was ten that year, ninety-six it was, but my sister Charlotte had already turned twelve, and she was, you know, growing up, shy about herself. It was hard for her, all of us, living in that one room.

"Anyhow, everything went to hell that fall. My mother had been taking in washing to have some money, you see, but he put an end to that. Then she just took off one day. We got home from school and the old man was in the shop working on a buckboard for some farmer or other. We could hear the baby crying and my sister went around back to see what she wanted. I watched the old man work for a while. He was a pretty good body man, I'll say that for him. Then I went around back. Charlotte was feeding the baby a bottle. She said she'd found her with her diaper all wet and filthy; the bed too. I asked after our mother, but she didn't know, so I went back around to the front and asked the old man where she was."

Boyer fell silent, his eyes wet and far away.

"What did he say?" Buckner prompted softly.

"He just looked at me for a long time, hard, as hard as I ever remember, then he said she went back to her people in Arkansas."

"How did she go? Train?"

"I asked him that. He said she walked into town. He figured she must've taken the train, though he said he didn't know where the hell she got the money. Anyway, she said not to follow her, none of us. She was through with us all."

"Had he tried to stop her?"

"I guess not, though he used to knock her around pretty good whenever he wanted to. He said if she was done with us, then we were done with her and he didn't want to hear her name mentioned in the house again. So we never did, around him, but my sister and me used to talk about her."

"You never saw her again?"

"No."

"Letters?"

Boyer shook his head.

"What happened after that?"

"Well, we tried to get by, me and Charlotte. She took care of the baby and I tried to take care of her. Course, we both quit school. I took to going through the old man's trouser pockets at night whenever he was home and asleep. I didn't get much, but I was able to buy food. I hunted and trapped for meat and sold the hides and furs, did odd jobs in town. We didn't do too badly, either, for a while. Then my sister left, too. Told me she just couldn't stand it anymore and took off."

"Where to?"

"I don't know. She wouldn't say." He was silent for a time.

Buckner nodded. His own sister had done the same thing when life at home had become too much for her. And they couldn't be the only ones. The city—St. Louis, Kansas City, Memphis, Little Rock, but mainly St. Louis—drew them, sucking the youth, the life, out of places like Corinth. He wondered if they found shelter there.

"And you haven't heard from her since?"

"No. Not once." His anger grew. "We were doing all right, the three of us. We could've made it, we *were* making it. But he ruined it all."

The two men were silent for a long time. Buckner could hear a hammer tapping on metal out in the shop. He was sweating from the heat in the office. Finally, he asked another question.

"So your mother left, then your sister, is that right?"

"Yeah."

"Then what?"

"Not too long after that, he brought me here to live with his brother, Henry. He lived over on Pacific." Boyer gestured off to the west. "He put me to work here in his shop, to teach me the trade the same way both of them had learned it, fixing wagons and carriages, then automobiles later because more people started using them. I worked here part time and went to school up to the eighth grade. Henry made me, said I couldn't run a business without knowing how to write and do sums. Then I worked here full-time after that. That was in 1900."

"How did that turn out?"

"Pretty good, I guess. Henry was a lot better than the old man, I can tell you that. He was a hard man: worked hard and expected me to do the same. But he never got drunk—he was death on booze—and he never knocked me around. Except when he caught me drinking. He was just as good a body man as my father, and a hell of a lot better teacher. He taught me everything. Then, when he died a couple years ago, he up and willed me the shop. So I guess I've got no complaints."

"What happened to the baby?"

"I never heard," he said with a shrug. "My father just dumped me here, never explained anything at all; I heard he dumped her with somebody."

"No other family?"

"Not that I know of. I guess I'm the last of the line."

"No wife and children?"

"That part of your investigation?"

"No," Buckner admitted.

Boyer nodded. "No, no family of any kind. Family just doesn't seem to be part of my life, I guess."

"What about the boy out there?"

"William? Hell, I'm not related to him!"

"No, but he looked like he was ready to fight me when he thought I was here to make trouble for you."

Boyer laughed. "I taken him on last year right off the county youth farm. He's been in and out of trouble for years. He cut up another boy in town when he was thirteen, but he got time off for good behavior, providing somebody would be willing to give him a job, teach him a trade. He lives with his aunt and uncle here in town now. Lawyer up at the courthouse that I've done some work for asked me if I'd give him a job, and I said yes. I guess I'm passing it along."

"Where were you on Friday?"

"That when it was done?"

"Yes," Buckner admitted, adding, "That is part of my investigation."

Boyer nodded. "I was here all day."

"When did you open up?"

"Six. Closed after dark. Me and the boy were working on a Chevrolet that had got rear-ended by a Dodge and I wanted to finish it up. I don't recall that we even stopped for supper."

"I guess he'll bear that out?"

Boyer got up and went to the door. "Come here a minute, will you?" he called. The boy appeared in the doorway, wiping his hands on the red rag. "Tell him what we did last Friday."

The boy turned his sullen gaze on Buckner. "You the police." It was a statement of fact.

"Yes," Buckner admitted. "I told you that. Deputy Sheriff in Corinth."

"Never been there," the boy said, as though it were a remote and uncivilized corner of the globe he had heard of and intended never to visit.

"Last Friday," Boyer prompted.

The boy glanced at Boyer, then at Buckner. "We worked on the back end of that Chevrolet."

"All day?" Buckner asked.

The boy nodded. "That all?" he asked sullenly.

"Yes, thank you," said Buckner.

"I'll be along in a bit," Boyer said. "We're most done here." The boy went back to work and Boyer turned to Buckner with a slight smile. "He doesn't think much of the police."

"Yes. I could see that."

"The story is that his daddy used to make shine up in the hills, and the state revenue people went up in there to burn him out and he got caught in the fire. His mamma died a year later."

"That'd do it," Buckner admitted. He got to his feet and joined Boyer in the doorway. "I guess that's all for now, Mister Boyer. Thank you for your help."

The two men shook hands and Buckner started across the shop floor and out to his auto, leaving the two in the shop exchanging glances and watching his retreating back.

Buckner drove back into town. He turned left and parked in front of a small drug store that advertised "Hot Coffee." Inside, the place was decked out like an ice cream parlor, with jailers and policemen from the courthouse sitting on white-painted iron chairs, their knees tucked under tiny tables with checked cloths. An old couple in church clothes shared ice cream sodas. They all looked like grownups who had wandered into a child's birthday party.

"Deputy! Join us."

Buckner saw the sheriff and a man in a khaki uniform sitting at a small table. He went over and sat down.

The sheriff waved over a young girl in checked gingham with a white apron.

"What can I get you?" she asked Buckner with a smile.

"I just came in for a cup of coffee before I head home. Black, no sugar."

"Can I buy you supper?" asked the sheriff.

"No, thanks. It'll make me sleepy on the drive home."

"Just be sure you don't drive off the road till you're over the county line," said the other man. His badge identified him as a deputy sheriff.

"You get anything out of Albert?" the sheriff asked. He turned to the deputy. "Deputy Buckner's here to talk to Albert Boyer about who killed his daddy."

"Somebody killed your paw?" the deputy asked; he sounded shocked, but his eyes twinkled.

"Boyer's daddy," said the sheriff. Buckner had the feeling of being in the middle of a well-rehearsed routine.

"Yeah," said the deputy. "Always check the kinfolk first."

The girl brought Buckner his coffee.

"I'm not sure how to take him," Buckner said.

"Was Boyer sober?" asked the deputy.

"Yes, but by the look of him, he wasn't last night."

"I expect not. Nor for many a night before."

"His father was a drunk," said Buckner.

"Something like that will run in a family," agreed the sheriff.

"Yes," said the deputy. "But I've seen it where the son of a drunk will be a real iron-clad teetotaler, too."

"Not this time," said the sheriff. "Albert's all right, and he's a good body man, but he drinks a whole lot. And he can be a pretty mean drunk." The deputy nodded agreement.

"Drove his wife to leave him," the deputy added. "Took the kids and went back to her people in Poplar Bluff."

"He said he didn't have a family," said Buckner.

"Not anymore, he doesn't," answered the sheriff. "He'd get drunk of an evening, and if he didn't get in a fight in town and spend the night in jail, he'd go home and knock his wife around."

Buckner nodded. Some things did indeed run in families, he thought. He also remembered the series of glances that had passed between Boyer and his employee. Were they lying to him about being in the shop on Friday?

He finished his coffee and reached into his pocket for money. The sheriff shoved a palm at him.

"Professional courtesy," he said, and called over his shoulder: "Put the coffee on my tab, Elsie."

Elsie, behind the counter, winked at Buckner. "Sure thing, Sheriff," she said.

"Much obliged," Buckner said, and went out.

The drive home, uphill most of the way, took longer than the drive down. He missed supper again, so he ate an apple, drank some milk and went to bed.

MONDAY, OCTOBER 25

ON MONDAY MORNING, Buckner began visiting the other body shops that served Corinth and the southern end of Highland County. There were three. At two of them, Louis Boyer was known only as a violent drunk. The third was "Dan's Auto Repair." It was just off the town square, not two hundred yards from his office. Dan Farmer, the owner, met him at the door. He was a handsome, smiling young man in a suit and a fresh white shirt. He did not have a speck of grease on him. Even his three employees, who bustled constantly while Buckner was talking with their boss, wore freshly laundered overalls. The shop floor was spotless.

Farmer had little to say about Louis Boyer.

"He does—did, now, I guess—a few jobs for those old boys that farm out that way, some of those ridgerunners down by the county line, too; mostly fellows he's known for years. And he did mostly wagons, with a few trucks; almost no autos. Me? I'm strictly autos. No money in wagons and too damned little in trucks, but if you can keep them automobiles looking new, your fortune's made." He smiled at the prospect.

"So he wasn't taking any business away from you?"

"Nope. Other way around. If anybody had a wagon or a

carriage they wanted worked on, I sent them up to Louis. Like I say, I'm strictly autos."

"You know of anybody that was mad at Louis for any reason?"

Farmer gazed off into the distance, pursed his lips, and shook his head slowly.

"I can't think of anybody in particular. I mean, other than the people he used to get into fights with. But, then, I didn't know him real well. I've only just been at this," he gestured toward the humming shop, "since I came home from the army. I fixed trucks for two years at Fort Riley." He grinned, then said, "But you know who might be able to help you out?"

He turned and called out a name and one of the three men in the shop stopped what he was doing and walked over.

"This is Franco. He might know something."

Franco was a large man with olive skin and coarse gray hair. The hand that shook Buckner's was as powerful, as relentless as a vise. He told Buckner that he had worked for Boyer for two days but left to escape the man's vicious temper. Other than that, he could add nothing to what Buckner already knew.

"Who would want to kill him?" Buckner asked at last.

"Almost anybody knew him," Franco said with a bitter chuckle.

That was the total of Franco's knowledge on the subject. Buckner thanked Dan Farmer and Franco and left.

That afternoon, he went to the lot behind the town hall and cranked up the county's flivver. It came to life immediately, as it always did. The old thing rattled as though it were about to shake itself apart, but Buckner had to admit that it would go at a respectable speed, and could take him places where only an army mule could follow, and all on one tankful of gas. What with the stories he had read in the papers of an oil shortage, he was glad of that.

The road took him to Pekin, about five miles west of Corinth. Pekin was little more than a grain elevator on the edge of the prairie, with a handful of houses huddled in its shadow. Max Blumberg had built the eight-story structure years before to serve the wheat farmers in the area, and he had financed a spur to connect the elevator to the main north-south rail line, the Kansas, Texas, and Pacific, giving those farmers, and himself, direct access to the world market. The homes that clustered around it belonged to those who served the elevator. Pekin had no other reason for being. It had no post office, no government, no stores or businesses, and Deputy Sheriff James Buckner was its entire police force.

Most of the houses in Pekin were one-story bungalows; all painted somebody's idea of sea green; but one was a white two-story frame with a screened porch running along the entire front. An angled line of poplars protected the north and west sides of the house from the wind, and a thick hedge stood in close to shield the windows. A tangled mesh of roses and honeysuckles climbing halfway up the walls had begun the slow process of dismantling the building. Buckner could see gaps between the clapboards where the invading plants had burrowed in. A gate in the hedge opened onto a flagstone walk that led to the porch. Buckner turned the doorbell and waited.

The door was opened by a small, cheerful-looking woman of about fifty. She had a book in her hand, one finger marking her place.

"Are you here about the room?" she asked pleasantly. "Please come in." She took Buckner's coat and hat and showed him through the front hallway, through a rope portiere, and into a small parlor. A large bay window overlooked the hedge, its floor-to-ceiling windows letting in enough light to brighten the room. A table in the window held several potted palms, as well as ranks of photographs in gilded frames. A curtained doorway led off into another room, where Buckner could see the corner of a bed and a large chest of drawers. Against the wall stood an upright pedal organ. There was a fire going in the fireplace opposite the window. More pictures covered the mantelpiece. Just to Buckner's right, a tall, narrow bookcase held a jumble of worn volumes of Dickens, Thackeray, and Scott, as well as complete sets of Hawthorne, Irving, and Cooper.

A tall grandfather's clock clunked loudly in a corner, and Buckner could hear at least two other clocks answering it from elsewhere in the house.

The woman sat in a large Turkish leather rocker by the fireplace and motioned to the smaller wooden rocker facing her.

"You can move that away from the fire if you like," she said as Buckner sat. She was wearing a woolen housedress and a heavy, dark green wool shawl over her shoulders. She opened her book and laid it face down in her lap.

"*Deerslayer*," she said, gesturing. "I usually like to read something adventuresome before I settle in for my annual Christmas reading of *Pickwick*. Such a comfort, don't you think?"

Buckner nodded. The room was stifling hot and so crowded with furniture, plants, pictures, and knick-knacks that he began to feel claustrophobic the minute he sat down. He also thought Natty Bumppo was a frontier incompetent, and Mr. Pickwick was a tiresome old fool, but he didn't say that either.

"Now," the woman went on. "The rent is five dollars a week for the room. I also serve supper six nights a week, and dinner on Sunday after church."

"I'm not here about the room," said Buckner apologetically.

"Oh? My heavens! Then why are you here?"

"I'm Deputy Sheriff Jim Buckner, ma'am. From Corinth."

The woman peered at him. "So you are. My, my. We've never been introduced, but I've met your mother on several occasions. How is she?"

"Fine, thank you . . . ."

"I hope your father is doing well."

"Much better, thank you. Ma'am . . . ."

"Please give him my best, won't you?"

"Yes, ma'am." Buckner waited for more, but nothing came, and an awkward silence filled the room.

"What did you want to see me about, then?" the woman said finally.

"About Louis Boyer."

"Louis Boyer?" She laughed quietly. "Oh, dear. I haven't laid eyes on him in years. Is he in trouble with the law again?"

"No. He's dead. Someone killed him."

"Oh, no." She shook her head sadly and looked down at the book in her lap for a long time. Finally, she looked at Buckner and asked, "What happened?"

"I don't know," he answered. "Somebody stopped by his shop to have some work done and found the body."

"And you're going to try to find out who killed him."

"Yes, I am."

"Why?" She seemed genuinely puzzled.

"He was killed in his shop, outside city limits, so it falls into my jurisdiction rather than Chief Bushyhead's," Buckner explained.

"No," she said with a little smile. "I mean, why are you bothering? Does anybody really care whether Louis Boyer lives or dies?"

"Obviously somebody does," Buckner answered. "Because they killed him."

"You didn't know Louis, did you, Deputy?" the woman asked.

"Only by sight."

"If anybody deserved to die, it was Louis," she assured him. Her tone was calm, even gentle, as though stating the obvious rendered the outrageous permissible.

"That really doesn't matter," Buckner said. "People can't go around murdering people."

"But I told you. I haven't seen Louis in years. You can't possibly suspect me."

So that was it, Buckner thought. He said, "No, ma'am, but I understand you once knew him very well. I've spoken with his son, Albert."

"Oh. Yes." She nodded. "Poor Albert. He always hated his father. Me, too, I shouldn't wonder. But that was years ago. Louis was easily bored, you see, and he loved his freedom. So when it appeared to him that I might represent a limit on that freedom, he turned elsewhere."

"How did you represent a limit on his freedom?"

"Well, I suppose I became too clinging, too demanding. And some men are so very skittish." She smiled.

Buckner suspected there was more, but decided not to push too hard.

"This is a lovely house," he said.

"Yes, it is." She looked around the room. "Blumberg built it, you know."

"Yes."

"He built the first grain elevator in this end of the county. Made a potful of money early, then retired to live in this place and amuse himself by speculating in the commodity market. Grain, mostly, of course. He did quite well, too, until the ought-seven panic wiped him out. He died two years later. The day Taft was inaugurated. Blumberg was a TR Progressive and he hated Taft with a passion, but I never believed there was any connection."

"He left you the house?"

"Yes. It was all he had to leave by then. That and memories of over ten wonderful years together." She leaned forward and winked conspiratorially. "Plus a little I'd set aside on my own."

"And you've lived here ever since?"

"Yes. I take in a boarder from time to time, to make ends meet, you know."

Buckner heard an automobile pull up outside, and in a moment the front door opened and closed. He turned to see a young woman of perhaps twenty-five stride into the room. She was blonde and trim-figured, in a navy wool skirt and white blouse. She carried a navy blue wool coat over one arm, and a leather case in one hand.

She paused when she saw Buckner standing by his chair. She went to give Angelina a perfunctory kiss on the cheek.

"Hello, dear," she said. "Elizabeth, this is Deputy Buckner. He is here to talk to me about Louis Boyer." The young woman frowned slightly at the name. "It seems someone has murdered him."

The young woman turned to contemplate Buckner; she looked him directly in the eyes for what seemed to Buckner an uncomfortably long time. Her face reflected mild disappointment at what she saw. Finally, she held out her hand and Buckner stepped forward to take it.

"How do you do," he said, smiling.

"Deputy," she responded, her expression unchanged. "So someone killed Louis Boyer. Do you think Angelina did it?"

"No. Not really. But she did know him at one time, many years ago. I was hoping she could provide me with some information on him."

"The Deputy has spoken with Mister Boyer's son, Albert, who told him about me," said Angelina.

"Really," said Elizabeth. There was a chill in her voice. "Well, then I'll leave you two alone. I have work of my own." She indicated the leather case.

"Work?" said Buckner.

"Either that or starve, Deputy."

"Where do you work?" Buckner probed. It still surprised him slightly how accustomed he was becoming to asking questions he once would have thought rude.

"I teach at the high school, Deputy. English literature and social studies. We're reading *Macbeth*. By William Shakespeare."

"Oh, yes." Buckner said, smiling.

"And right now I have to grade thirty essays on Lady Macbeth's motivation."

"I always thought she just wanted to be Queen of Scotland. Or maybe king."

"There's more to it than that, Deputy, I assure you. Psychological motivations, social pressures. She was more ambitious than her husband, but because women in that time were denied access to normal political channels . . ."

"She was more squeamish, too."

"I beg your pardon?"

"'Had he not resembled my father as he slept, I had done it.'"

"Very impressive, Deputy."

"Regimental theatricals," Buckner said modestly. "I played Lady Macbeth at Fort Bowie in 1911."

"You seem tall for the part."

"I was the junior noncom, and nobody else would do it. But I always felt she really wanted to kill her father. What would the psychologists say to that?"

"I'm sure I don't know." She nodded curtly, her short hair falling forward to brush her cheeks. "Good day." She strode out.

"She's very pretty," said Angelina.

"I expect every boy in her class has a crush on her."

"Yes, I expect so."

"She doesn't seem to like me, though," Buckner admitted.

"I'm sorry about that. She didn't mean to be rude, really. She just doesn't like hearing about Louis Boyer."

"What's she got to do with Louis Boyer?"

The woman sat for a long time, looking at the pictures that surrounded her. The hands folded in her lap were thin and spotted with age, but still shapely, resting quietly with fingers intertwined. At last she lifted them and gripped the arms of her chair as if for support.

"It was a very long time ago, Deputy. You must understand, the nineties was the worst time this county ever had. You probably don't even remember, you must have been just a boy."

"Yes, ma'am. I remember my father bringing home chickens, live ones, and fruit, firewood, things people had given him when they couldn't pay him in cash."

"That's because there wasn't any. The big banks had called all their loans. Wheat prices went through the floor. The stuff rotted on the ground right next to Blumberg's elevator because he didn't have room to store it all, and farmers couldn't afford to ship it. And yet people in the cities were going without bread. Naturally, some folks blamed him—because he was a Jew and all—but he wasn't getting rich. Oh, he made a bundle in the red hot eighties, and again after ninety-eight; but through the nineties, he just barely got by."

"I thought you were, uh, with Louis Boyer during those

years."

"I was Louis Boyer's mistress for two years, until the fall of 1896." Her tone was blunt, matter-of-fact. Buckner compared it with Antonia Clay's and wondered about the effect Louis Boyer had on women. His recollection of a stumbling, drunken lout seemed so different from the handsome, dashing young man they had once been infatuated with. Still, Antonia Clay had said that the men she knew disliked Louis Boyer instinctively, while women, just as instinctively, responded in exactly the opposite way.

Angelina Robideaux continued. "But I always preferred having a man in my life, and I was never without one for long. I decided it was time for me to settle down, and Blumberg and I hooked up that winter. Just about twenty-four years ago. He wasn't handsome, by any means, certainly not as handsome as Louis, and no spring chicken either, I can tell you. But he owned this house, and his own business, however badly it was doing, and in those times, that meant a lot. And he didn't mind that I brought along an extra mouth to feed."

"Elizabeth? But I thought . . . ."

"That she was Blumberg's?" The woman laughed and got up. From the mantelpiece, she took several of the small framed photographs and handed them to Buckner before resuming her seat. The first photograph showed a pleasant-looking, dark-haired man wearing a dark suit and a Homburg. He had kindly dark eyes, a broad nose over a thick moustache, and a wide, smiling mouth. The next showed the man with a much younger Angelina, the two of them posed in a studio against a painted backdrop of trees. Angelina, quite pretty, looked like a Gibson girl, with her hair piled up on top of her head. The dark-haired man stood next to her, half a head shorter, beaming contentedly at the camera, his arm around her waist.

The third photograph was taken in front the house. The paint looked fresh, and no vines embraced the walls. Blumberg and Angelina stood on the bottom step of the porch, and, standing between them on the next step up, holding one of their hands in each of hers, was a little girl of about seven, wearing a short white dress. Her hair, almost white in the photo, fell long and loose over her shoulders. Her clear gray eyes gazed steadily into the camera; her lips were set in a determined line that Buckner recognized immediately.

Buckner nodded and returned the photos to the woman.

"Pretty obvious, isn't it, Deputy?" she said, placing the pictures on the table at her elbow.

"Yes, I suppose it is. But if Blumberg wasn't the father, then . . ."

"Why, Louis Boyer, of course."

"Oh, yes," said Buckner, feeling foolish. "That was why Boyer wanted to be quit of you," he went on. "He really was pretty rotten, wasn't he, to treat you that way."

"You don't know the half of it, Deputy."

"What do you mean?"

"She wasn't my daughter, either."

"What? I don't understand."

"Obviously. Elizabeth was the third child of Louis Boyer and his wife, Victoria, who had the most beautiful blonde hair I had ever seen in my life."

"You took in Louis Boyer's daughter?" Buckner said. He remembered Albert Boyer's description of him and his older sister trying to take care of a baby without a mother. He had said he did not know what had happened to the baby. Had he lied? And if so, why?

"Yes. After Victoria left, there was no one else. The two older children could not have taken care of an infant for long. So I did. That's why he threw me over. Because I wouldn't abandon the baby. I was just lucky Blumberg loved children."

"So Blumberg married you and the two of you raised Elizabeth as your own."

"Married! We were never married, Deputy. It would have been impossible."

Buckner stared at her in astonishment.

"Quite impossible. He was a Jew, after all, and I am Catholic."

"So the three of you, without any ties, not of law or religion or blood, lived here as a family?"

"That's right, Deputy," said Angelina. "It was a very practical relationship for us all, really. It solved so many problems. Elizabeth needed a home; I always seemed to need a man around; and Blumberg needed a family. Jews put a lot of stock in family, you know."

Buckner nodded vaguely. Where did everybody go to church, he wondered.

"We were quite happy, I can assure you. Blumberg and I were never able to have children of our own. So it was just the three of us, together for over ten years. And now it's just Elizabeth and me, though I can't believe she'll be with me much longer. Some young man will marry her and take her away. But that's only as it should be, of course. She's young and full of life, and I am old, now, and I have only memories. Most of them quite wonderful, but not all. Not all."

After a moment, Buckner asked, "Does she know? Have you told her?"

"Yes, I told her once, years ago. About the time that picture was taken. And she learned more as she grew up. Children can absorb only so much at various ages, you see: the older they get, the more they can deal with. She knew that Blumberg and I weren't married, and weren't her real parents. We discussed that often, over the years. But after I told her about Louis Boyer, we never discussed it again. She didn't ask, and I didn't bring it up. I must admit I did not paint a very pretty picture of her father."

"Did she ever try to make contact with him?"

"Not that I know of. I certainly would have discouraged it. And by the time she was older, he was—well, he had gone down so, that I believe she would have been quite repelled by just the thought of him. And the contrast with Blumberg was extreme, I assure you. Blumberg really was the kindest, gentlest, most loving man I have ever known in my life, Deputy."

Angelina fell silent and looked up. Buckner turned and saw Elizabeth standing in the doorway, a loaded tea tray in her hands. She had plainly been standing there listening, though for how long, Buckner could not say. When their eyes met, she stepped into the room and set the tray on the table in the window. She poured tea from a large silver pot into three dainty, translucent cups, then brought the tray over, offering it first to Angelina, then to Buckner. There was cream and sugar, but Buckner ignored them. He'd had tea only infrequently since the war, and he always drank it black. Elizabeth then returned the tea tray to the window, picked up one of the chairs there, and placed it next to Angelina, facing Buckner. She got her own cup of tea and sat down.

"Talking can be such dry work," she said. The corners of her mouth tilted up in something like a smile. "I thought you might like someone to help, as long as she brought refreshments. I hope you don't mind."

"Thank you, Miss . . ." Buckner paused.

"Blumberg, Deputy. Angelina's right. He did love me. And in return, I took his name. Although," she turned to Angelina, "it isn't strictly true that I had no contact with Louis Boyer. I spoke to him once, several years ago, before I went away to school."

"Oh, dear," said Angelina. "I wish you hadn't."

"I wanted to know, to satisfy my curiosity. You had told me so little about him, I had a sort of outline in my head, and I had seen him around town, of course. Anyway, I wanted to fill in the outline."

"Did you visit his shop?" Buckner asked. The two women looked at him as though surprised that he was still there.

"No," Elizabeth answered. "I met him quite by accident in town one day. He did not seem to be drunk, and was fairly clean. But he smelled like a distillery, and his clothes were all disheveled and tattered. His hair was wild and he hadn't shaved in a week at least. I decided to seize the opportunity, so I stopped him and asked to speak with him. He demanded to know who I was and I said I was his daughter, Elizabeth.

"Well, he just laughed at me. He said he only had two children, and they were named Charlotte and Albert. Then he stopped and just stared at me for the longest time, his eyes, which were terribly bloodshot, got colder and colder. It was as though he were seeing me for the first time, then he said, 'You *are* her brat. By God, you look just like her.' Then he cursed something awful, at me or my mother, I'm not sure which, and turned and walked away. And that was the only time I spoke to my natural father."

"I tried to spare you that, dear," said Angelina, taking the girl's hand in hers.

"I know," said Elizabeth coolly. She withdrew her hand from Angelina's embrace. "Thank you, but I didn't really need protecting. I didn't exactly understand everything he said; and he certainly glared at me, and spoke to me with anger and hatred. But I thought he was more pathetic and feeble than frightening. There on the street, in broad daylight, with people passing by, there was nothing he could do to me there."

"Well," said Angelina. "No harm done, I suppose. You went off to the normal school at Cape Girardeau and that was the end of it."

Buckner wondered if she had known her brother was living in the same town, struggling with at least some of the curses that afflicted their father.

They finished their tea in silence.

"What about your, ah, your real family?" Buckner asked. "I mean, your blood kin. Your mother, your brother and sister. Did you keep in touch with any of them?"

"Oh, no, Deputy," Elizabeth said. "I never knew any of them, really. Angelina told me that they were good to me and tried to take care of me, but just couldn't. I don't bear them a grudge; but I have not tried to find them, either."

Buckner glanced over at Angelina, who seemed to be peering at Elizabeth, as though she could not see her clearly. Probably needs glasses, he thought, and is too vain to wear them.

"What did happen to Victoria?" he asked her.

"All I know is, she left," Angelina said, turning to face him. "Louis told me that she went back to her people in Arkansas.

Once he even told me she had the tuberculosis and went out to Arizona to recover. But I never really knew."

"Did she have any friends that you can remember?"

Angelina shook her head. "He kept her pretty close. I don't believe he liked her having anything to do with anybody but him." She thought a moment. "There was somebody, though, now I come to think of it. There was a colored woman, did washing in town. She had children the same age as Charlotte and Albert."

"How did she know Victoria?"

"For a time, Victoria did washing, too. To make a little money. The two of them would work and the children would play together, up at the shop. They worked there because there was plenty of space to hang the wash to dry. They must've done that for a couple of years. Then Boyer put a stop to it."

"Why?"

"Oh, lots of reasons. He told me he didn't like having his wife work. Said he didn't like having a nigger around the place, didn't trust her. So when one of his tools went missing, he blamed the poor colored woman and ran her off. But I believe it was because the two of them started making some money. He took most of Victoria's share, of course, but she always managed to keep some back, and he didn't like that. I think he was afraid she might save up enough to take the children and leave him. She did, eventually, only she didn't take the children."

"My mother abandoned me, Deputy," said Elizabeth, as though repeating a litany. "Max and Angelina never did. I'll always be indebted to them."

"I suppose so," said Buckner, getting to his feet. He retrieved his coat and hat from a chair by the entrance. Elizabeth got up as well. "I'll show myself out. Thank you for your help, both of you."

The two women looked at each other.

"One thing more," Buckner said. "Who was the Negro woman that Victoria worked with? Do you remember her name?"

"Oh, no. I never knew her, Deputy."

"All right. Thank you, then."

Buckner went out, stopping on the porch to put on his hat and coat. The late Blumberg's grain elevator cast its enormous shadow across the front of the house and the yard. Elizabeth followed him out onto the porch and into the yard, saying nothing, her face blank and impenetrable.

He started up the county's Ford and drove back to town, leaving Elizabeth standing in the shadow, watching him drive away.

He ate supper at home that evening, which pleased his mother, despite the fact that he and his father got into a discussion of the coming election.

"I do not think that politics is a suitable discussion for the dinner table," she said in protest.

"But you should be interested in this," Buckner said. "Women will be voting this time."

"Ridiculous," said his father. "Nothing a woman says above a whisper is worth listening to."

Regina Long Buckner gave her husband a long, cold look, but said nothing.

"In her last letter, Martha Jane said it was about time women achieved the full political equality denied them by the Founding *Fathers*," said Buckner. "She underlined 'Fathers' twice."

"That is just another thing your sister is wrong about," his mother huffed. "Women had more influence over politics without the vote, when they could stand above the fray, make rational evaluations, and act accordingly through the men in their lives."

Buckner's father snorted at that, but said nothing.

"Now," continued his mother, "they will be cajoled, threatened, pandered to by grubby office-seekers and their hired hucksters, just as men have been for over a century. They will join the common herd, and their unique position will be lost forever."

"How will you be voting then, Mother?" Buckner asked innocently.

She turned and looked at him down her long Roman nose

for a full thirty seconds before answering.

"I believe the ballot in this state is secret," she said.

Buckner, wondering briefly how she would feel if she knew Doctor Peck shared similar views, changed the subject.

"Angelina Robideaux asked me to say hello. I was out that way today."

"How kind of her. Did you meet her daughter, Elizabeth?"

"Yes, only she's not her daughter."

"What do you mean?"

Buckner explained.

"Good heavens!" exclaimed his mother.

His father just laughed.

"But Elizabeth is very pretty, nonetheless," his mother went on.

"Yes," Buckner admitted. "But kind of chilly, like she's standing back watching you all the time, thinking, taking you apart and looking closely at the parts."

"The very same thing you do yourself," said his mother triumphantly.

"But it's my job. She does it because it's her nature."

"You are entirely too choosy," his mother said. "You keep that up, and you'll never get married."

When her son did not respond, she got up and began clearing the table. Buckner's father took out two cigars and offered one to his son.

"No, thank you. I've got to go out."

"Business or pleasure?" asked his father.

"Business."

The old man nodded and went to the front room. Buckner got his hat and left the house.

He walked through town. The shops on the square were closed and dark. He could see lights, and occasionally hear music from a piano or a Victrola, but there was no one on the street. He kept going until he reached railroad tracks. They belonged to the Kansas, Texas, and Pacific Railroad, which everyone along its right of way called The Katy. The Katy gave Corinth producers access to world markets and provided Corinth consumers with the latest in everything from everywhere. It brought people to town and carried them away. And it neatly divided the town into two sections, one white, the other black.

Stone crossed the tracks and the field beyond and stepped up onto a sidewalk. If the white part of town had gone to bed for the night, here were people on the streets, couples in fine clothes walking up and down, greeting each other, enjoying the crisp, pleasant evening air. The shops in that part of town were open and doing brisk business, especially the ice cream parlor, which was full to bursting with families and couples, people spilling out onto the sidewalk, laughing and talking.

They grew silent as Buckner walked along, turning to watch him until he passed, curiosity, suspicion, and hostility unconcealed, then resuming their activities. Buckner noticed, but paid no attention.

Up ahead, he saw a man in a worn policeman's coat, at least a size too small, and an old-fashioned high police helmet. He carried a short billy, and the badge on the front of the coat shone in the light that spread into the street.

Buckner stopped and waited for the man to come up to him.

"Evening, Constable."

"Deputy," said the man, touching the billy to the brim of his helmet. He looked over Buckner's shoulder up the street. "You sure can put a damper on some people's fun."

"Yes. They don't see me over here very often, so they're not used to me."

"Not used to any white policemen, unless it's something bad." He looked at Buckner and asked softly, "Is it something bad?"

"No." Buckner smiled. "I'm just after some information. Besides, you know I don't have jurisdiction over here."

"That's right; and I do. But folks over here know who's in charge, and they know it ain't me. White police can come here and take over any time they want." The officer changed the subject. "Say, speaking of white policemen, you sure kicked over a hornet's nest in the police department over there."

"I did?"

"Yes. Upset Chief Bushyhead something fierce, you messing with one of his blind pigs. Vince Marolis is a special friend of the Chief's, or didn't you know that?"

"No," Buckner admitted, "I guess I didn't."

The constable chuckled. "You don't want to mess with those boys, Deputy. They's a lot of them, and ain't but one of you."

"Thanks for the warning. Speaking of special friends, is Elroy Dutton open for business tonight?"

"Sure. Every night. That man's in a terrible rush to get rich. That where you going to ask your questions?"

"Yes." Buckner refused to say any more.

The officer nodded, unoffended, and smiled. "Then I'll leave you to your business," he said. With another brief salute, he resumed his patrol.

Buckner continued down the sidewalk and turned in at the door of a barbershop. An old man sweeping the floor was the only sign of life. Buckner smiled at the man's startled expression and nodded a greeting. The old man, seeing who it was, recovered, nodded back. Buckner headed for the stairs. He heard a small bell chime somewhere. There was a door at the top, and Buckner could hear music and laughter through it. He did not knock, for the peephole had slid open, and a single eye contemplated him.

"I need to see your boss," he said bluntly to the peering eye.

"Business or pleasure?" rumbled a voice from the other side of the door.

"My concern, not yours, Buster," Buckner answered testily. He liked Buster personally, but sometimes he was just a little over protective of his employer.

"Mine if you want to get through this door, Deputy."

"I'll explain that to your boss when I get him out of bed tomorrow, say around six in the morning."

The peephole slammed shut. After two minutes, the door swung open. It was thick oak, backed with steel plate, but it moved easily on heavy-duty hinges.

A tall, slim, elegantly dressed man stood in the doorway with a much larger man looming just behind him. The slim man held out his hand.

"Deputy," he said.

"Good evening, Mister Dutton," said Buckner, shaking the offered hand. "How are you, Buster?"

The big man at Dutton's shoulder nodded without smiling and returned to the bar.

Buckner followed Dutton across a large, simple, well-lighted room scattered with small round tables. The one piece of elegance was a long mirrored bar that ran along one entire wall. At a polished upright piano, an elderly man dressed in overalls, heavy work boots, and a battered straw hat, played a slow, almost dreamy variation of "Maple Leaf Rag." People sat crowded around the tables, or lined up at the bar. They continued to talk, but quietly, and they openly followed Buckner's progress across the room to an empty table in a back corner. This table was larger than the others, and had a green cloth cover. A vase of flowers sat in the middle of it. Buckner and his host sat down.

A young man in a short, white waiter's jacket appeared as though he had risen through the floor.

"Anything for you this evening, Deputy?" Dutton asked.

"I'll have a beer," Buckner said.

Dutton nodded to the waiter, who disappeared. In moments, he was back with a champagne bucket and a bottle chilling, which he deposited at Dutton's elbow. He went away again and came back with a crystal flute and a large schooner of beer. He gave the flute to Dutton and, almost as an afterthought, set the schooner in front of Buckner without actually spilling any of it.

Dutton nodded and Buckner said thanks. When the waiter had gone, Dutton poured champagne into the flute and raised it in a toast.

"To justice," he said, grinning slightly.

"To justice," said Buckner lifting his schooner and taking a long drink.

"You don't think it'll hurt your chances in the election to be seen drinking in a colored speakeasy?" said Dutton.

Buckner looked around the room. The customers seemed to have resumed their previous level of enjoyment. He could see a few white faces.

"Not enough voters here," Buckner said. "Besides, isn't this near-beer?"

Dutton laughed. "Hardly. I buy that direct from a good German brewer up in St. Louis. It's the real thing."

Buckner drank again. "Amazing," he said. "Sure tastes like near-beer. Anyway, I'm off duty, and I have no jurisdiction here in town. As several people have reminded me lately."

"Yes. Your smooth working relationship with the municipal police seems to be operating better than ever."

Buckner grunted. They drank in silence for a few minutes. Finally Dutton spoke.

"I don't mind you dropping by, Deputy, but was there anything in particular you wanted to see me about?"

"Maybe I just wanted to relax for a few minutes," Buckner said. "Did that ever occur to you?"

"I can't say it ever did, no." Dutton poured more champagne. "You have the reputation down this end of the county of being a hard man. Hard on other folks, but hard on yourself mostly."

Buckner frowned at that. "What load of horse manure," he said.

"Maybe," said Dutton. "But I've talked to folks that knew you before the war say you changed over there. Say they haven't seen you laugh since you got home."

"You know anybody didn't come back different?" Buckner asked. "What about you? I've heard people say before you went to France you were just about the laziest nigger in Corinth."

Dutton's eyes flared angrily, but Buckner only returned a humorless, challenging smile.

"But since you came back," he continued, "you've been nothing but business. They say you're aiming to be the first Negro governor of the state."

"Have to be able to vote, first," said Dutton, not disguising his bitterness. "Besides, business is where the power is in this country. Businessmen own politicians, not the other way around. And money's always green, no matter what color wallet it's in. Especially as far as Republicans are concerned."

"They have to get into office first," Buckner said.

"They will. You watch."

"Maybe up North, but not here. Not in any of the Rebel states."

"You know, Deputy," Dutton said. "You're right about one thing. Before I went to France, I didn't see anything in my future. But I came back believing in change. And part of that change is going to be taking some of what you people have had all your lives and giving it to black folks who've never had anything."

"What if white folks don't want to give it to you?"

"I didn't say anything about giving; I'm talking about taking." His tone was fierce, and his eyes flashed.

Buckner raised his schooner. "Here's to change, then." He drained it. Already his head was telling him it was not near beer.

"You want another?" Dutton asked.

"No, thanks; I may be off duty, but I'm still working. I need to ask you a question."

"All right."

"I'm trying to find a woman, a Negro woman, who used to do laundry around town."

"For white folks?"

"Yes. And for a couple of years she worked together with a white woman, Victoria Boyer, up at Louis Boyer's place on the Jackson Road."

"This the Louis Boyer that got himself killed the other day?" Dutton made a point of knowing as much about white folk' business as about black folks'.

"Yes. This woman was in business with Boyer's wife for a while. Then Boyer accused her of stealing and chased her away."

"I didn't know Boyer was married. When was this?"

"Sometime in the mid-nineties, I think."

Dutton laughed. "How old do you think I am, anyway? I

wasn't even born until ninety-three." He continued laughing. People at the tables turned to stare.

"I just thought I'd ask."

"All right. I'll ask around, too. What do you want with her?"

"Victoria Boyer ran off not too long afterwards, abandoned three children to their drunken, violent father, and just left. I'm trying to find out where she went."

"You think she might've come back and killed Boyer?"

"Oh, I don't know about that. I'm just after information."

"All right," Dutton said. "I'll see what I can find out for you."

"Thanks." The two men got to their feet.

"You can stay if you like," Dutton said. "Have another beer. Maybe I can find somebody to keep you company."

Buckner grinned. "Another time, perhaps."

Dutton nodded and showed Buckner to the head of the stairs. They shook hands, and Buckner descended. As he sketched a brief wave to the old man with the broom, the black policeman emerged from the shadows. Buckner halted.

"You might want to go home by another way, Deputy," he said.

"All right," Buckner said. "Why?"

"Couple fellows been hanging round this side of town, looking for you, asking questions bout you. White fellows. Big white fellows."

Buckner frowned slightly. "Do you know them?"

The man hesitated briefly before nodding.

"Who are they?" Buckner prompted.

"Corinth police officers," the man answered softly.

Buckner nodded, though his confusion only grew.

"Thanks for the advice," Buckner said.

The policeman shrugged. "I just don't think it'd be a good thing for me if a friend of Mister Elroy Dutton's got hurt over this side of the tracks. Even a white friend."

Buckner thanked him again and left.

After the heat and the smoke and the beer, the night air was pleasant and cool. There were fewer people out now and he walked in silence. He turned north and circled around the center of town, coming up to his house from the opposite side.

Buckner stood in the darkness and watched the house for several minutes. He saw no sign of other watchers, no unexplained shadows. Soon he went into the house and went to bed. As he lay on his back staring into the darkness, he wondered why two policemen were looking for him. Had he angered Chief Bushyhead so badly? He hoped not.

Finally, he drifted off to sleep.

TUESDAY, OCTOBER 26

THE DAY DAWNED bright but cold. Buckner was awake early and at his desk by seven. Sheriff Aubuchon had him scheduled to post the last of his handbills today, then to meet with the town Democratic Committee to plan the monster rally that was to be held on Saturday. Instead, Buckner went over his sketches and his notes from Louis Boyer's shop, making sure he had in his mind a clear picture of what the place had looked like, so that, as he gathered more evidence, he would have an accurate context in which to evaluate it. The sketches, originally suggested by Aubuchon, had become a basic element of his work. The ability to sketch terrain accurately, to take careful notes about enemy activity, had helped make him a valuable scout in the army. Now these same skills made him a better policeman.

He shook his head at the stick-figure representation of Louis Boyer lying on the floor of his shop: too bad he still couldn't draw people.

About ten, he heard a soft tap on his office door. He looked up. Willis Johnson stood there next to a bucket, a mop in his hand. He grinned foolishly and fixed Buckner with his good left eye. The bulging, wandering right eye stared off into space.

"Come to mop your floor, Deputy," he said loudly, with a glance back down the hallway.

"Fine, Willis. Come on in." Buckner got to his feet and prepared to leave to give the man room to work. But Johnson was not mopping. He sidled over to Buckner, his good eye on the doorway.

"Deputy," he hissed. "I got a message for you."

Buckner stopped, his hat in his hand, and waited. The man put his bucket down and began working. He kept his head down, and talked out of the side of his mouth. Now the right eye, cloudy and blind, stared up at Buckner.

"Elroy Dutton wants to see you."

"Now?"

"Yes."

"At the barber shop?"

"No. Ibo Mary's house. Round behind the AME Church."

"All right," Buckner said. He looked around. There was no one in sight. "Why are we whispering?"

"Be my job, they see me getting too friendly with you."

"Oh," said Buckner. "Well, then, thank you, Willis." He left the courthouse.

He knew exactly where the church was. A solid, square, red brick building with a modest white wooden steeple, it occupied a corner of a residential block not far from Elroy Dutton's place of business. There was a cross over the door, and squares of brightly colored tissue paper had been pasted over the plain square windowpanes, making do for stained glass. A ladder leaned against an outside wall. A man in denim overalls stood on it, chipping old paint from a windowsill.

"Excuse me," Buckner said. The man turned and smiled. A clerical collar rose from the top of the overalls.

"Yes, Deputy," he said. His voice was full and rolling and Buckner could hear the latent power in it.

"How are you today, Reverend Coyle?" he asked."

"I'm tolerable," said the man. "How are you?"

"Pretty good."

"And how is Mrs. Buckner?"

"My mother is as she always is, Reverend."

"I'm delighted to hear it. She is a fine lady, your mother. Please tell her for me that we would be honored and pleased to have her worship with us again sometime."

"I'll be sure to tell her," Buckner said. Again? His mother had Presbyterian roots reaching all the way back to the English Civil War. When had she started going to a different church, a black church? Giving them the big dining room table and chairs was a simple act of charity. Several people in town wondered aloud why she couldn't have given it to her own, white, church, but Buckner's mother had never paid the least attention to fools. Still, he struggled to imagine his very Presbyterian mother, truly one of "God's frozen people," worshiping with Reverend Coyle's considerably more relaxed and demonstrative congregation.

"Can I help you with something, Deputy?"

"I'm looking for Ibo Mary's house, Reverend."

"That would be Mary Carpentier. Two doors down," the man said with a slight sniff and a lifting of his nose. "Behind the house with the blue trim. She casts her spells in a run-down shanty back in the alley."

"'Casts her spells?' Is she a competitor, Reverend?"

"Only in the minds of children and unbelievers, Deputy. My regards to your mother." He turned his back and resumed his work.

Buckner thanked him and walked on. Beside a neat two-story house with blue trim ran a narrow dirt path. Buckner turned down it and followed it to the alley that ran behind the houses on that block. He walked between yards of bare, swept dirt and laundry drying on lines. Children shouted and dogs barked, and careful dark eyes watched him through kitchen windows and from behind freshly washed sheets. At the end of the yards, just off the alley, was a small building made of rough planks covered with tarpaper. There were no windows, and the door was a blanket over a low opening. Elroy Dutton was pacing nervously back and forth in front of the building, pausing now and then to brush invisible dust off his immaculate dark suit. Buster stood placidly to one side, his elbow resting on the roof of the shack, a cigar in his mouth, his hat on the back of his head. He watched his employer's pacing with relaxed amusement.

"You damn sure took your time," Dutton said when he saw Buckner.

"Couldn't you just telephone me, like a normal person?" Buckner asked.

Dutton stared at Buckner in surprise; Buster grinned around his cigar. "I could if I wanted everybody on the Corinth police department to know my business," Dutton said.

"What does that mean?"

"You don't know they been listening in on your telephone conversations?"

"Well, I know that Givens, or somebody, is sitting right there every time I use the telephone," Buckner said.

"And why the hell do you think you still don't have a telephone of your own? It's not just the county. Every time the request comes back down to the city, Bushyhead squashes it. Hell, it's his building, the city government's anyway, and if the Chief says they don't need another telephone in the building, then they don't get another telephone. Especially if it's *your* telephone."

"But why would they listen in on my conversations?" Buckner asked. "I never talk to anybody about anything but business."

Buster made a low gurgling sound that Buckner thought might be laughter. "They don't listen in all the time," Dutton said. "But they've been listening a lot lately. Ever since that little dust up at Vince Marolis's place."

"I have a feeling everybody in town knows about that."

"Deputy," Dutton sighed heavily. "What everybody knows is that you caught one of Bushyhead's men picking up the weekly payment. The Chief's furious about that. He runs a real tight operation over on that side of town. Prohibition hasn't hurt him any; in fact, he's raised his prices on booze now that it's unconstitutional, but it has complicated things for him. You've complicated things for him."

"How have I done that?" Buckner protested. "I'm not blind. I know what he's got going. But I'm just not interested in his deals with bootleggers. And I have no authority over what goes on inside city limits."

"He's involved in a lot more than deals with bootleggers, Deputy. Every crooked thing that happens on that side of town, the police department gets a percentage. Do you mean you really didn't know that?" Dutton seemed truly surprised.

"Well, yes, I guess I suspected," Buckner admitted. "But Sheriff Aubuchon went out of his way to make sure I understood when I took this job, there was to be no crossing of the line, no sticking my nose in the town's business. I'm a county officer. I've got more than enough to keep me busy without worrying about Chief Bushyhead and his boys. I'm no threat to them."

"I don't think he sees it that way anymore," Dutton insisted. "I think the Chief's the kind of man that figures, if you're not with him, you're against him. The fellow that had the job before you, he was a local boy. Bushyhead handpicked him because he could be counted on to mind his own business, and keep the Chief informed about the Sheriff's office. But you, you're Aubuchon's boy. You got this job because Aubuchon's friends with your pa. Then you turned out to be as independent as a hog on ice, and twice as stubborn. Bushyhead can't tell which way you're going to jump, and that makes him nervous. Now, with that fracas at Vince Marolis's the other day, he's really getting worried, especially with the election coming up."

"The election?" Buckner asked. "What's that got to do with anything?"

"It's got everything to do with everything." Dutton was growing exasperated at Buckner's innocence. "Vince Marolis is Bushyhead's link to St. Louis. We're only seventy miles away. If the Chief can convince Marolis that he's got Corinth wrapped up tight, then that'll mean a partnership with some very powerful people. People who can keep him supplied with booze and provide muscle whenever he needs it. One of the ways he can prove how powerful he is, is by guaranteeing the election." Dutton was warming to his subject.

"The problem in this county, from the Chief's point of view, is your boss. Not only is he fairly honest, for a cop, but the last thing he wants to see is the big boys from St. Louis coming in here and taking over. The Chief would like nothing better than to retire Sheriff Aubuchon, just to get him out of the way. That's why he's been working hard for Foote."

Buckner watched, vaguely baffled, as Dutton talked on. He had always felt that a high, opaque curtain hung between himself and the rest of the community, but he had always attributed it to his experiences in the army and the war, things that set him off from them. But, as Dutton was now trying to make clear to him, there were aspects of life in Corinth that set them apart from him.

Dutton was still talking.

"Now, you're the best thing the Sheriff's got going for him down this end of the county. Folks take you for a fair man; and solving that murder case last year marks you for a smart man, too. Here you've got another murder. Nobody gave a hoot in hell about that white trash Louis Boyer, but if you don't bring in his killer, it'll hurt Aubuchon and help Foote. So don't expect any support from Bushyhead's office. Worse, if you start feeling like you got cross-hairs on your back, don't be surprised."

Buckner remembered the warning from the black policeman about the men looking for him.

"I guess I've already got that feeling," he said.

"Good. Might keep you alive."

"How do you stay out of his way?" Buckner asked.

"I stay on my side of town, Chief stays on his," Dutton said tersely.

"Your side is still Corinth," Buckner said. "It's still his bailiwick. Where do you fit in all this?"

"I don't compete with the Chief," said Dutton, "and he doesn't compete with me."

"What about the big boys from St. Louis?"

"They're mostly Irish and Jews, a few Italians, like Marolis. As a rule, they don't much care for people of my complexion. They'll take our money, but they like to be in charge of things. Let's just say, if they take over, I don't think I'll be able to count on their good will."

"So you like things the way they are, dividing up the town with the Chief."

"Well . . ." Dutton shrugged.

"You've even got a couple of Negroes on the force . . ."

"Who work my side of town," Dutton pointed out.

"Still, it must be a pretty convenient arrangement for you," Buckner said.

"I hope you don't have any trouble with it," Dutton said lightly.

"Is that why you got me over here?" Buckner asked. "To explain life and crime in Corinth to me?"

"No," Dutton said. "Not that you don't need it. You may have been hell on the Apaches, and on the Boche, too, if everything I hear about you is true, but you don't know a damned thing about Republicans and Democrats."

Buckner grinned. "I'm learning fast," he said.

Dutton aimed a thumb at the little house nearby. "You said you wanted to talk to the woman that used to take in washing with Victoria Boyer twenty-five years ago. Well, this is her."

Buckner raised his eyebrows. "Thanks," he said, and ducked his head to enter the shack. Dutton grabbed his arm.

"Better let me go first," he said.

Buckner stepped back. "Fine." He pulled the blanket aside. Dutton went in. Buckner followed. Buster waited outside.

It was just as well: there would have been no room for him anyway. It was almost completely dark in the hut. The only light came through cracks in the walls, and from a kerosene lantern that sat on an upended box and emitted a soft, yellow glow. The place was stuffy and hot. Buckner, bent nearly double, could see a small stove and a wood box, full to the top with fresh kindling. There were piles of books, magazines, and newspapers everywhere. On the far wall hung a crucifix flanked by pictures of black people, who might have been saints, in worshipful poses, and under them were rows of candles. A cracked, white, shallow dish sat on a small shelf. It held a smudged substance in the bottom, the residue of something burnt. Buckner peered at the crucifix: the figure of Christ, with crown of thorns and upraised eyes, was black, with clearly delineated African features.

Next to the lantern, huddled in a broken-down easy chair, sat a tiny old woman. She was engulfed in blankets and quilts, but even standing up, Buckner estimated she would be no more than four and a half feet high. He could see part of her head peeking up, with a few sparse clusters of gray hair over bare scalp, and her narrow, sharp chin and nose. The old woman's eyes were dark but completely clear, with small flames in them radiating intelligence and a fierce energy.

Elroy Dutton, who could almost stand upright in the cramped shack, went over and knelt beside her.

"Grandmother, this is the man I told you about, the one who wants to talk to you about Victoria Boyer." Dutton spoke softly, but Buckner could hear that he spoke differently, deferentially, and with a thick, dark accent at once recognizably rural and completely alien to the polished, elegant saloonkeeper Buckner was familiar with.

The old woman abruptly raised a shriveled hand, closed her eyes, and sketched the sign of the cross. She said something in a high, thin voice, but Buckner could not understand her. He looked at Dutton.

"She says her spirit is troubled," Dutton said.

"Hers?" Buckner asked, pointing.

"I don't think so," said Dutton. He turned to speak to the old woman, then relayed her answer to Buckner.

"Victoria Boyer's spirit."

"Victoria Boyer's dead?"

Dutton turned back to the woman and whispered to her. The old woman frowned at him, shook her head, and spoke for a long time.

"She says everybody's got a spirit, don't have to be dead. She won't talk about that," he said. "She says you come here for other business, so get to it."

"That's all? She talked a pretty long time to just say that."

Dutton looked away, embarrassed. "She also apologized for having to meet you here. I invited her to meet you at my place, but she won't go there because it is a house of sin."

"She's right about that," Buckner said.

The old woman talked some more. The more she spoke, the more Buckner was able to make out a few words, enough to realize that she was speaking some combination of English, French, and another language, and all of it in a thick accent, made nearly unintelligible by the fact that she seemed to be entirely toothless.

Dutton, saying nothing, was looking up at Buckner. The three of them waited in the half-darkness. Buckner felt drops of sweat gather in his armpits and slide down his ribs. Finally, the old woman jabbed Dutton on the shoulder with one skinny, prompting finger, and he began to speak.

"She says she doesn't know what's become of me, I used to be such a nice little boy, and now all I do is help people to drink and have sex and destroy their souls."

Buckner raised his eyebrows.

"That's just a summary," Dutton said.

"I'll bet," Buckner said. "So what about Victoria Boyer? Will she tell me about twenty-five years ago?"

"I think so," Dutton said.

Ibo Mary began to speak. Elroy Dutton passed her message on to Buckner. As the woman spoke, Buckner found himself listening less to the words and more to the tones and rhythms of her voice. To his surprise, he began to understand her. He asked some questions to guide her, and her story came out.

"This was long after the slavery times, and all the soldier boys had gone home. My husband died, my third, and I didn't have nobody to look out for me, so I had to look out for myself. I didn't mind that, I have looked after myself for most of my life, even when I was just a child and belonged to M'sieur Carpentier on his big farm up on the Fourche Renault. I always could look after myself, working around the house or in the fields. I could walk the corn as good as any man, and all day, too, but pretty soon I began to follow my mother around while she did the washing for M'sieur Carpentier and Madame and the young ones. Then the war came and all that stopped. The people all run off and my mother died, and I worked hard to live. Farmed and trapped, hunted and fished. Buried three husbands; birthed eleven children and buried four of them. The rest all gone away now.

"After my husband died, Lemuel that was, I come into Corinth and started taking in washing for the white folks over on the other side of the tracks. The white folks was having a hard time, they said, there wasn't no money and no jobs, but some of them still needed somebody to do their cleaning up. Seems like some white folks just can't do for themselves, no matter how poor they get. They didn't pay much, but I didn't need much. Most of my children was all grown and gone by then, it was just me and the two little ones, Henry and Alice. Now they gone too."

Buckner found himself leaning forward, listening intently as the old woman told her tale.

"Then I come to learn about a white woman was taking in wash up north of town, on the Jackson Road. I seen her one day, coming into town. She had a donkey and a cart and she'd go round to the houses of the white folks and take their laundry and carry it back up to her place, then the next day she'd bring it back and pick up some more.

"This white woman had long yellow hair, and all the white men said she was beautiful, but she looked so tired and beat down to me. She had her two children helping her, a young boy and a young girl, and they loved her so much, especially the girl, who followed along after her mama and tried as hard as she could to walk just like her and talk just like her. I never seen anything like that. All I knew was that there wasn't barely enough white folks' washing to go around, and that her and me was cutting into one another's business. So I talked to her one day and said we should go partners. She had the donkey and the cart, but she had never taken in washing before, and besides, she said she had two children that loved her and tried to help, but they was wearing her out. I was still young and strong and had done plenty of washing in my time, and we decided the children could play together and maybe help us a little, because, you know, two can watch children easier than one. She agreed, so we went partners.

"We was together near two years. We worked out a pretty good system, and it wasn't too long before practically every family in town that could afford it was giving their washing to us. This white woman, Victoria was her name, was real easy to work with. She didn't say much and she was always very respectful to me, but it was like she was sad all the time. She had been raised proper by some big family in Arkansas. They was supposed to have a lot of money, but they all died and come to find out they didn't have nothing but debts. That made her husband mad, on account of he had planned to get his hands on that money. Now he taken to going around with other women, and he kept most of the money she made doing washing and spent it on liquor. And he beat her whenever he come home drunk, blaming her for him not having any work, like a man will do. So she had plenty to be sad about. Except for her children. They was her darlings. They'd all play round the yard when we was doing the wash, her two and my two, and sometimes they'd ride to town with us on the cart and help us take the washing back. When they got older they began to help more with the work. She always had time for them and hovered over them like a mother hen. Wouldn't let her husband come near them children if she was around, she'd just go at him if he ever tried to bother them children. I didn't understand it; she could protect them little ones, but not herself.

"I used to ask her why she didn't take the children and leave and she said she didn't have no place to go. She didn't have no kinfolk close by, nobody to protect her if he come after her; the children was too young to be moving around. Then she was pregnant again and couldn't run off. I tried to tell her about the slavery times, how women would run off and leave their families, or sometimes whole families would run off together, that sometimes things was just so terrible, you had to get away, even if you was leaving a lot behind and wasn't going to nothing that you knew of.

"That was about the time when her man chased me off. I don't know if he heard me telling her to try to get away or what; said it shamed him, having his wife taking in washing with a nigger woman. So I went, though I didn't want to. I'd got to where I liked them children; liked her, too. Last time I seen them was up on the Jackson Road, standing in the yard there, sheets and bed linens flapping in the sun; all three of them, her and the children crying, tears running down their faces, waving goodbye to me."

"I was crying," the old woman said. "Henry and Alice, too."

She ended her story and sat in silence, watching Buckner closely.

"She did leave him, finally," Buckner asked.

The old woman's burning eyes fixed his, penetrating them. "That's what *he* said," she announced suddenly, in a high, clear, unaccented voice. She added, "Talk to the daughter."

Buckner thanked the woman as Elroy Dutton got to his feet.

"Thank you, Grandmother," he said.

The old woman spoke quickly to him in a low voice.

"I'll think about that, Grandmother," Dutton answered.

On their way out, Dutton slipped a thick wad of bills into a coffee can by the door.

Back outside, the sun blinded them, and the sharp autumn breeze reminded them of how hot it had been in the shack. Buster had finished his cigar and lighted another. The three men walked down the alley together.

"What was that last about?" Buckner asked.

"Oh, she wants me to marry and settle down and start a family."

Buckner pushed his hat back and scratched his sweaty head.

"Yeah," he said. "My mother hands me that line pretty regular. Whenever she can't think of something else to say."

"What about what she said? That help you any?" Dutton asked as they stood at the end of the alley. Children played baseball in the dusty street, using trash barrel lids for bases and a pick handle for a bat.

"I'm not sure," Buckner answered. "I'll have to think about everything she said. How reliable do you think her memory is? She must be eighty."

"Closer to ninety," said Dutton. "She told me once that she had seen her birth date written down in the Carpentier family Bible: eighteen thirty."

"So when she was 'young and strong' and taking in washing with Victoria Boyer, she was sixty." Buckner shook his head. "Is she really a conjure woman? Is that why they call her Ibo Mary?"

"They call her Ibo Mary because that's what she wants to be called," said Dutton. "She claims her father and mother were full-blooded Ibo, kidnapped from Africa and smuggled into Louisiana by the Lafitte brothers. They were bought right off the boat and came up here with the Carpentier family in the twenties. Mary was born on the Carpentier place ten years after that. She said they named her Mary Carpentier, but she says ever since the war—her war, not ours—she's been free, so she gets to have whatever name she wants. As for her being a conjure woman," Dutton shrugged. "Lots of folks come to her for cures. She uses old-time remedies, roots and herbs and things like that, but I don't think she casts any spells."

"Yes, she does," said Buster. "My little girl used to have stomach aches something terrible, then I taken her to Ibo Mary, and she said some words over her, and she stopped having them pains."

Dutton nodded. "I remember that, Buster. I suspect that the

words she said over your daughter were something like, 'Stop eating green apples, child.'" He laughed. Buster just frowned around his cigar and shook his head.

Buckner thanked Dutton and Buster and parted from the two men and crossed the tracks into the other side of Corinth.

He felt as though he were leaving one world, alien and mysterious, and entering another, familiar, comforting. But how comforting was it really? And how different? Elroy Dutton was operating an illegal drinking and gambling establishment, as were several businessmen he knew on the white side of town. He was now sure who the white businessmen were paying off, and he assumed Dutton must be paying somebody as well. But who? White police? What was Dutton's relationship with Bushyhead? How did Dutton know that the police, the white police, were listening to his telephone conversations? And why did Dutton tell him? In fact, why was Dutton helping him at all?

But more than that, what nagged at Buckner, tugging softly at a corner of his mind and popping into consciousness in quiet moments, was the image of a suitcase full of a little girl's clothing. What that might mean was something he did not want to think about at all.

He kept walking, toward the town square, around behind Coy's Drug Store. He climbed the stairs, knocked on the door, and entered.

He found Jeff Peck sitting at his desk, drinking.

"That smells like good bourbon," said Buckner from the doorway.

"Does that surprise you?" asked Peck.

"A little. I didn't know anybody was making anything like that around here."

"They aren't here, but they are in Canada."

"Then here's to our friendly neighbor to the north," said Buckner, sitting and pouring. It was a little early, and he had not eaten since breakfast, but Buckner wanted a drink just then.

"That's right," said Peck. "You're sort of an adopted Canadian, aren't you?"

"Sort of. Though they didn't seem to care where I was from when I enlisted in their army in 1915."

"'He that sheds his blood with me this day shall be my brother,'" Peck intoned.

"Absolutely," said Buckner, sipping his drink. The whiskey was good, but it went down with a shudder.

"You don't agree with our Great Experiment?" Peck asked, referring to Prohibition.

"No, and it's awkward as hell. I'm not much of a drinker, but I do like to take a drop from time to time, and now it's illegal." The moral ambiguity of prohibition disturbed Buckner's hard-edged sense of right and wrong.

"And you an officer of the law." Peck shook his head.

"Yes," Buckner agreed morosely. "But I spent the morning with Elroy Dutton, a man I know for a fact is breaking that law. He did it in my presence without a by-your-leave. I helped him do it. But I needed his help on something, so I couldn't exactly arrest him for selling booze to me."

"But your being with him, accepting his aid, implies your sanction of his other activities."

"It seems that way to me. But if I couldn't talk to anybody who drank, then I'd have to become a hermit, and I couldn't do my job that way."

"But now you're all tangled up with Chief Bushyhead over what he's doing." Peck grinned at his friend's dilemma.

"Yes, but that's about him taking money to look the other way. I don't do that."

"No," said Peck. "You just take payment in kind. Like help from Elroy Dutton. What are you going to say to Dutton when he comes asking you for a favor?"

"I don't know." Buckner shifted uncomfortably in his chair. "Tell him he's already been paid, I guess. After all, I didn't arrest him."

"He may not see it that way."

"I understand."

"What did he help you with?"

"I'm trying to find out what happened to the Boyer family back twenty-five years ago. He took me to meet an old Negro woman named Ibo Mary . . ."

"The conjure woman?"

"You know her?" Buckner was surprised.

"I've heard of her. My colleagues in the profession devote a great deal of energy to condemning her."

"Dutton says she uses herbs and roots to heal folks."

"Nothing wrong with that from a medical point of view," Peck said. He aimed a thumb in the direction of his examining room and the bottle-lined shelves. "That's where most of that stuff comes from. It's just processed and packaged by chemical companies for profit. Ibo Mary makes it available to people who can't afford the bottled variety." Peck drank some more whiskey. "But what do Ibo Mary and Victoria Boyer have to do with each other?"

"Back in the mid-nineties, Ibo Mary and Victoria Boyer were in business together, doing washing. I tried to get her to tell me where Victoria is now."

"What did she say?"

"She wouldn't talk about it, but she made it pretty obvious that she thinks Victoria's dead. She didn't say how she knew, either." Buckner told Ibo Mary's story.

"But Victoria finally did run off after the third child was born," said Peck, refilling both glasses when Buckner was done.

"I don't know," said Buckner. "Ibo Mary told me that she tried to get Victoria to run off, but that Victoria told her that she didn't have any kinfolk at all, so that if she did run off, she had no place to go, nobody to protect her. Besides, Ibo Mary seemed convinced she would never go off and leave her children. And when I told her that she'd run off anyway, she just looked at me and said 'That's what *he* said.'"

"Meaning what?"

"Like I said, she wouldn't tell me."

"So where does that leave you?"

"I don't know." Buckner thought a while. "I'm beginning to

get the feeling that if I can find out exactly what happened to Victoria, I'll be well along in finding exactly what happened to Louis."

"Why do you say that?"

"Because, if she's alive, she might be able to tell me something that would help me."

"If you can find her."

"Yes." Buckner continued, thinking aloud now. "And if she's dead, which I think is the case, maybe that will tell me something, too. But any way you look at it, I have to find out what happened to her. That's where this whole thing begins."

"You're sure of that?"

"I *feel* it."

"The science of criminology," Peck said.

"Art," Buckner corrected. Peck laughed.

"Who might know about her?" he asked.

Buckner shrugged. "She was from down in Arkansas. And she and her children lived up there north of town, almost completely isolated, practically Boyer's prisoners. Ibo Mary seems to have been closer to her than anybody else during that time."

"You need to talk to Boyer's children," Peck offered.

"I've already talked to two of them, Albert and Elizabeth. Albert said he came home from school one day and his mother was gone; and Elizabeth was just a baby. But Albert's been in Cape Girardeau for the past twenty years, and Elizabeth grew up as the daughter of a Jewish grain elevator owner in Pekin."

"Albert didn't have to stay in Cape Girardeau the whole twenty years," said Peck. "He could've come back any time he wanted to, including last Thursday, to smash in his father's head."

"He certainly hated his father," Buckner agreed. "But I don't think Albert knows for sure what happened to his mother; and," he went on, his tone reflecting his confusion, "If he killed his father because of that, why wait until now?"

"I don't know," Peck admitted. "What about that sister, Charlotte? She was the oldest. She might be able to tell you something."

"If I could find her. She ran off, too, and nobody seems to know where."

"Mother ran off, then the daughter." Peck thought a moment. "Any chance she kept in touch with her brother and sister?"

"Both Albert and Elizabeth say not."

"Any chance they're lying?"

"Sure, but why? Elizabeth says she never knew Charlotte or Albert. Albert and Charlotte were fairly close, but that was twenty-five years ago, and a pretty bad time, the way Albert tells it. And Elizabeth was never a part of any of that. According to her, she had a wonderful childhood with Angelina and Blumberg. Who weren't married, by the way."

Peck shrugged. "All you've proved," he said, "is that they wouldn't have much reason to try to find her; I'm talking about her finding them."

"I didn't really ask either one of them about that."

"Maybe you should."

"Maybe I should," he said, getting up. "Thanks for the whiskey."

"You're welcome." Peck poured the contents of Buckner's glass into his own.

Buckner left, heading for the town hall and the Ford.

As he was driving to Pekin, he realized that Elizabeth would still be at school. But maybe that was just as well. If she was in contact with Charlotte and Albert, she had said nothing about it the day before. Perhaps Angelina would be easier.

The older woman must have seen him come up, for she was standing in the doorway by the time he got onto the porch.

"Deputy," she said. "Back so soon?"

"Yes, ma'am," Buckner said. "I'm sorry to bust in on you like this. I just need to ask you something, then I'll be on my way."

"Come in," she said. "You're not interrupting anything important."

When they were seated once again before the fireplace, Buckner asked his question.

"Do you know where I can find Charlotte Boyer?"

Angelina looked at him steadily, a slight smile lifting the freshly rouged corners of her mouth. "Now, what makes you think I know where Charlotte Boyer is, Deputy, after twenty-five years?"

"I'm not convinced you do," Buckner admitted, returning her smile. "But Elizabeth might. And you might be able to tell me something about Elizabeth that will tell me what I want to know."

"What makes you think so?" It seemed to amuse her to fence with him.

"Oh, I'm just guessing."

"No," she said. "I mean, even if I do know, or could guess, where Charlotte is, what makes you think I'd tell you? After all, Deputy, if Elizabeth knew, she certainly didn't tell you, even though you gave her plenty of opportunity yesterday. Perhaps it's just something she wants to keep to herself."

"Maybe," Buckner agreed. "But I'm investigating a murder. That's most of what I do: go around and ask people rude questions about things they'd rather keep to themselves."

"Do you get many answers?"

"Enough. Sometimes people understand that I'm just trying to put criminals in jail, and they help me. Some people seem to be carrying things around with them, like a heavy pack, and they're glad to have someone to unload on. Sometimes they don't want to help me but they do anyway, by what they don't tell me, or the way they lie."

"I haven't told you any lies," said Angelina. She did not seem offended.

"I don't believe you have," Buckner responded. "But Elizabeth was very careful to say that her brother and sister had not sought her out; but when she said that, you looked surprised."

"I thought Blumberg had taught me how to play poker better than that," she said, blushing.

"You do all right," Buckner admitted. "Has Elizabeth been in touch with Charlotte?"

"I don't know, for certain, Deputy. Honestly, I don't."

"But you think so."

She hesitated, then spoke. "All I know for certain is that, starting about her twelfth birthday, Elizabeth began asking about her real family. I took that to be perfectly normal, since she obviously wasn't ours, and we never tried to fool her into believing she was. I was honest with her, as I told you, while trying to protect her. I do know that, for years now, she has gotten letters and picture postcards from all over. St. Louis, Kansas City, even New York City. All sorts of places."

"Have there been many of these?"

"Just on her birthday. And not every year, either, for many years. But she's gotten more lately. I mean at other times besides her birthday. "

"Is she still getting them?"

"In the last four years, she's gotten two from Jackson."

"Only two?"

"Only two that I know about. Usually I pick up the mail; it gives me a reason to go to town. But lately she picks it up, since she's in town, and she wants to be helpful. Consequently, I wouldn't see what mail she got."

"Two from Jackson in the last four years," said Buckner.

"Yes, and that was the first time she ever got two from the same place in a long time. Of course, I don't know who they were from. I've tried never to pry into Elizabeth's personal life."

"Did she answer them?"

"I don't know. Honestly, I did not try very hard to find out. I think I did not want to admit to myself that Elizabeth might try to find her real family."

"Do you think that is what she has been doing?"

The woman shook her head, but said nothing. Her face was red, and her eyes glistened with tears. Buckner felt sure he would learn nothing more from Angelina that day.

He stood up and thanked her. She showed him to the door and he drove back to town. He parked the Ford at the curb in front of his house and ran inside. His mother was out and his father dozed quietly in his chair in the front window. Buckner did not disturb him. He ate an apple and some bread and drank some milk at the table in the kitchen. He brewed a pot of coffee and drank a cup. As he was pouring another, his father walked in and filled a cup, and the two of them sat together drinking coffee.

"How've you been?" Buckner asked.

"All right, considering," his father answered.

Buckner nodded and drank coffee.

"You know," he said. "Sometimes I can be an awful fool."

"Glad to hear you finally agree with me," his father answered. "You been foolish about anything in particular?"

"About what goes on in this town."

"I thought local goings-on was your job."

"I guess it is, but I've been having a hard time admitting it to myself. I've tried to build a wall between the town and the county, and ignore what went on in town. Maybe I need to start looking a little closer."

"Not a bad idea."

Buckner glanced at his watch; school would be letting out soon. He said goodbye to his father, left the house, and drove the short distance to the school. He sat at the curb with the Ford idling vigorously.

The new high school had been built in 1912. The town had grown, and so had an interest in education. The square, stolid, two-story red brick building seemed a fitting emblem of the community's progress. Buckner had attended high school in a four-room clapboard building in Jackson, and always believed he'd gotten a pretty good education. He wondered if this fancy new school produced better students.

At 3:30, a loud bell rang, and seconds later the doors flew back and what looked like hundreds of boys and girls exploded through them and out onto the sidewalks. Immediately they broke up into little groups that formed and scattered and reformed, usually around some pretty girl or big, good-looking boy. Buckner noted that the farm kids, in denim overalls and gingham dresses, clustered together, separate from the town kids, in their suits or middie blouses and skirts. It was a warm Indian summer afternoon, and most of the students carried their coats and sweaters over their arms or tied around their shoulders. Footballs arched between groups of scrambling boys; the girls watched them and turned to talk, their heads leaning together. They would look back at the posturing boys and laugh. Just watching them made Buckner feel old, and when he got out of the Ford, his bad leg seemed stiffer than usual.

Inside the building, Buckner was stopped by a tall woman with smiling, direct eyes.

"Can you tell me where I can find Elizabeth, ah, Blumberg?" he asked.

"You're James Buckner, aren't you?" said the woman, holding out her hand.

"Yes," said Buckner, puzzled. He grasped her hand. Her grip was firm and, to his surprise, exciting.

"I'm Judith Lee." She laughed pleasantly at his confusion. "We met two years ago, at a Red Cross fund-raising dance. Martha Jane and I are great friends."

"Oh," said Buckner. He could not remember ever seeing this woman before in his life, which surprised him, for she was very pretty. "I apologize for not recognizing you. You're a teacher."

"I'm the assistant principal," she corrected him.

"Of course," said Buckner. He could feel himself blushing. "What happened to Miss Roach? I'm sorry, but you don't seem, I mean . . ."

"Old enough?"

"Well, yes," Buckner admitted. "That is, not old enough to be an assistant principal."

"You're very kind. Several members of the school board agree with you, but they thought Miles, I mean Principal Wagron, needed a more energetic assistant than Miss Roach, who is sixty-three, after all. So they retired her and hired me. I managed to convince them that twenty-eight isn't particularly young."

"I suppose not, but doesn't your husband mind?"

"I expect he would, if I had one," she said, laughing.

"I see," said Buckner.

"Yes," she said. "I hear that tone in your voice. 'Another emancipated woman.' But you didn't think your sister would be friends with any other kind, did you?"

"Not really."

"We're not such a bad lot, once you get to know us." Her eyes glittered with something like a challenge. "We're certainly a great deal more interesting than the more traditional sort."

"I suppose," Buckner said.

"But surely you must find the old-fashioned sort of woman terribly dull; after all, you've been to France."

"Yes, I have, but I don't see what that has to do with it. I didn't go there to meet women."

"I know," she said in a matter-of-fact tone. "Martha Jane told me everything, all about what a hero you were, and how you got hurt. But you must have met some French girls, and nurses. I can't believe they were blushing violets."

"I suppose not," Buckner agreed. His discomfort was growing, and he was desperate to change the subject. "Can you tell me where Miss Blumberg is?"

"I'm keeping you from your business," she said. "Forgive me." She smiled.

"Not at all," answered Buckner. Her smile seemed to suggest that forgiveness was not what she wanted. Was his sister this way with strange men? He hoped not.

"Elizabeth is in Room 102, down the hall that way." She pointed.

"Thank you," said Buckner, still looking at her.

"You're welcome," said Judith Lee with a nod and a satisfied grin. She turned and walked through a door marked "Office." Buckner, frowning and shaking his head, went in search of Room 102.

The door to the room stood open, and Buckner entered. Afternoon light slanted through high windows. The walls were covered with maps of Italy and England and pictures of literary figures. Elizabeth Blumberg stood at a small podium at the front of the classroom, reading aloud in a clear soprano voice from a thick volume.

"'Yet who would have thought,'" she said, her voice tinged with horror, "'the old man to have had so much blood in him?'"

She certainly sounded genuinely frightened to Buckner.

At desks in the front row sat three young men gazing fixedly at their teacher. They hardly noticed Buckner as he stood in the doorway. They watched her with wide eyes, bemused expressions, and blushing cheeks.

Elizabeth saw him and stopped. She closed the book. "That will be all for today, gentlemen," she said.

"But, Miss Blumberg . . ." began one boy.

"We can work on this tomorrow, if you like, Edward," said Elizabeth with quiet firmness. "That is all for now."

Instantly the three young men gathered up their books and papers and, with many a backward glance, left the room.

"Budding scholars?" said Buckner, smiling.

"I doubt it," she answered. Her voice was now flat, her face expressionless, and her eyes watched him closely. "How may I help you, Deputy?"

"I need to ask if you know where your sister is." He stepped toward her, closing the door behind him.

She stared at him, her eyes widening slightly. "What makes you think I know that?"

Buckner did not want to tell her what Angelina had said, so he said nothing, simply stood and looked down at her, permitting his size and grim expression to threaten her. She did not seem threatened, but she did take a step back and to one side so that the podium stood as a barrier between them. She looked past him, at the closed door, then up at him, watchfulness clouding her eyes now.

"You have heard from her," Buckner said.

"Yes." She turned and went to a window.

"Recently?"

"No. Not for a year or more." She continued to look out the window as she spoke. The yard, which had been full of students earlier, was empty now.

"But before?" Buckner pressed her.

"Yes."

"Often?" His question came quickly.

"No. Sometimes not for two or three years." Elizabeth's voice was sad. "And then only a picture postcard from someplace far away."

"Letters?" His tone was flat, impersonal.

"Yes. Once in a while. She seemed to want to confide in me."

"What do you mean?"

"Well, the post cards were always quick and cheerful, just a few lines. The letters were longer, sometimes filled with news of her doings, sometimes . . . tormented." She looked directly at Buckner now, her eyes large and luminous, her thick, dark lashes wet with tears. She blinked them at him. "Oh, I think she has had a very hard life, Deputy."

"Did you keep any of the letters?" Buckner avoided any indication of sympathy.

"No. I still have some of the post cards, because of the pictures. But I couldn't keep the letters. They were too sad. They made me feel guilty, almost, that I had grown up with Angelina and Blumberg, and not with . . . him . . . my father."

"Because the family was so poor?"

"Yes, but more than that." She hesitated, her own face red now.

"What?" Buckner insisted, pushing her.

"I don't know," she shook her head violently, as though to drive out Buckner's questions. "I'm not sure," she insisted. "She didn't say, really, in any of the letters. I don't know." Her voice was tighter now, and colder, as she regained a measure of self-control.

Buckner nodded. He shifted tactics now, shaping his face and voice into expressions of sympathy and kindness.

"All right," he said softly, smiling slightly. "Do you have any idea at all where I might find her?"

"Deputy," Elizabeth pleaded. "I don't want to hurt my sister. I want you to stay away from my family altogether."

"I understand," said Buckner. "But a man has been murdered."

"A terrible man!" said Elizabeth, her voice harsh. She came closer now, still keeping the podium between them. "A man who drank and treated his family terribly, a man nobody liked and nobody will miss. What can we have to do with that?"

"I don't know. But I have to find out who killed Louis Boyer."

"Why? Who cares?" She was gripping the podium with one hand, and her knuckles were white, her eyes hardened against fear.

"I guess I do," he answered.

"Then you're the only one," she said harshly.

"Yes," he agreed. "That's why the county pays me."

"It's too bad you can't earn your money in a more respectable way, Deputy," Elizabeth said coldly. "But, in any case, I'm not going to help you do it if it means jeopardizing my family's peace of mind."

They stood and watched each other for a minute. Finally, Buckner turned and left the room. The halls were dark now, quiet, empty of students and teachers. School had been out for barely half an hour, but everyone had fled as though from a plague. The afternoon sun streamed through windows and the classroom doors, casting long rectangular blocks of light onto the hallway floor. From somewhere in the building, Buckner could hear the sound of a bucket clanking and the wet splash of a mop. He smelled chalk dust and sweeping compound.

Assistant Principal Judith Lee had not left. She stood outside the office door, leaning with one shoulder against the wall, her arms folded, making no attempt to conceal the fact that she was waiting for him. When she saw him, she smiled and came toward him. She wore a navy blue skirt, white blouse, and navy blue sweater. Although the outfit seemed designed to disguise the fact, Buckner saw that she had an attractive, slim figure. Her dark hair was bobbed, and she her large pale gray eyes that watched him from under level brows.

"Did you find Miss Blumberg?" She spoke lightly, making conversation.

"Yes." Buckner was in no mood for chitchat, but something held him there.

"I'm sorry it didn't go well."

"It went all right."

"Oh." She frowned slightly. "You don't look like it did."

"It went fine," said Buckner sharply. "I'm sorry. Bullying young girls is new to me." He paused. "There are times," he finally said, "when I don't care much for being a police officer." He walked through the front door; she stayed with him, matching his long stride.

"Then why do you do it?" She actually seemed to want to know.

He stopped sharply, turned, and looked at her. "I do it because I'm good at it!" he said. "And because it's something that needs doing. Was Elizabeth Blumberg here on Friday?" he asked abruptly.

"Of course."

"Are you sure?"

"It's my job to know if one of my teachers is absent, Deputy," she said firmly. "Besides, I gave her a ride home at the end of the day. Her automobile wouldn't start." She laughed. "Terrible things, aren't they? Automobiles, I mean. We get so dependent on them that we're crippled when they don't operate properly."

"Thank you," said Buckner. He jammed his hat on his head and walked to the Ford.

She followed him, refusing to be put off by his bad mood. She watched as he cranked the Ford to life and put her hand on his arm as he was getting in.

"Yes?" He turned, one foot on the running board.

"If you'd like to discuss this matter further," she said, her pale eyes watching him closely, "I live at the corner of Maple and Jefferson. The brown house with the rose bushes across the front."

"Rose bushes? Sounds like Sleeping Beauty's castle," muttered Buckner.

"Not at all," said Judith Lee.

He got in and she stood and watched until he had driven away. Then she smiled and went back inside the school.

Buckner drove to the town hall and went inside, continuing up to the second floor and through a door marked "Coroner's Office." A short woman, with hips and thighs so wide they made her rather small upper body appear as though it belonged to someone else entirely, stood before the open drawer of a file cabinet. With studied casualness, she stopped what she was doing and slowly turned her head.

"Good afternoon, Deputy." Her voice conveyed the weary patience of a dedicated public servant. "Something I can get for you?"

"I hope so. I need to look at the death records for 1896."

"Really?" She raised her eyebrows, perhaps her first animated expression of the day. "Anybody in particular?"

"I don't know for sure. I expect it'll be listed under Unknown White Female."

"All right." The woman smiled slightly. "I'll get the book."

In a moment, she returned, carrying a large volume in both hands. She set it on the counter. The red leather binding was old and crumbling, and produced a fine, dry powder that permeated the air around it.

"Is there somewhere I could sit down to read this?" Buckner asked.

"I suppose," she answered, gesturing toward a desk by the window.

Under the woman's interested eye, Buckner walked around the counter and sat at the desk. He opened the book and started at the first entry, January seventh, 1896, written with black ink in a clear, spiky hand. The pages were thick, creamy white, gold-edged, and lined in faint, light blue. He took a large bandanna from his hip pocket and brushed the red powder from his hands as he began to read.

At first he read quickly, following his finger as it tracked down the list of names. But as he began to read more of the entries, he found himself drawn into the stories contained in the terse, official language, and his progress slowed. Two hours later, he had reached December, surprised at the number of people who had died in that year, and the variety of their passings. Young brides drank lye; farmers fell into machinery and were chewed to bits; brother butchered brother over the next pull from the jug. Some people even died of old age. And some did not. One old woman sat bolt upright in her coffin during the most solemn part of her funeral and demanded to know when supper was.

But as interesting as these people were, none of them was Victoria Boyer.

In all but a handful of cases, the deceased was well known, with numerous relatives and friends to provide identification. There had been seven corpses that year, however, that had gone into nameless graves. Three were men, found dead along the railroad tracks. One body belonged to a woman who had frozen to death in an unused shed near the edge of town. No one had known she was there, but several people remembered seeing her around town that autumn. She had been at least sixty when she died. Another body was that of a newborn baby girl, found in a pile of trash in an alley in town.

Which left two. One was a female found floating in the Osage River after the spring floods, her features eaten away by water and the creatures that lived in it. She had apparently been shot to death; a local doctor found a .38 caliber bullet in her body. The other was the partially decomposed body of a woman found in a shallow grave by a man and his son who had gone deer hunting. The rib cage and legs of the corpse were crushed.

Buckner wrote down the details of both cases in his pocket notebook and closed the large volume. He sat and stared out the window, trying to make sense of what he had learned. If Victoria Boyer had left town, the unidentified bodies meant nothing. If she had died and her body had never been found, he had nothing. If she had simply gone south a few miles, running desperately to get away rather than to go somewhere in particular, and had died in another county, he had the same problem.

"Excuse me, Deputy," said the clerk. "Are you ready to look at 1897 now?"

Buckner looked up. "1897? Why would I want to look at that?"

"I don't know, I'm sure," she said. "But the last one in here looking at death records looked at 1897 next. He went all the way to 1900."

"Last one? Who was that?"

"That detective fella that works for Baxter Bushyhead."

"Harris?"

"Yes, that's the one."

"He was looking at this book?"

"Yes, six weeks, two months ago. I only remember that far back cause nobody ever wants to look at these, and now here's two in two months."

"Did Detective Harris say why he wanted to look at them?"

"No more than you did, Deputy."

Buckner grinned sheepishly. "Sorry. I'm trying to find out what happened to a woman named Victoria Boyer. She disappeared in 1896. Her husband told everybody at the time that she had gone back to her family. Sometimes it was Jefferson City, other times it was Arkansas. But someone told me that she didn't have any family at all, not in either place. This same person also led me to believe that Victoria Boyer is dead." Buckner's smile now became warmer, more engaging. "I realize you must've been little more than a child at the time, Nell, but do you remember anything about that?"

The woman laughed raucously. "Not bad, Deputy," she said as she calmed down. "Not bad at all. Harris just offered me money." She wiped her eyes. "I'll take sweet talk anytime. In fact, I had been in this office for three years in 1896, and I remember it quite well. The middle of the depression, folks around here were barely getting by. There were tramps everywhere, and people up and left their families all the time, men and women both. Sometimes they thought they were doing them some good, going to find a decent job and send money back, save them the extra mouth to feed. Mostly they just got to where they couldn't take it and left. If this Victoria Boyer said she was going off to live with her kinfolk in 1896, she'd be like a whole lot of other folks who did the same thing, and were never seen again."

"So she really could have gone off," Buckner said. "But how could she have survived?"

"If she took to the rails and wasn't damned tough, and careful, and lucky, then she could have ended up dead and buried anywhere between here and California." She thought a moment. "Which Boyer was this, anyway? There must be a dozen or more of them around here, even more over in Washington County."

"This was Louis Boyer's wife."

"The body man, had that shop up on the Jackson Road? He got himself killed the other day, I hear."

"Yes, he did."

She shook her head. "Don't believe I ever knew them," she said.

Buckner got up. "I can't honestly say you've helped me, Nell." The woman shrugged. "But it was interesting to hear that Detective Harris was trying to find to find out what happened to Victoria Boyer, too."

"You never heard that from me, Deputy. There's an election coming up, and I need this job. The Democrats lose, and I'll have to stay home and cook dinner for Clyde and them damned kids of mine."

Her laughter echoed down the dark hallway as Buckner headed straight for the police department, where he found Detective Harris on his way out.

"Have you got a minute, Detective?" Buckner asked.

Harris paused and looked at him suspiciously, but said nothing.

"I believe you might have some information that would help with a case I'm working on," Buckner said, still trying to appear friendly. "The Boyer killing. I thought we might compare notes."

"What makes you think that?" Harris's tone was jeering, offensive.

Buckner said, "I could really use the help."

"I don't think that would be a good idea," said Harris, brushing past him and heading for the stairs.

"Thank you," Buckner called after him.

He went down the hall and spoke to Desk Sergeant Givens.

"I just ran into Detective Harris on his way out the door. When will he be back?" he asked.

"Not till tonight. He usually takes Tuesday daytime off."

"Why is that?"

"Cause he works Tuesday nights. Especially toward the end of the month."

"What time does his shift start?"

Givens looked at Buckner suspiciously. "Why do you want to know, Buck?"

"I need to talk to him about this Boyer case I'm working on. I think he can help me."

Givens nodded, apparently satisfied. He said, "He goes on at six."

"Thanks." Buckner said.

"You're welcome."

Buckner reached for the telephone, then, remembering what Elroy Dutton had told him, changed his mind and went upstairs and out. He walked across the square to the Chamber of Commerce offices, where Sophia Malcolm, as secretary to T.T. Court, township Democratic chairman, oversaw the local election headquarters. She was bundling handbills, and Buckner sensed an element of panic in her actions.

"What?" she snapped as he stood waiting.

"Is T.T. in?"

"No!"

"All right. Just tell him I won't be able to meet with him to plan the rally on Saturday. I'm in the middle of a murder investigation."

"Louis Boyer's?"

"Yes."

Sophia sniffed. "You missed the luncheon. One of these days, Deputy, you're going to figure out what's important and what's not."

Buckner stood looking at her, his face expressionless, until she blushed and looked away.

"Just tell him."

"I will."

"Thank you."

He caught up on his paperwork until dusk, then went to Coy's Drug Store for a sandwich and a cup of coffee. As he ate, he considered various approaches to Detective Harris. Obviously, a direct and friendly strategy was not going to work. He was going to have to try something else.

He returned to his office to look up Detective Harris's address, and to wait for time to pass. At five forty-five, he left his office and headed home. He went through the front door of the house, straight on and out the back, with barely a nod to his parents, who were setting the table for dinner.

He was not certain that he was being watched, but he knew he couldn't risk the possibility. He continued through the neighbor's back yard, and out onto the street behind. He circled around and waited. In a moment, two men in ill-fitting suits took up positions in the shadow of a large tree some twenty yards from his house. Buckner smiled and headed across town and took up his own post outside a small clapboard house. When Harris's short, heavy figure emerged, Buckner waited a bit before following him. He followed him for several hours as he made his stops. At each stop the same routine occurred. Harris would knock softly on a shadowed door; the door would open a crack while whispered words were exchanged; then Harris would slip inside, to emerge, eventually, and move on to the next door.

Sometime after midnight, Buckner watched Harris step into the dark alley behind a small hardware store. He casually looked both ways, and headed out onto the square. Buckner followed, and caught up with him on the street.

"Hello, Detective," Buckner said, suddenly coming abreast of the man.

Harris jerked violently and stared at him with startled eyes. His hand flew to his pocket, and then stopped.

"Goddammit, you son of a bitch, what the hell do you think you're doing, sneaking up on me like that?"

"Didn't mean to scare you, Detective," said Buckner, smiling.

"You didn't scare me," said Harris. "But you could get hurt, creeping around like that."

"I'll keep it in mind," Buckner said.

"What do you want?" Harris demanded as they walked along.

"Why, I want to talk to you, Detective," said Buckner in a soothing tone. "And there's no point in looking around like that. Those two boys the Chief has set on me are standing outside my house right now, waiting for me to come out."

"Get the hell out of my way," Harris said quietly. "I'm not afraid of you."

"That's fine, Detective," said Buckner, his friendliness slipping away. He clung to his friendly tone, however. "You tell me what I want to know, and we can just forget about the places you visited tonight."

"What do you mean?" The two men stopped walking. Harris narrowed his eyes. One hand brushed his side pocket.

"I mean that I followed you tonight on your rounds. You visited practically every illegal drinking establishment in Corinth—and there's a lot more of them than I thought—and collected the police department's protection money. That's what you're holding onto in your coat there." Harris's hand dropped to his side. "Now, these places are operating in violation of state and federal laws, and you're helping them to do that. I have a friend in the state attorney general's office over in Jefferson City who thinks he owes me a big favor. If I ask him to, he'll be more than happy to come over here and drop on you like a ton of bricks."

Harris stepped back and suddenly punched Buckner hard in the stomach, catching him off guard. As Buckner doubled over, gasping for breath, Harris clubbed him with his fist on the back of the neck. Buckner put out a hand to keep himself from falling. Harris brought a blackjack from his back pocket and raised it over his head. A voice called out and Harris looked up. Someone was coming across the square, through the darkness toward him.

"Hey!" called the figure. "What's going on there?"

Harris returned the blackjack to his pocket, turned, and ran across the square.

Jim Buckner looked up in time to see a dim shape disappear around the corner of the town hall. Then somebody was helping him up.

"Are you all right?" said the voice. "Say! Deputy Buckner! What's going on here?"

"Nothing," said Buckner, breathing deeply. He recognized the acned face of George DePew, the projectionist at the small movie house on the square. He must have been headed home after closing up for the night. "Thanks, George," he said. "Sorry, don't have time to explain." He inhaled deeply to clear his head and started off the way Harris had gone.

"You're welcome," George called out. The man stood for a moment in the dark and now empty square, then turned away and resumed his walk home.

Buckner stopped in the dark shadows of the town hall and listened. He could hear no running footsteps, no barking dogs. He looked at the ground. It was packed bare earth, and showed no clear prints. He walked along the wall of the building. The corner of the building was just ahead. Buckner's feet clomped loudly, announcing, he hoped, his arrival at the ambush site. As he reached the corner, Buckner bent double and dove forward, somersaulting to come to his feet. He heard the blackjack slash the air behind him. He turned and struck Harris hard under the ribs on the left side as the detective was straightening up to attempt another blow. Harris folded up with a whoosh. Buckner struck him twice in the left kidney, with hard, pounding blows. Harris fell to his hands and knees, the blackjack landing on the ground next to him. Buckner picked it up and put it in his pocket. Harris was reaching for his hip and Buckner punched him in the kidney twice more, as hard as he could, all of his weight driving down behind the fist. Harris collapsed and lay on the ground. His breath came in thin wheezes.

Buckner placed one foot firmly on Harris's left wrist and held it down, grinding it into the dirt. Then he took Harris's right arm and bent it double behind his back as he reached into the man's hip pocket to remove the pistol he found there. Buckner shoved it into his belt. Then he turned Harris over and thrust him into a sitting position with his back against the wall. Harris sat bent forward, clutching his mid-section and moaning. Buckner went through his coat pockets and removed a badge in a leather case, and a thick envelope. These he put in his own hip pocket.

"Jesus Christ," Harris gasped after a time. "What did you do to me?"

"I expect you'll be pissing blood for a week," Buckner said cheerfully. "Now, if you don't want to end up in a hospital, talk to me."

"Fuck you," Harris muttered. "Bushyhead'll have your hide for this."

"No, he won't," Buckner said. He shoved Harris's head sharply against the wall and held it there, his hand around the man's throat. The ripe melon sound of Harris's head hitting the wall made Buckner's lips draw back over his teeth in a kind of grin. Harris's eyes were full of pain and fear, and he was making gurgling sounds in his throat.

"You listen carefully, Detective Harris, and stop cursing me." Buckner's voice was soft, caressing, his grip on Harris's throat just tight enough to make his breathing difficult and speech painful. "The minute the state and federal authorities come in, Bushyhead will drop you like a hot potato. Suddenly this whole payoff scheme will be your own private little operation. The Chief will be surprised and shocked that one of his own men, someone he has trusted and worked with for so many years, could be involved in something like this. And he will, with much sorrow, let justice take its course, and the big shots here in town that back him up will nod their heads and sip the fancy bourbon that he sells them, and do nothing. You will be left high and dry, Detective Harris."

There was a long silence as Harris looked up at Buckner, realization dawning in his eyes. He nodded. Buckner released his grip and sat back on his heels. He could feel his bad leg tightening up.

"Yeah, he'd sure as hell do something like that." Harris thought a long time before going on. "All right," he said softly. "It doesn't matter. You'll never be able to stop him. He's got too much money, too many important people behind him, like you said. You're just asking for trouble, but I'll tell you what you want to know about him."

"I'm not after Chief Bushyhead. That's not what I want to talk to you about."

"What's this all about, then?" Harris was genuinely mystified.

"I just want to know what happened to Victoria Boyer."

"What?" Harris was surprised and confused.

"Victoria Boyer. She used to live around here, but she disappeared twenty-five years ago."

"Twenty-five years ago! What makes you think I know anything about somebody that's been dead for twenty-five years?"

"So that's what Ibo Mary meant," said Buckner, nodding. "She did die."

Harris said nothing and turned his face away. Buckner waited a moment. "Look," he said in as friendly a tone as he could manage. "I'm working on a murder investigation. You seem to have some information that might assist me. Why don't you give me a little help?"

"Why should I?" Harris's belligerence was losing its edge.

Buckner shook his head. "You just haven't been paying attention, Detective. You need to tell me what I want to know for two reasons. One, we're both police officers, and we should cooperate; two, if you don't, I'm going to pound your head into that wall some more until one or the other gives out. I'm betting your head will go soft before the wall does. What do you think?"

"Jesus," said Harris under his breath.

"Come on, now, Detective. Make this easier on both of us. Think of it as professional courtesy."

Harris looked off into the darkness for a long time before he spoke.

"I'm not sure, but I think Louis killed her," he said finally.

"What makes you say that?"

"Some evidence; some guessing." Harris paused and considered. "I think it all started when Louis found out Victoria was pregnant. He was living pretty much full time with Angelina Robideaux, and only going to the shop to work, which wasn't very often, since he wasn't getting much work by then. But he must've been doing more than just working or sleeping it off, I guess. Anyway, after he found out Victoria was going to have another baby, I think something snapped. He chased off Ibo Mary and her pickaninnies. Then Elizabeth was born that summer. Not too long after that, I believe Louis killed Victoria."

"How?"

"I think he ran over her."

"Why do you say that?"

"Because of the condition the body was in. Let me finish." Harris resumed his story. "Louis killed Victoria sometime in late August, early September, dragged her off in the woods and buried her. Then, later that year, a couple of things happened. Charlotte took off. This actually suited Louis, since he didn't want to have to worry about children; and it made it easier for people to believe that Victoria had run off, too: like mother, like daughter. Then he sent Albert to his brother in Cape Girardeau, which got rid of him. But then something else happened that he hadn't exactly counted on."

"Angelina took Elizabeth to raise."

"Right." Harris smiled slightly. "You have done some work."

Buckner ignored that. "So Louis drops Angelina because she won't give up the baby, and the last thing he wants messing up his life is a baby. But then what?"

"Simple, when you think about Louis."
"He took up with another woman."
"Right."
"But, who?"
"An octoroon named Mabel Yellin."
"He took up with a Negro woman?" Buckner was surprised.
"Yeah." Harris was disgusted.
"Where's she?"
"Dead, now. Died not too long after I talked to her. Hell, she was dying *while* I was talking to her, practically. Coughing all the time, wheezing, couldn't hardly breathe. Anyway, she told me that she and Louis were together for about a year after he left Angelina Robideaux. But the important part is that, in December, not too long after they took up housekeeping, Louis started cussing and carrying on over a newspaper story he read. She asked him what it was and he told her to keep her damned mouth shut or she'd get the same."

"What did that mean?"
"She told me. He was reading the newspaper one day; then he jumps up, throws it on the floor, and starts cussing. Then he started drinking. It wasn't long before he was drunk and asleep on the floor. That's when Mabel read the newspaper. He'd only been looking at the front page, so that's where she looked. She found a story about two hunters, a man and his son, who came across a body out in the woods south of town."

"The partially decomposed body of a woman, with crushed chest and legs," said Buckner.

"Right. It was too chewed up to tell who it was, but it was wearing a dress. And they sort of had to guess that it was a white woman, but they were pretty sure of that, because there was some blonde hair still attached to the scalp. The coroner's office decided she'd died from being run over by an automobile and whoever did it was afraid of getting caught, so they dragged her off into the woods. Anyway, the county buried her."

"Did this Mabel know who it was?"

"I think she guessed. Louis had told her about Victoria leaving him, but when she read that story, along with what he said to her, she just added it up and decided he'd killed her."

"And she kept quiet about it all this time?"

"Hell yes. After all, she was pretty sure the man was a murderer."

"Why'd she tell you?"

"Like I said, she was dying. Maybe she wanted to square things. I don't know." Harris shrugged. "I gave her some cigarettes and some money, for food or whatever she needed. Maybe she was just grateful."

"That's all pretty circumstantial," Buckner said.

"I told you, it was mostly guess work."

"Wouldn't hold up in court."

"Couldn't hardly even get a warrant on that," Harris agreed. "Not that it matters now."

"Why were you interested?"

"What do you mean?"

"I mean, why were you looking into the disappearance of Victoria Boyer?"

Harris hesitated, then shrugged. "I was paid to."

"Paid? Who by?"

"Woman up in Jackson."

"Who?"

"I don't know her name. She showed up in town one day last summer and wanted to hire me."

"Why you? And why *hire* you? You're a city employee, aren't you?"

Harris nodded. The movement seemed to hurt him. He winced. "Sometimes I do outside work. Hell, this sort of thing, looking into a twenty-five-year-old murder, doesn't come under my usual duties. Besides, I got four kids that eat like a span of mules, and the city doesn't exactly pay me a lot."

"Don't you get to keep some of the money you collect for Bushyhead?" Buckner asked.

"The Chief keeps most of it."

"So poverty led you to a life of crime," said Buckner.

"Fuck you, Deputy," Harris muttered. "Not everybody in the world is born rich."

Buckner smiled. "That's right; I'm just an eccentric millionaire playing deputy sheriff for fun. But you haven't said how the woman found you," he prompted.

"I have a friend on the force up in Jackson. He sends work my way and I do the same for him."

"So this woman, whose name you don't know, just appears in town and asks you to find out what happened to Victoria Boyer."

"She telephoned me and I met her down here."

"Did she pay in advance?"

"Half in advance; half on delivery."

"You took the information to her?"

"Yes."

"In Jackson?"

"Sure, where do you think?"

"Where in Jackson?" Buckner was getting exasperated. "Her home?"

"No. We met in a restaurant up there, the Emporia Cafe."

"So you never found out her name and you never found out where she lived," said Buckner.

Harris blinked and dropped his gaze. Buckner watched him and thought a moment.

"But you followed her from the restaurant, didn't you?"

Harris shrugged and nodded. "I guess I been a cop too long."

"I expect you have," agreed Buckner. "What was her address?"

"So you can go up there and squeeze some money out of her?" Harris said. "From the size of the house she lives in, she's got plenty."

"So I can find out who killed Louis Boyer," said Buckner patiently.

The two men looked at each other in silence. Finally Harris spoke.

"I don't see why you're bothering. Louis Boyer wasn't nobody at all."

"I know. What's the address?"

"1415 Grand St." Harris looked at Buckner and leered. "She lives there with another woman."

"Thank you," Buckner said. "Why didn't you tell me all this when you found out Louis had been killed? Or today on the stairs? You must have figured there was a connection."

"What difference does it make what I thought?" Harris said, some of his old resistance returning as he recovered. "I'm a city cop; sheriff's office doesn't mean shit to me. I figure you can do your own damned legwork. You're really just kind of a joke around the office, you know that? Big war hero got lucky last year and doped out a murder; you think that makes you a cop. You don't know the first thing about being a cop. You and that fat turd you work for can do your own damned investigating."

Buckner got stiffly to his feet and looked down at Harris. "But you did help me out after all, didn't you," he said.

"Only because you sucker-punched me."

Buckner nodded and turned away.

"Hey!" called Harris. "What about my stuff? I thought you said you weren't after Chief Bushyhead. If I don't come back with the money, it'll be my neck."

Buckner turned back. He took out the blackjack and pistol and looked at them. Then he looked at Harris.

"I'll be keeping the envelope," he said. "As for these, you sure you want these back?" He took a step forward. He was smiling his strange grin, and he felt a thrill racing through his body. "You want me to give you back your toys and then you can face me and see if I sucker-punched you?"

Harris leaned back into the wall and made a pushing motion with both hands. "Never mind," he said. "Forget it."

Buckner nodded and walked away. His heart had stopped pounding by the time he got home. He saw the two men watching from the shadows and waved to them as he went up the front walk and into the house. He went to bed and fell asleep at once.

WEDNESDAY, OCTOBER 27

THE NEXT MORNING, Buckner took the train to Jackson. The ride was brief and pleasant. He slept the whole way.

Once in Jackson, he went straight to the County Sheriff's office. The office occupied most of the second floor of the county court house; the Jackson Police Department took up the rest. The jail was on the floor above. The office was a warren of tiny rooms, anterooms, and alcoves with desks shoved into them. Normally quiet, the office was alive with activity, most of it directed at getting Elmer Aubuchon reelected. Clerks and officers strode about urgently with stacks of posters or fliers in their hands; phones rang; sergeants shouted orders. One deputy concentrated on gluing red-white-and-blue ribbons to little buttons with the Sheriff's picture on them. Buckner looked around for any law enforcement activity. At the booking desk, under a large, red, white, and blue "Reelect Elmer Aubuchon" banner, three dapper young men in tight suits and plug hats sneered around their cigarettes at the desk sergeant who was taking their valuables. Two arresting officers stood nearby. Their eyes were red, their uniforms were wrinkled, and they looked like they had not slept in a week. At a bench along the wall, a young woman in an astonishingly short lavender satin party dress with a large dark stain down one side sat staring morosely at something in the middle distance. The knee of one of her dark silk stockings was ripped out, and the skin was torn and bleeding. Next to her was an older woman, hands thrust deep into the pockets of a long, dark coat, man's shoes on her feet, who concentrated on the floor.

As the arresting officers led the three dapper young men away, the booking sergeant looked up.

"Hey, Buck! You come up here for the monster rally?"

"Rally?"

"Yeah. Tonight. Over at the auction barn. Lieutenant Governor's coming in. Sheriff's giving a speech."

"Uh, no. I'm looking into a murder. Sheriff in?"

"That's you, ain't it, Buck?" said the sergeant with a friendly smile. "All business. Sheriff, too, now I think about it. Just different business."

"Is he in?" Buck repeated with growing impatience.

"No, as a matter of fact, he ain't. You just missed him, though. He's headed out south of town to post some handbills."

"I thought that's why he had deputies," said Buckner sarcastically. He turned and hurried for the door.

He managed to catch his boss at the county garage just as he was pulling out. The Sheriff, he noted, drove a new Packard.

"Howdy, Buck!" he called, waving a chubby hand out the window. "What're you doing up here?"

"I need to talk to you, if you've got a minute."

"All right." The sheriff stopped the automobile and got out.

Elmer Aubuchon wore a faded tweed jacked over a tie-less khaki work shirt buttoned to the neck, denim overalls, and heavy work boots. He weighed over three hundred pounds and was the fattest man Buckner had ever known. He was also enormously strong and agile, and Buckner had once seen him, on a bet, kick the top of a door while standing *in* the doorway. He had seven children, all boys and all big. His wife, Sarah, might have weighed a hundred pounds, with flatirons in her apron pockets.

Aubuchon's hand went automatically into a pocket and

emerged clutching a brown paper sack. He reached into the sack and took out a piece of red hard candy. He slid it into his mouth, and sat down on the running board, causing the Packard to tip dangerously. A warm smile spread his thick, shining lips.

"Want one?" he asked, holding out the tattered sack.

"No, thanks," Buckner said.

"The red ones got cinnamon in 'em," the Sheriff said with a grin. "Hot stuff!" He sucked noisily as if to prove it. "Now what can I do for you, Buck?"

"I'm in the middle of something down in Corinth, and I wanted to talk to you about it. Did you get my report?"

"Yes. This that Boyer killing?"

"Yes. I'm looking for Charlotte Boyer."

"Who's Charlotte Boyer?"

"The victim's daughter."

"She involved somehow?"

"I don't know for sure," he confessed.

Aubuchon just nodded. Buckner had known commanding officers who hung over their subordinates' shoulders, watching everything closely, offering advice, suggestions, orders on how to do it right. Elmer Aubuchon picked men he thought could do the job, and then let them do it.

"And she lives here in Jackson?" he asked.

"So I've been told."

"You check the city directory?"

"Not yet," Buckner admitted. "I've got an address. I wanted to stop by and talk to you first. Let you know I was in town on business."

Aubuchon nodded. "I appreciate it. You think you'll need any help on this?"

Buckner shook his head. "I'm just going to talk to her. Find out what she's got to say for herself."

Aubuchon looked relieved. "Want to talk to Pinch?" he asked.

Eldon Pinch was the county prosecutor.

"Not yet," Buckner said. "Hell, all I know for sure is that somebody killed Louis Boyer."

"Think she done it?"

"Got no proof she did."

"Got any proof anybody did it?"

"Nope."

"Too bad. What're you going to do?"

"Keep looking for sign, I guess; talking to people."

"All right, Buck. But I hope you aren't forgetting to campaign."

"No," Buckner lied.

"Now, what's this about you having a run-in with the police down there?"

"Bushyhead come whining to you about that?"

"Yes." Aubuchon began to crunch his piece of candy. "Look, Buck, I know Baxter Bushyhead's a pretty poor excuse for a police officer, but he was a good one once, and he's the stud duck in Corinth, and we've got to work with him, so you've got to try to stay off his toes."

"I'm doing the best I can, Sheriff," Buckner protested.

"He said you rousted one of his officers."

"That's not exactly what happened. I walked into the Dew Drop Inn and saw Vince Marolis and Bushyhead's hired man, Harris, exchanging an envelope. They both got real embarrassed, then real upset about it. I have to figure Marolis pays Harris to look the other way whenever he passes that back room of his. It's beginning to look like the Chief is involved in everything crooked in town."

"Only if it's lucrative. Baxter's not a law enforcement officer anymore, he's a businessman. If it don't turn a profit, he ain't interested. One of these days, he's going to get tripped up in one of his little money-making schemes. But until then, just try to stay out of his way, can you? Especially until the election's over. I need a man down at that end of the county, but I haven't got the budget to keep one down there on my own. If I don't have Bushyhead's cooperation, I don't have the Corinth substation. It's that simple."

"All right, Sheriff."

"Buck, the election's only a week away. I know this ain't your cup of tea, but let me tell you, I've been doing this for years, and those last few days before the election can make the difference. I want you to wrap up this murder investigation quick as you can. The minute you've got yourself a likely suspect and enough evidence to get an indictment, you turn the whole thing over to Pinch's office. You've got more important things to do. Don't forget, if I'm out of work, you are, too." Aubuchon chuckled. "Not that I expect to be, of course. Hell, this county ain't voted Republican since Reconstruction, and that was only because them goddamned Yankee soldiers lined folks up at bayonet point, black and white both, and marched them off to the polls and made them vote that way."

"I'll keep working on it, Sheriff," Buckner said.

"All right. Don't forget to campaign, though." He got up and took out another piece of candy. He put it in his mouth and got into the car.

"I won't Sheriff."

"I'll do what I can to protect you from Bushyhead, Buck, but there's only so much I can do, even under the best conditions. You're down there and I'm up here, and he's got a rock-solid power base there in Corinth. And now, what with the election less than a week away, the first thing I've got to worry about is beating Foote. Anything else has to be in second place." Aubuchon spread his enormous hands in a gesture of helplessness.

"Thanks, I'll manage on my own," Buckner said, realizing that he had no choice.

He went around to the front of the Packard to crank it and was surprised when Aubuchon waved him away.

"Watch this," he cried.

Suddenly, with no apparent effort on his part, the Packard sprang to life.

"Got a starter button right in here on the floor," the Sheriff said. "Pretty fancy, huh?"

Buckner stepped back and Aubuchon, grinning contentedly, drove off. Buckner turned back toward the center of town.

He had been born in Jackson, and had lived there until he left for college at sixteen. Since then, over fifteen years ago, he had hardly spent thirty days inside the city limits. During that time, Jackson seemed to have changed completely. The whole pace of movement had increased. What was once little more than a village of wagons and horses had grown into a real town of rattling, buzzing automobiles and trucks. Pedestrians moved more quickly now, hurrying along sidewalks, dashing across the streets. There seemed to be more people around, too. Downtown actually felt crowded. And the people had changed. He still saw men in dark, shapeless suits or overalls and work boots, women in long dark dresses; but more people seemed to have dressed from the pages of the latest magazines. The sleepy little county seat was becoming a real city. Buckner crossed the square and turned up Grand Street. Before he had gone a block, he was back in the small town of his youth. Here, along the tree-shaded streets, little had changed except for the chugging of flivvers. The oaks and maples and elms were shedding bright leaves now, and for a moment, Buckner walked along in the gutter, scuffing dry, rustling mounds of them along before him. He smiled at himself and returned to the sidewalk. The big, rambling houses along Grand sat well back from the street, vast front yards creating a barrier, a safe margin. His friend Morgan Springer had lived in that house, a pretty good left-handed pitcher as Buckner remembered him, but hopelessly tongue-tied around girls. He wondered what had happened to him, but he didn't knock on the door to find out.

He walked north. The fourteen-hundred block was farther out than he remembered. The houses were newer up this way, not quite so big nor quite so far back from the road, and he was soon in a neighborhood he didn't recognize at all until he noticed a side street, Murphy Avenue, and he remembered. This had all been Hiram Murphy's dairy farm when he was a boy. Murphy's milk wagon rumbling down the early morning street, the steady clop-clop of the horse, had been one of the sounds that had awakened him as a child. That was all gone now, replaced by new homes. Where did folks get their milk from now? he wondered.

By the time he found the house he was looking for, Buckner could see the corn fields that extended beyond the north end of town. He turned in at a neat white picket fence and followed the fieldstone walk across a neatly trimmed lawn that had recently been raked clean of leaves. The house was not as imposing as Harris had suggested. It was a two-story clapboard with a wide screened porch. Buckner could see a woman sitting motionless in a swing on the porch, watching him come across her yard and up her steps. She was tall and had light brown hair worn unfashionably long and falling in waves to her shoulders. She wore a long wool dress and high shoes and a heavy wool sweater in whose folds she warmed her hands. Her brown eyes turned up at the outside corners; so did her generous mouth. She was smiling at Buckner as he came onto the porch. Surprised, he just stood and stared at her.

"By God!" he said. "Serena Hastings. What are you doing here?"

"Hello, Buck," the woman answered, still smiling. "I live here."

"You do? Isn't this 1415?"

"Yes, it is."

"But I'm looking for Charlotte Boyer."

The woman's smile dimmed slightly, and she watched Buckner for a moment before making some kind of decision.

"She lives here, too."

"Oh. Is this a boarding house?"

"No. We own it."

"You and Miss Boyer?"

"Well, I do. You remember that big old place on Madison?" Buckner nodded. "That was fine for my brothers and sisters and me, but after Susan, the baby, got married and moved to California, my folks got lonely in it and they bought this one. Then they both died in the epidemic."

"I'm sorry." Buckner remembered in a rush. Serena was the oldest of a half-dozen children of the wealthiest banker in town. He had been to that house on Madison many times, to visit Serena, and for parties.

"Thank you. Anyway, none of my brothers wanted this house, so I ended up with it. It was one of the reasons I decided to move back to Jackson. So here I am, the prodigal returned, and nobody to greet me with a fatted calf." She smiled. "Oh, and she isn't Charlotte Boyer anymore. Her name is Charlotte Tilly. It was her mother's name," Serena Hastings added.

"I see," said Buckner, not sure that he did. "Well, is she here?"

"No. She had business in town."

"When do you expect her?"

"I really can't say. Perhaps not until this evening. What did you want to see her about?"

Buckner hesitated. "I have some bad news for her, I'm afraid," he said. "May I sit down?"

Serena Hastings smiled again and moved to one end of the swing.

"Of course. I beg your pardon, Buck. We just took in the furniture for the winter, and this is all that's left."

"Aren't you cold?" Buckner asked as he sat.

"No, not really. It's peaceful, and the swinging soothes me and that keeps me warm." She continued. "What is your bad news?"

"Oh. Miss Boyer's . . . Tilly's . . . father is dead. Murdered"

"I see," she said, nodding, frowning slightly. After a moment she said, "Just recently?"

"Last week," Buck said. "I didn't know Miss Tilly was living up here or I'd have come sooner."

"Well, I'm sure Charlotte will appreciate your calling." They sat together in silence for several minutes. "By the way, why are you the bearer of this news? Is that what you do now?"

"Sometimes," he admitted. "I work for the county. I'm a deputy sheriff."

"Oh. So you're not just bringing news; you're here to ask questions, as well."

"Yes, I am."

The silence returned. At last Buckner spoke.

"It's quite a surprise, seeing you after all these years, Serena. I thought you had moved to Kansas City."

"I did. And I lived in Chicago, too, for a time. That's where I met Charlotte."

"Really," Buckner said.

"Oh, yes. It was quite a coincidence, in fact. I was working as a secretary for an insurance company, and a new girl came to work at the desk next to mine. We got to talking one day and discovered we were both from Highland County. This was before the war, late in 1915."

"The war had been going for a year by then," Buckner said abruptly.

"Yes, of course," she admitted. She did not hear, or chose to ignore, the anger in his voice. "But America wasn't in it then, so it doesn't really count, does it?"

"I suppose not," Buckner agreed, gritting his teeth. But the men who were dying then are still dead, he thought to himself, and the maimed are still . . . . He stopped. Serena was speaking.

"Anyway, Charlotte and I hit it off right away, and we've been friends ever since, first in Chicago, and now here."

Together? thought Buckner, saying "Then you moved to Jackson?"

"Yes, right after the Armistice. We both decided we'd seen enough of the world. I'd been to Europe; Charlotte had been all over the United States. We'd saved some money and my father left me some more, so we came down here and took over the house. And here we are." She leaned back in the swing. "And how have you been all these years, Buck? What have you been doing? Have you been a deputy sheriff all this time? I never would have thought you would make a good policeman."

"I know several people who might agree with you," Buckner said.

"I suppose I assumed you would be a doctor, like your father."

"So did he."

"You were always so serious, I remember, always so diligent

in your studies. You didn't seem to care a thing for dances and parties or flirting. You were always tucked away in your own little world. Several of my girlfriends, I recall, tried very hard to attract your attention, with no success at all. It quite drove them mad." She laughed.

"I suppose," muttered Buckner. This kind of talk made him uncomfortable. That was not how he remembered his years in school. It had seemed impossible for him to think about anything but girls, much less schoolwork.

"You got my attention, Serena," he said.

"Yes," she admitted with a laugh. "And I wasn't even trying to." She turned her gaze to the front yard. "Oh, look. Here comes Charlotte now."

Buckner turned and his mouth dropped open. Even at a distance, and through the front porch screen, Buckner could see what Louis Boyer must have looked like a quarter of a century ago. The same dark hair, the same piercing eyes, the same good looks, had been softened and feminized only slightly. What had been blurred in Albert by alcohol was clear in Charlotte Boyer: she was beautiful.

She came up onto the porch with an armload of packages. She nodded and smiled at Buckner before she dropped the packages by the front door. She went to Serena Hastings, who had risen to greet her. The two women embraced warmly and kissed each other on the cheek.

"How was your day?" Serena asked, her arms still around Charlotte.

"Wonderful, thank you."

They sat together on the swing, leaving Buckner standing.

"This is Deputy James Buckner, Charlotte. He came up from Corinth to see you."

"Yes?" said Charlotte softly, turning her wide eyes up at Buckner and smiling.

"I have some bad news, ma'am."

"Go on."

"I'm afraid your father is dead, ah, Miss Tilly," Buckner said.

Charlotte said nothing at all, did not move, only continued to watch Buckner, her eyes wide, her smile now frozen in place.

"Oh?" she said, her voice trembling only slightly. "Then he finally did drink himself to death."

"Not exactly, Ma'am. Somebody killed him."

Charlotte's smile faded.

"Really?" was all she said.

"Yes, ma'am."

"You seem puzzled, Deputy," Charlotte said. "Did you expect me to break down in tears?"

"Well, no," Buckner admitted.

"I hadn't seen my father in years. I left home when I was no more than a child, and I have been making my own way in the world for a long time now. It is not easy to be on your own at the age of twelve, Deputy, I can assure you. Especially if you are a female. I cut my hair, of course, and was able to pass myself off as a boy fairly easily for a while, but that did not always improve my situation."

"Where did you go?"

"Oh, many places, Deputy; many places. It was difficult at first, because there was so little I could do. But I learned." She laughed. "I learned how to be a carpenter's helper; I've made cigarettes and sewn flowers on hats for rich women. I've worked on a dairy farm and in a coalmine. I've been all over the country, too. Chicago, New York, New Orleans, Cleveland. I had to learn to protect myself at all costs. But it has been an exciting life."

"It sounds lonely, too," said Buckner.

"In a way, I suppose so," she agreed. "I met many people, though. Most of them were just ordinary people; some of them were very wicked and evil. And some were perfectly wonderful."

She smiled at Serena, who was watching Buckner closely.

"Did you miss your family?" Buckner asked. "Your home?"

"I barely had a family, Deputy. Don't you understand? He made it horrible, then he destroyed it. We kept moving around from place to place when I was little, then we finally seemed to have settled down in that shop on the Jackson Road. But you couldn't call that a home, really. We all lived on top of one another, he and my mother in one bed, my brother and I in the other. And you simply cannot imagine the filth. My mother tried to keep the place clean, and us, to dress us and wash us so we wouldn't look like hillbillies, but he laughed at everything she tried to do."

As Charlotte spoke, she leaned toward Buckner, her face cold and still.

"He wouldn't let her have any money, you see. He kept it all for his fancy women. He would come home at any hour of the day or night, stinking of liquor and sex. He would wake her up and try to force himself on her. Sometimes she tried to fight him off, then he would beat her and . . . ."

Serena laid a hand on hers. She paused, and sat back in the swing.

"Finally he drove her away. I was very angry with her for a long time. I believed she had abandoned us. But, as I grew older, more experienced, I came to understand her, to understand better what she had to put up with. I found out that there are things so horrible that a person simply cannot put up with them any longer. You have to either do something about them, or you have to run away. Then I didn't blame her so much. After all, I had done the same thing."

"But you did try to keep in touch with your family, what was left of it, over the years, didn't you?"

"Occasionally. Post cards mostly."

"But you didn't see them, visit them?" Buckner asked.

"Oh, no. I'd made a new life for myself by then."

"Not even after you moved here to Jackson?"

"No."

"You're sure about that?" Buckner persisted.

"Charlotte has already answered that question," Serena interrupted coldly.

"You didn't, for example, hire a detective to look into your mother's disappearance twenty-five years ago?"

Charlotte looked surprised.

"No. Of course not. Why would I do that?"

"Good question," Buckner said.

"I think Charlotte has answered enough question, Buck," Serena interrupted.

Buckner turned and smiled at her.

"I don't know about that," Buckner answered.

There was a long silence. The two women looked up at him. Buckner's leg was beginning to hurt, and he still had a long walk back to town. He waited for a reply. Finally Serena Hastings spoke.

"Charlotte, darling," she said. "Would you go inside? I'm afraid you'll catch cold out here."

Charlotte looked at her friend for a long time before getting up and moving toward the door. Then she remembered her packages and turned to them. Buckner stepped forward, scooped them up, and handed them to her.

"Thank you," she said, avoiding his eyes.

"You're welcome," he answered. He opened the front door for her and she passed through it and was gone. He closed the door behind her and turned back to Serena.

"Where was she last Friday?"

"Here. With me."

"All day?"

"Yes. All day."

"Serena, I don't believe you."

"I don't care if you do or not." Her face glowed with righteous defiance. "If necessary, I will swear to it in court, and there's nothing you can do about it."

Buckner nodded and put his hat on. "Maybe," he said. "If she's involved in this, you're not doing her any good by covering up for her."

Serena Hastings did not answer. She sat motionless on her swing and looked Buckner directly in the eye, unflinching and unfrightened, her lips drawn into a thin, tight line, her arms folded across her breast. She looked as cold and hard as iron.

Buckner shook his head, stepped down off the porch, and walked back to town, leaving Serena Hastings guarding the front door of her home.

He stopped by the sheriff's office, but the place was empty except for a deputy at the booking desk. Even the banner was gone.

"Where is everybody?"

"Gone to the auction barn to put the finishing touches on the decorations."

"The criminals too?"

"What?"

"Nothing. Sheriff over there, too?"

"No. He's still out putting up handbills."

"Did he campaign this hard in sixteen?"

"Sure." The man looked puzzled. "Oh. That's right. You weren't on the job yet."

"No. Before my time."

"Yeah. He always campaigns this hard, even if there's nobody running against him. He just likes it I guess."

"Well, what if somebody decides to break the law?"

"Gee, Buck. Take it easy. You want to keep your job, don't you?"

"I want to *do* my job, not just keep it."

He turned and walked out.

The waiting room at the Katy station held perhaps a half-dozen people. Buckner sat in a dark and empty corner and dozed until the westbound chuffed in. He boarded the car and sat in the first unoccupied seat he came to. As the train started moving, he sat upright in his seat and tried to think about the Boyer case. He fell asleep, and did not wake up until the conductor touched his shoulder.

"Corinth, Deputy," he said as Buckner came awake with a spasm that startled the man into a mumbled apology.

It was getting dark as Buckner stepped down onto the platform and went into the deserted waiting room. He crossed to the ticket window.

"How many trains a day do you have stopping here?" Buckner was fairly sure of the answer, but he wanted to make certain.

"East bound or west bound?" asked the thin, pale young man from his stool in the tiny booth. His eyes remained glued to a magazine on the desk before him.

"West bound, from Jackson."

"Weekdays or weekends?" The young man's voice droned in a combination of boredom and annoyance that grated on Buckner's temper like a blade across bone.

"Weekdays."

"Two."

"When do they get in?" Buckner struggled to keep his voice level.

"Well," said the young man. He raised his head and gazed into space, weighing each word carefully, "When they're on time, they get in at nine-forty in the morning and four twenty-three in the afternoon."

"You get a lot of passengers?"

"East bound or west bound?"

"Down from Jackson," Buckner said, adding quickly, "On weekdays."

"Today was about normal for a weekday."

"Thank you," Buckner said with exaggerated politeness.

"Welcome," said the clerk, returning to his magazine.

Buckner walked out into the cool evening. He looked at the town spreading out around him. He had spent so much of his life in military camps, with their strict lines of men and equipment, comings and goings ordered by voice or bugle or shrill whistle, that the contrast was still sharp to him. Even after three years, this life seemed a chaotic jumble of things, buildings, streets, dropped anywhere, and people flying off in a thousand different directions, commanded by no common purpose, only their own desires, interests, whims. He did not disapprove of it, or even dislike it; he just felt remote from it. He hadn't been born a soldier, after all; but nearly ten years of military life, especially those last two in France, seemed to squat like a shadow, heavy across his past, preventing him from seeing clearly what had gone before, clouding even his present. This sense of apartness from the people of the town was his only acute sensation, felt, almost seen, because of that old life. A result, too, he had to admit, of his role of law-enforcer. So he was still the solitary scout, patrolling, watching for the comings and goings of the enemy. Whoever that was.

Buckner went home by an entirely new route, pausing often to check his back trail, avoiding dark corners, watching his house from deep shadows before crossing the street and going in.

He heard a sound and went into the front room. He found his father sitting there, smoking a cigar in the dark and looking out of the window. Buckner accepted the cigar the old man offered him and pulled up a chair. As he sat and lighted his cigar, his father watched him.

"You expecting some kind of trouble?" he asked.

"What makes you think that?" Buckner responded.

"Well, I saw you standing across there by the corner house for about fifteen minutes before you came on in. I just wondered if you were expecting somebody to be waiting here to surprise you."

"I'm just being careful," Buckner said.

"Of what? Injuns? Germans? Your mother?"

"Maybe I don't want to lose my fighting edge," Buckner said.

His father laughed until he began to choke on his cigar smoke and had to gasp to catch his breath.

"All right," he said at last. "Whatever you say."

They smoked quietly for a long time before the old man spoke again.

"You working on that Louis Boyer murder?"

"Yes."

"Know who done it?" Buckner knew his father to be a highly educated, extremely well read man who, despite all that, still talked like an untutored mountaineer. Whether this was intentional, as a way of remaining close to his patients, or out of pure orneriness, Buckner never knew.

"I think so."

"Done anything about that?"

"No."

"Why not?"

"Because I can't get the killer to the scene of the crime."

"How far's he got to come?" Since his father's recovery from his debilitating stroke, the old man's fondness for challenging him in conversation had returned. Buckner clearly remembered having to defend at the dinner table virtually every position he took on practically any subjects. Any failure of factual evidence or logical argument was met with scorn.

"From Jackson, if I'm right."

"Automobile?"

"Doesn't own one or have access to one, as far as I can tell," Buckner answered.

"Train?"

"Well, sure. But there's still over two miles from the Katy station to Louis Boyer's place."

"That's not a long walk," the old man pointed out.

"No," Buckner responded, his mind racing to the defense. "But you run a hell of a risk of being spotted all the way from the station, up there, then back to the station, where you have to wait around for the train back to Jackson. Besides, the timing of the train isn't right. You'd have had to come in the night before, if you wanted to get up there early in the morning." He realized he had forgotten to ask the obnoxious ticket agent about trains leaving Corinth for Jackson. He knew of two, but perhaps there were others. He began to feel as though he were bailing out a sinking ship.

"You could have somebody drive you," his father proposed, clearly enjoying the game.

Buckner thought about that. "Yeah, maybe" he conceded. "Then you've got an accomplice to worry about."

"I don't know for sure," said the old man, "but my impression of the matter is that any number of people would have signed up to be an accomplice in murdering Louis Boyer."

Buckner thought of the two women sitting in the porch swing in Jackson and tried to envision them as partners in crime, in murder. If that's what they were, his investigation was doomed to fail. Serena Hastings had lost none of the characteristics that had attracted him to her years before. She had always been very pretty. Now her prettiness had softened into a genuine beauty, while her intelligence seemed as sharp, and her self-control as solid, as ever. Moreover, that control now seemed to extend to Charlotte.

"I'll tell you one thing," Buckner said, more to himself than to his father. "If Elizabeth Blumberg has any guilty secrets, about anything, she will never divulge them to me; and if Charlotte Tilly has any, she'll never divulge them as long as Serena Hastings is there to stiffen her resistance."

"Who are all these women?"

"Charlotte and Elizabeth were born Boyers. Louis was their father."

"You think one of them killed their father?"

"I think it's more than likely."

"Why?" his father challenged. "What solid evidence have you got to make you think that?"

"I don't know, for sure. None, I guess." Buckner admitted. "But I hadn't been in Charlotte's company for more than a few minutes before I found myself thinking: She did it. I never worked it out; the thought just popped into my head. The trouble is, I can't tell where it came from. I do know that, as soon as I heard that Boyer had children living in the state, I thought there might be a connection. And I got to thinking, so even more as things went along, especially after I found out that Boyer's wife was gone, that he had probably mistreated the children, that there had been no one close to him for years."

"You sound pretty sure of yourself," his father said.

"Well, it isn't my first murder, don't forget." Buckner sounded more confident than he felt. "I suspected Albert Boyer at first, but it looks like he has an alibi. Of course, so does Charlotte. And Elizabeth never really knew Louis Boyer at all, so I'm having trouble coming up with a motive for her. Then I met Charlotte. She seemed calm enough, but I could feel her hatred of her father the way you can feel heat from an oven even with the door closed. And then there was the way she looked when I first told her someone had killed him: just cold as December. Plus the fact that she lied to me about knowing what happened to her mother and about writing to her brother and sister. She had no particular reason to do that."

"All right," said his father. "Where does that leave you?"

"No place at all," Buckner admitted. "What I know, and what I believe, proves nothing. Because I still haven't answered the obvious question: Why did she wait a quarter of a century to come home and kill her father? Was she nagged all those years by the suspicion that he had killed her mother?"

"And how did she get to the shop on the Jackson Road?" asked the old man.

"Yes," Buckner agreed. "And if she did get there somehow, how on earth will I prove that? Is there a witness somewhere who doesn't want to get involved for some reason?"

Buckner thought about the building on the Jackson Road, tucked into its little corner of cornfield, remote from any other building, isolated, squalid, with trash piled by the back door.

Buckner stopped and considered.

"You know," he said finally. "I think I might just be able to locate a witness after all, although I'm not sure it's anybody who would be very anxious to step forward and testify in court."

"Who is it?"

"Can't say." Buckner shook his head.

"Getting secretive on me?"

"No. I mean I don't know who it is. Yet."

"Then how can you be sure there is such a person?"

"Well," Buckner admitted. "I'm guessing about that, too. But I think it's a safe guess."

"What makes you think so?"

"Because Louis Boyer was a drinking man."

Buckner stubbed out his cigar and left the room.

THURSDAY, OCTOBER 28

BUCKNER SPENT A restless night filled with vague dreams. He was outside a French farmhouse, confronting a gang of motley, starving children. They wanted something, needed his help, but there was a Hun patrol in the area and he seemed paralyzed with indecision and fear. Then the French children became Indian children, somewhere along the Mexican border. They were hungry and alone, but he still could not help them. Finally, he woke up sweating and lay on his back and staring up into the darkness until he fell asleep again.

It was barely dawn when Buckner got up, dressed, gulped coffee, and left the house. He had people to see, but he knew none would be up at this hour. Instead, he went to his office and got his pistol, a box of shells, and a handful of targets. Then he drove to the quarry outside town and practiced shooting for two hours.

He seldom carried the pistol, leaving it with its leather holster and green web belt, locked in a drawer in his desk. But he practiced with grim faithfulness at least once a week. He believed it was part of his job to be a good shot, and he was deadly accurate with either hand up to forty yards. Beyond that, with a handgun, he knew it was pure luck, but the thought of shooting someone by mistake haunted him. And so he practiced.

After he had finished shooting, he collected his brass and returned to his office. He cleaned the pistol and put it away, then walked across the town square to the drugstore. He spotted the brakeman's cap at once and went down the line of coffee drinkers to take an empty stool.

"Morning, Benny," he said. He sipped the coffee that appeared before him.

"Morning, Buck," said the old man. He wore the same heavy gray wool trousers and shirt he always wore, regardless of season, and brown work boots with thin white socks that hung loosely around his bony ankles. As usual, he hadn't shaved in several days.

Buckner said nothing more. They sat and drank their coffee in silence. Conversation along the counter that morning was muted, each man sat huddled over his steaming cup, and no one intruded on Buckner's silence. Finally, Benny put a dime on the counter, got up, and headed for the door. Buckner quickly finished his coffee, paid, and followed him. He caught up with him at the corner.

"Ask you a question, Benny?" Buckner asked, falling into step with the old railroader.

"Sure, Buck."

"You ever hear of Louis Boyer buying moonshine?"

The old man thought carefully for a moment, then spit a stream of tobacco against the wall of the drug store.

"I believe I might've heard something about that," he said slowly.

"Know who it was supplied him?"

"I don't believe I do. Why? You planning on going after moonshiners now?"

"No. I'm just looking for information."

"Well, I don't have any for you; you know them woods is full of fellows making illegal brew. But I know who you might talk to, though."

"Who?"

"Walter Greene."

"The man that works at the stable?"

"That's the one."

"Thanks, Benny."

"Don't mention it."

He found Greene cleaning out stalls.

"If it's a little nip you're looking for, Deputy," said Greene, pitching a dripping mass of steaming, brown straw into a wheelbarrow, "you can try my cousin. He's got a little place in the hills up behind Taylor. Makes pretty good stuff, too."

"I don't want a nip, Walter," Buckner insisted. "And I don't want to arrest anybody." His eyes, assaulted by the sharp ammonia smell, were watering like faucets turned on full. He wiped them with his sleeve. "All I want to know is the name of the man who supplied Louis Boyer with his shine."

Walter Greene peered at Buckner for a long time. "You sure that's all you want?"

"I'm sure."

Greene gazed thoughtfully down at the full wheelbarrow beside him and chewed slowly at his tobacco cud. Reaching his decision, he spat definitively and nodded.

"All right, Deputy. But you never heard this from me, understand?"

"Fine, Walter. Just give me a name."

"Neb Healy. Lives way south of here, just inside the county line, near Burning Stump, though I believe his operation's over in Texas County."

"That's down by Clear Creek Gulch," Buckner said.

"Yep."

"I know where you mean." He headed for the door. "Feed up the bay, Walter," he called over a shoulder. "I'll be needing him first thing tomorrow morning."

"Right, Deputy."

Buckner kept going. Out in the stable yard, he turned and looked south. He could just see the blue line that marked the mountains. Ozarks, the French had called them, The Arches. They began at the Highland County line and rose south and southwest across the southern part of the state and down into Arkansas and Oklahoma. Thick tangles of trees and thorny underbrush clung to the rocky sides of steep ridges, home of five-foot rattlers, of copperheads as thick as a man's arm, of secretive bobcats and even more secretive humans, who were the most dangerous of all.

Buckner knew these people well. Town folk, people in the city, called them ignorant and backward, but they had only clung to a way of life that ignored the twentieth century in favor of the nineteenth—the *early* nineteenth. They were hunters and gatherers and subsistence farmers, growing crops more for consumption than for profit. They lived without electricity, telephones, plumbing, internal combustion engines. Often their weapons were their only modern possessions. "They nursed their idiosyncrasies and took no advice," Old Bullion Benton had said of them before the Rebellion, and they still kept the modern world at arm's length and more.

That was what Buckner admired in them, their absolutely uncompromising you-be-damnedness. Of course, they also made and sold whiskey, which meant that they were breaking county, state, and federal laws, and now were violating the Constitution as well. But they also grew their own tobacco and cured it and mixed it with bark and smoked or chewed it like the Indians before them. They got their metal implements from local smiths and their medicine from local herbalists. If they needed cash, which was seldom, they could sell a hog fattened on acorns, or whiskey processed from their own corn, and the one activity was no more illegal to them than the other. But it did make them alert to the activities of lawmen.

Buckner did not relish the thought of trying to penetrate that world just to ask a man a question, but if he got the right answer, it could help resolve the Boyer murder, to his satisfaction, if no one else's.

He prepared carefully. Clear Creek was one of a dozen small watercourses that fed into the St. Francois River as it began its run south into Arkansas, where it eventually flowed into the Mississippi. Buckner was certain he could locate it, but he was not sure where Neb Healy lived. He could not afford to go stumbling through the brush on a hunting trip. It could get him shot.

The assessor's office, upstairs in town hall, gave him a United States Geologic Survey map based on information provided by the St. Joe Lead Company, which had mapped the county during the nineties in its relentless pursuit of ore. With the aid of the map, Buckner quickly pinpointed Clear Creek, and managed to narrow down the location of Healy's place to a couple of possible sites. There were no improved roads into that section of the county, just a few sketchy lines indicating logging trails and footpaths. He committed that portion of the map to memory, and returned the original to the assessor's office. The clerk thanked him.

"Map's a good thing to have," he said, chuckling. "Wouldn't do to get lost in the woods."

Buckner smiled and left. One thing he never worried about was getting lost in the woods.

He looked at his watch. Lunchtime. He went to a sundries shop on the corner of the square and bought a pound of Prince Albert tobacco and several packs of papers. Then he went home to eat a sandwich.

He met his parents on their way out the door.

"Where are you off to?" he asked.

Both were heavily swaddled in coats and scarves, and his father leaned on his mother's arm.

"Going to get the mail," his mother said. "What are you doing home?"

"I thought I'd take a break from Mrs. Coy's menu. Is there any roast pork left?"

"Yes. In the ice box," his mother replied.

Buckner stood on the front porch and watched his parents walk off down the street.

After lunch he slept, waking after dark.

He got up and put on his heavy, olive drab sweater with the high turtleneck collar and his old campaign hat and the high-topped officer's boots he had rescued from the supply tent at Fort Huachuca years ago. He had kept them pliable with frequent oil treatments ever since, and they fit like moccasins. He took along his heavy, sheepskin-lined moleskin coat, and a burlap bag containing biscuits, a full canteen of water, and the pound of tobacco and the papers. The night air chilled him as he walked to his office, and he pulled on the coat. In the office, he unlocked the desk and buckled on his pistol and two spare magazines of .45 caliber ammunition, then sat down to wait. He did not plan on shooting anybody, but sometimes it was best to carry a weapon among people who went about fully armed as a matter of course.

Just before midnight, he went to the stable and woke the night man, Walter's son, Waldo.

"Thought you weren't going until morning," he said.

"Changed my mind," Buckner said. He got the big bay gelding out of the stable and tied the coat to the back of his new saddle and the sack of goods to the front.

He had recently abandoned the old 1904 Modified McClellan he had used for years in favor of a "new" 1912 experimental model that a friend still in service had sent him. The new saddle was a good deal more comfortable to sit, he had to acknowledge, but he was skeptical about its ability to stand up to a two-week campaign in the desert.

He smiled and shook his head as he mounted and rode south through the darkness. He only had about twenty-five miles to go, and it wasn't through desert. That stage of his life seemed over for good, and there was a part of him that missed it; or maybe he just missed being young and strong and healthy as a stud horse in springtime. No matter. Now he had different work to do. And he wanted to do it as quietly and as carefully as possible. He wasn't chasing Yaquis or gunrunners or Villistas anymore. The people he was going among were in many ways like those Border outlaws, and certainly quite as dangerous, but he was going to talk only, and he needed to be able to explain that before someone shot him.

He quickly passed beyond the few lights of town that remained lit. The sky was overcast and starless and the air was still. His eyes adjusted quickly. He moved the bay into a trot and listened for anything rattling or clinking. He heard too much, and reined in and dismounted. He took a roll of black electrician's tape from his coat pocket and wrapped several places on bridle and saddle, then remounted and rode on. He trotted the bay for a short distance before nodding to himself in satisfaction.

It was cold, and Buckner turned up the collar of his coat, thankful that he'd thought to wear a sweater as well. But it was a damp cold that seemed to soak right through to the marrow of his bones, like the French winter, and he shivered. He dropped the reins on the bay's neck and let him pick his own gait while he shoved his hands deep into his pockets and diverted his mind to other things. To his surprise, he found himself thinking of Judith Lee. Why hadn't he remembered her? he wondered. She was certainly pretty enough to remember. Of course, he had met her during a time in his life when his sister was enthusiastically tossing attractive young women into his path almost daily. Most of them passed virtually unnoticed. Still, he thought he would have remembered Judith Lee.

As the bay ambled comfortably along the road leading south, Buckner kept an eye on the distant line of hills, darker against the darkness. Although the black mass did not seem to have gotten any closer, Buckner turned the bay off the road after about two hours, and followed a line of trees that paralleled it along the edge of a cornfield.

After another hour of riding, when his eyes began to make out individual trees in the hills ahead, Buckner dismounted and led the bay at a slow, careful walk. A few miles inside the tree line, where the ground began to rise sharply before him, he stopped and listened. He dismounted and left the horse and went on alone, well above the trail and the creek bed that ran along it, moving even slower now and soundlessly through the dark. He stopped and listened again for a long time, then went on, a silent shadow in the night.

FRIDAY, OCTOBER 29

DAWN FOUND BUCKNER, stiff and cold, squatting in wet leaves behind a large rock halfway up a slope overlooking Clear Creek. Below him, behind another rock, he could see a figure in a long fur coat and fur hat, a Mauser over one arm, carefully watching the trail that ran along the creek and softly bouncing up and down on his toes to keep warm. His breath rose up over his head like a soft white plume.

The sun was coming up over the rim of hills and the mist was rising and burning off as it warmed. Morning was working its way into the valley. Buckner waited for it, and when he decided there was light enough for good vision, he raised both hands high over his head and stood up.

"Morning," he said in a loud, clear voice.

The figure whirled and tried to bring his rifle to bear, but the sudden move took his feet from under him, and he sat down heavily on the wet, slippery leaves. He did not drop the Mauser, though, and Buckner remained motionless, hands in the air, as the young man, his face flushed bright red, regained his feet and his composure and aimed the rifle directly at a spot between his eyes.

"Who the hell are you?" He was young, just in his teens, his face spotted with acne. He was surprised, embarrassed, almost, but not particularly frightened. "What the hell do you want here? Get your hands up." He stopped, his embarrassment growing, as he saw that Buckner's hands were already up. "What do you want?" he repeated.

"I want to talk to Neb Healy. My name's Jim Buckner. I'm from down in Corinth."

"Buckner? You that new Deputy they got down there?"

"Yes," Buckner admitted, though he had been in the job for three years, and the newness was wearing off fast.

"What the hell do you want here?"

"I told you. I want to talk to Neb Healy."

"You ain't going to collect no taxes up here, Mister," the boy said. "You ain't going to arrest nobody, neither."

"I'm not here for that," Buckner said evenly. "I came to talk."

"'Bout what?"

"Not your concern."

The young man frowned under his fur hat, uncertain what to do.

"Why don't you take me to see Neb Healy? He'll straighten this out."

"How'd you get up here?" the young man asked.

"I rode here."

"Where's your horse."

"I left him back down the trail a ways."

"How'd you know where I was?"

"I heard you, I guess." Buckner shrugged and grinned. "Or smelled you. I'm not sure, really."

The young man glowered at Buckner now, his embarrassment turned to fury.

"Don't feel bad about it," Buckner said. "I've been sneaking up on people since you were in short pants."

"All right, goddammit. Let's go get your horse, then we'll just see what Neb has to say to you."

Buckner nodded. "Can I put my hands down?"

"No," snapped the young man, and followed Buckner off down the trail, his Mauser at the ready. As they got to his horse, Buckner only hoped the young man would not trip and fall and shoot him, or the bay, by accident.

The trail followed Clear Creek through steep, wooded terrain. Buckner led his horse, with the young man just behind. After about two miles, the ground opened out into a small park, perhaps a hundred yards long and twice that wide, before closing in once more to form a dark, constricted corridor through the woods. At the north edge of the open area, Buckner saw an aging gray dogtrot house with a new tin roof; opposite it was a new log barn that had been covered recently in the same material. A Jersey cow, freshly milked, gazed calmly at him from the barn's central corridor. The creek ran between the two buildings, bubbling over rocks as though happy to be in the sunshine. There was a truck patch beside the house, and a dozen or more chickens scratched in the dust of the yard.

Buckner saw no sign of any kind of whiskey-making apparatus, but a corncrib near the barn was almost full of fresh ears, and fresh wagon tracks led from it into the woods.

As Buckner and the young man approached the house, the door swung open and a heavy-set man with an iron-gray beard and hair stepped into the yard. He carried a Winchester pump 12-gauge shotgun, butt forward, in the crook of his left arm as casually as he might have carried a milking bucket earlier in the day.

The man waited for Buckner and his escort to cross some invisible line before speaking.

"Morning, Jamie. What you got there?"

"Morning, Paw," said the young man. "He . . ."

"The boy got me dead to rights," said Buckner, interrupting loudly. "Had me in his sights practically the minute I put my foot on the trail. Let me get right up close, where he couldn't miss me if he tried, then stepped out, cool as you please. I never even saw him."

"That true, Jamie?" said the man.

Buckner ignored the boy's surprised look and said, "Like an Apache, Mister Healy."

"All right, then," Healy said, smiling. "Go on back down the trail, son. I'll see what it is the Deputy here has to say for himself." Although he had never met Healy, Buckner was not surprised the man knew about him. He might choose to live in a remote corner of the mountains, but it would be to his advantage to know the goings on of the flatlanders.

With one more glance and a confused frown in Buckner's direction, Jamie Healy turned and slung his Mauser over his shoulder and strode back into the woods.

"You can put your horse in the barn," Healy said to Buckner once the boy was gone. "And give him a bucket of oats if you're of a mind."

"Thank you," Buckner said. A few minutes later, he returned to the house. Neb Healy was seated in a ladderback chair beside the door, his shotgun across his lap. There was a second chair next to it. Buckner noticed that the building was located to catch as much of the low sun as possible during the winter months, yet tucked back under the trees so that it would be shaded when the sun was high in the summer. Buckner sat and unbuttoned his coat. He had his burlap bag with him, and he opened it and took out the tobacco and papers. These he handed to Neb Healy.

"Peace offering?" Healy asked with a broad smile, taking the offered goods. "Or a bribe?"

"Sure," Buckner admitted. "Why not?"

"No reason at all." Healy reached into his mouth and removed a wad of tobacco and threw it beyond the corner of the house, where one of the hens had it before it hit the ground. The others stood around and squawked jealously. Healy took out a paper and shook tobacco into it. When had built his smoke, he lighted it and offered the makings to Buckner.

"No, thank you," Buckner said. "I'm purely a cigar man when I smoke, and then only of an evening."

Healy nodded and inhaled deeply. "Stuff we grow up here

ain't to my taste for smoking, so I usually mix in a little molasses and chew it. This here's prime, though." He drew on the cigarette again, consuming half its length, his features lost in the thick smoke. He reached back and knocked on the door of the house. In a moment, a tall, rail-thin woman with a narrow, sharp face opened it and looked out.

"What do you want?" she asked, not unkindly. She wore a long sweater over a faded wool dress, and had big, gnarled, work-reddened hands.

"Bring us some coffee," said Healy.

The woman closed the door without answering, but in a few minutes returned with two enameled cups full of steaming coffee.

"Thank you," Healy said, taking them and handing one to Buckner.

The woman disappeared through the door.

The two men drank their coffee in silence while Healy finished the first cigarette, fashioned another, and got it burning. Buckner relaxed and let the liquid and the sun warm him as his eyes slowly scanned the clearing and the surrounding wooded hills. He looked for lines and curves not made by nature, movements not made by wind. By the time he had finished his coffee, he was certain that at least two men with rifles stood watching in the shadows, one directly opposite where he and Healy sat, and the other off to the right where the hills and underbrush closed around the creek and trail.

"How's Elmer been doin'?"

"Pretty good. Campaigning hard."

"He always does." Healy paused. "Henry Bonney married Hattie Long sometime back. She's yore cousin, ain't she?"

"My mother's second cousin, actually. But all the Longs down in this neck of the woods are my mother's kinfolk."

"That's what I heard."

They sat in silence for a while.

"You're a bit early," Healy said at last. "We wasn't expecting you until later today."

Buckner nodded, not at all surprised that news of his coming had preceded him.

"I've got to be back to town this afternoon," was all he said. Healy did not respond.

"How's business been lately?" Buckner asked.

"You mean since the Amendment?"

"Yes. Bootleggers cutting into your business much?"

"Not enough to notice. I've got a long list of customers that have been with me for years. Long before Prohibition. They've got a taste for what I provide. Making store-bought liquor harder to get doesn't mean a thing to them."

"It doesn't seem to mean much to anybody around here."

"No, it doesn't. The dagoes make their own wine; the krautheads and the bohunks make their own beer. Rich folks have got the money to pay for the stuff they like, legal or not. So now they're paying premium prices because the stuff they like has to be bootlegged in from Canada or some such place." Healy laughed.

"And you sell to folks like Louis Boyer."

"Sure," Healy admitted. "That why you come up here? It sure wasn't just for the ride."

"No, sir," Buckner admitted. "It surely was not."

"Bad leg?" Healy asked, glancing down.

Buckner realized that he was massaging the back of his leg. The action had been unconscious and he at once withdrew the hand.

"Yes," he admitted, wondering if he did that a lot.

"I heard you got shot during the war," Healy said. "Seems like that's what you get when you go sticking your nose into somebody else's fight."

I was a soldier, Buckner thought; going to the war was my job. But he remained silent.

When he did not respond, Healy went on. "Well then, Deputy, what do you want to know about my old friend Louis?"

"I just need to ask you a couple of questions," said Buckner.

There was no point in circling around the issue with Healy, he decided.

"You think I done for him?"

"No."

"You think I know who did."

"Do you?"

"No."

"All right."

"What, then?"

"Were you selling shine to Louis Boyer?"

"Yes."

"How could he afford it? He didn't look like he had a dime to his name."

"He paid when he could," Healy said. "Like most of my customers. Old Louis and me go way back. Back to when he first come into this area. We used to tomcat around. Back when I had the energy for tomcatting." He chuckled. "We drank together, played cards together. Got in fights together, too." Healy unbuttoned his shirt and pulled his collar open. Buckner saw a long scar, fully half an inch wide, beginning near the shoulder and running across the collarbone before disappearing near the sternum. "Fellow from over in Madison County done that to me because I was sporting with his wife. I expect he'd've killed me if Louis hadn't caved in his head with a shovel. Anyway," he shrugged, "like I said, we went way back, and I always believed I kind of owed old Louis."

"All right," Buckner said. "Did you deliver two jars of shine last Friday morning?"

"Well, I don't know what day it was, for sure, but I did make some deliveries up that way last week. I may have dropped off two bottles for Louis. Why do you ask?"

"They were still sitting on his back steps when I went out there to look at his body on Saturday morning. He was killed on Friday morning. I figured if you'd delivered them before he was killed, he would have taken them inside."

Healy nodded. "But I could have made that delivery any

time between when he was killed and when you got there. That's a whole day."

"That's true," Buckner admitted. "But if you'd delivered them before Boyer got up that morning, he'd have seen them there on the stoop and put them inside. If you arrived later, say after he was dead, you'd have looked around, found the body, and gone on your way without leaving anything at all. So the only way you would leave two jars of shine on the back stoop for me to find was if there was someone with Louis when you got there."

"Not bad, Deputy, not bad at all."

Buckner laughed. "Well, this is a pretty cold trail, no doubt about it, but I've got to follow it until it plays out, or it'll nag at me. Did you usually talk with him when you made your delivery?"

"Usually."

"But not this time?"

"No."

"Why not?"

"I heard voices."

"Boyer's?"

"Yes."

"Did you see anybody?"

"No. Didn't look too hard, neither. I dropped off the two jars and went on my way."

"Did you look at all?"

"What do you mean?"

"I mean, did you look into the yard of his shop? To see if you could see who he was talking to?"

"Yes," Healy admitted. "But only for a minute."

"What did you see?"

"Nothing. There was nobody there. I guess whoever it was must've been inside the shop."

"But what did you see," Buckner repeated. "In the yard, I mean."

"Just the usual junk Louis always had there. You know, old wagons and automobiles and pieces of automobiles."

"What kind of autos? What kind of whole autos, not pieces."

"I don't know," Healy said irritably. "I'm not much of an expert on them things."

"What did they look like?"

"There was that big gray one with the headlights shot out of it that he's had there for years."

Buckner nodded. The Pierce Arrow. "Anything else?"

"There was a kind of a little one."

"Little one?"

"Yeah. Built low. Shaped kind of like a bullet."

"What color?"

"I don't know," Healy shrugged. "Dark. Blue, maybe, or black. I didn't pay much attention."

"Anybody in the little one?"

"I couldn't tell. It was facing away, and had a kind of a high back."

"All right. Did you hear what Boyer and his visitor were talking about?"

"No," Healy was getting exasperated. "Listen here, Deputy. I just came up to the house through the cornfield, like I always do . . ."

"Didn't the owner of the cornfield mind?" Buckner interrupted.

"Doubt it," Healy said. "I'm the owner."

"Oh."

"Got to get my raw materials from somewhere, and I can't get it to grow in these hills." He smiled. "Anyway, like I said, I came up to the house through the field. I could see the yard from back a ways, through the rows, you know. I didn't see anything or anybody. Then, when I got close, I heard voices, so I just checked to see if anybody was around, didn't see anybody, left the jars on the step, and went back through the field. That's all."

Buckner nodded. "That may be enough," he said. "Would you testify to this in court, if you have to?"

"Oh, I don't know as I'd do that, Deputy," Healy said. "I don't care for no courts."

"Not even if it will help punish whoever it was killed your old pal Louis?"

Healy snorted. "My old pal Louis was a rough old boy, Deputy. The rest of us from that crowd kind of settled down as we got older so that some of us, me for example, are even kind of respectable. The ones that didn't, like Louis, paid the price. Louis couldn't stop boozing and he couldn't stop tomcatting and it caught up with him." He shrugged. "Whoever it was done for him was just collecting on old accounts. Putting whoever that was in jail would be a waste of time."

"I could subpoena you," Buckner suggested with a smile.

"You'd have to find me to serve it," said Healy, returning the smile. His teeth were big and brown and reminded Buckner of a horse's teeth. "You think you're going to need my testimony that bad?"

"I don't know yet," Buckner admitted.

He got up and slung his bag over his shoulder.

"That's all?" Healy asked, looking up.

"That's all."

"You want some more coffee? For the ride back?"

"No, thank you," Buckner said. "You've been mighty helpful, but I have to get back to town."

Healy got up and walked Buckner to the barn, waiting while he took the oat bag off the gelding's nose, replaced the bridle, and led the horse out into the yard. Buckner tied his bag to the saddle and mounted.

"Thank you again for your hospitality, Mister Healy," he said.

"You're welcome, Deputy," Healy answered. "And thanks for doing my boy that favor. He's young yet."

Buckner smiled. "He does all right," he said and rode across the field and into the dark woods. Two miles down the trail, he stopped.

"Thanks," said a voice from somewhere in the gloom.

"You're welcome," Buckner answered, and rode on.

* * *

In the daylight, and with no need for caution, Buckner rode quickly. The sun and the motion of the horse warmed him finally, the chill leaving his fingers and toes last of all. By noon, he was back in Corinth. He cooled and put up his horse and returned to his office, stopping briefly at Coy's to get a ham sandwich wrapped in paper and a Coca Cola.

As he was crossing the square on the way to his office, Buckner heard someone call his name. He turned and saw David Estes come striding toward him. He stopped and waited.

Many people said that David Estes was the best lawyer in the county, certainly the best in Corinth. Not yet forty, he was slim and handsome, well dressed and smiling, and wanted to be governor. Most people were confident he could have any office he wanted.

Buckner had gotten to know Estes on the township council of defense during the war. His wound had brought him home, and the family's economic condition had brought them to the house in Corinth, and Buckner to the job of Deputy Sheriff. When America finally entered the war in the spring of 1917, Buckner found himself serving on a multitude of boards and committees designed to mobilize the reluctant population into Mr. Wilson's campaign to make the world safe for democracy, even if they had to subvert democracy to do it. And so Buckner and Estes had frequently worked together to explain the confusing new draft law to young men uncertain of their obligations and unconvinced that they should die to rescue J.P. Morgan's loans to England. Estes had been fair and kindly in those dealings. As he often told Buckner, "It doesn't do anybody any good if the federal government throws these boys in jail for draft dodging." Buckner found himself agreeing with the attorney, and the two had formed a smoothly functioning relationship.

"How are you, Buck?" said Estes, smiling.

The two shook hands.

"Pretty good. How about yourself?"

"Fine. Just fine. Couldn't be better." He glanced at the sandwich and Coca Cola Buckner was holding in his left hand. "I won't keep you from your lunch, Buck. I just wanted to ask how you're doing with the Boyer investigation."

"Not too well, I'm afraid," Buckner, admitted.

"No suspects?"

"Oh, no. I've got a couple of suspects. No evidence; no witnesses. I can't put my suspects at the scene of the crime."

"He was killed out there at that shop of his, wasn't he?"

"Yes. There's not much else out that way to begin with, and with the corn as high as it is this year, that shop of his might as well be on the moon, for all anybody can see of it."

"Yes. It's going to be hard to get an indictment without any solid evidence."

"I know," Buckner admitted.

"Well, I'll be seeing you," Estes said, turning away. Buckner started for his office, but Estes had turned back. "One thing, though, Buck."

Buckner waited.

"I hear you've been having a little trouble with the police department. Something about a jurisdictional dispute?"

"I wouldn't call it that," Buckner answered.

"Whatever it is, Buck," said Estes, smiling even broader now, "you take it easy. Everybody likes you around Corinth, and we're pretty well satisfied with the job you've been doing as deputy sheriff, too. But Baxter Bushyhead's been chief of police here for longer than almost anybody can remember. He's got a lot of important friends, and he runs a nice, quiet town. Keeps the local businessmen happy; hell, keeps everybody happy. Not that it matters. He's not an elected official; he's appointed by the town council. He doesn't have to worry about getting reelected next week." He patted Buckner on the shoulder, still smiling. "You see what I mean, Buck?"

"Yes, I guess I do," Buckner admitted. The friendly hand on his shoulder made him shiver.

"That's fine, just fine," Estes said. He turned abruptly and walked away.

Buckner went to his office and ate his sandwich and drank his now warm Coca Cola while sitting at his desk. He thought about his encounter with Estes. David Estes was one of the handful of men who made things happen in Corinth. None of them were on the town council, of course. Judge Hubbard, Ted Linderman, and the others had no need of political office. Or, like Estes, they aimed much higher. But they ran things. And now it appeared they had dispatched Estes, their youngest member, to warn Buckner about interfering with Chief Bushyhead's operation. Were they part of it? Buckner wondered. Were they in charge of it? Or did they just want to keep things quiet while they took their cut?

However he looked at it, Buckner realized that his entanglement with the police department meant trouble for him. He only hoped it would not trip him up before he could solve Louis Boyer's murder.

When he finished eating, he threw away the paper and set aside the bottle to return for the deposit. He stretched and yawned and thought about trying to catch up on the sleep he had lost. Instead he took out his .45 Colt. It was clean, but he wanted something to occupy his hands. As he was removing the magazine, Jeff Peck walked in.

"Going target shooting?" he asked, sitting in the chair in front of Buckner's desk. He held a cup of coffee in a hand that trembled only slightly.

"No. I just got back from a talk with a moonshiner named Neb Healy."

"Ah, yes. Manufactures a high-quality product, I hear. Did you make a purchase?"

"No. I figure to keep on bumming free drinks from my friends."

"Sound policy. Save money that way. Where did talking to Neb Healy get you?"

"Healy was supplying Louis Boyer with moonshine; had been

for years. He made a delivery the morning Louis was murdered. He says he saw a roadster in Louis's lot that morning."

"Just a roadster? No people?"

"Said he didn't see anybody around the place, but he heard voices. So he left his two jars of shine and went on home."

Buckner kept his eyes on Peck as he spoke. At the same time, he field stripped his pistol, his hands moving confidently and quickly. He placed the pieces on his green blotter. He even emptied the magazine and stood the fat little bullets in a neat row across the top. Peck watched him work.

"You like everything nice and tidy, don't you?" said the doctor.

"Sometimes," Buckner admitted, looking at the line of pistol parts. "At least I don't lose anything that way."

"You a hundred per cent sure about that?" Peck asked.

"Yes," Buckner said with finality. "Besides, it's the only way I know how to work." He got out his cleaning rod, patches, and oil.

"How many times you figure you've done that?" Peck asked.

Buckner pushed an oily patch through the barrel of the pistol. "With this piece?"

"With any."

"I don't know," Buckner said, shrugging. "Thousands, I guess."

"They sure can make a mess out of the human body."

"I suppose so," Buckner admitted. Firearms had been so much a part of his life for so long, and now he seldom carried one. He hadn't made a conscious decision to stop; he had simply found that his job seldom required a weapon, and he fell out of the habit with as little thought as he had fallen into it.

"So, whose roadster do you think it was?"

"My guess is that it belonged to Albert Boyer."

"That's just a guess, though. You've got no actual proof."

"No," Buckner admitted.

"You think Albert drove up here and killed the old man, then drove home?"

"Not by himself," Buckner said.

"Then Charlotte did it?"

"Not by herself."

"All right," Peck continued after some thought. "Here's how I see this thing. You're convinced Charlotte went to her father's shop, probably driven there by her brother, Albert, in his fast racing automobile. That while she was there, she murdered her father by smashing him on the head with a piece of pipe. Then she went home, either driven there by her brother, or on the train. Is that correct?"

"Yes, that's about it," Buckner answered.

Peck took a sip of his coffee. He grimaced.

"This is terrible stuff," he said.

Buckner carefully wiped clean the pistol's long main spring. "Well," he said after setting it carefully down on the blotter, "what do you think?"

"Looks plenty clean to me," Peck said, "considering how little you use it."

"I don't mean this," said Buckner.

"I know," Peck acknowledged. "But I don't have an answer to your question. You still haven't explained why she waited twenty-five years to get revenge."

"I think it's because she did not know for sure that her father had killed her mother. I think Victoria's disappearance hit her hard. She loved her mother; her mother doted on her and protected her from her father, or tried to. I think she hated her mother for running off and leaving her. She went from loving her mother to hating her almost overnight."

"You've got no proof of that," said Peck.

"I've got no proof of any of it," Buckner responded sharply. "I'm trying to answer questions in my mind. I want to get this sorted out so that I can get a handle on what went on out there last Friday morning. I'll worry about building a case later."

"Sorry," said Peck, not sounding sorry at all. "I didn't mean to try to inject a little logic into your argument. Go on."

"Her mother abandoned her," Buckner continued. "Her father was a brutal drunk who lived openly with another woman.

Conditions at home drove her away, despite whatever sense of responsibility she might have had toward her sister and brother. And over the years, whatever she was doing, I think her mother's disappearance was always there, eating away at her. She began to wonder what had really happened. I think she was always drawn back to this area, and when she got involved with Serena Hastings, she let that pull take over and moved back to Jackson with Serena."

"Involved?" Peck said.

"Well, I don't know what else to call it."

"Sounds like they're lovers," Peck observed.

"I didn't ask," Buckner grumbled. "Besides, I don't see why you think that; you didn't see them. Maybe they're just good friends, and you just have a dirty mind."

"Maybe," Peck admitted. "But I've read my Krafft-Ebing. The point is, this is all a fiction you have constructed inside your head. You still don't have a shred of proof of any of it. And I don't think you're going to be able to get any."

"I might. If I can crack Albert. He either lent his auto to his sister, or drove her himself, which is more likely. I doubt if she can drive an automobile." He thought a while. "There's no direct train line between Jackson and Cape Girardeau, and I don't think Charlotte took the train to St. Louis, then down to Cape Girardeau, then drove to Louis Boyer's with Albert, then back to Cape Girardeau again, to take the train. I think Albert drove straight to Jackson, took her to their father's shop, then drove her home again. In that fast roadster of his, with his racing experience, it wouldn't have taken him any time at all."

"But all you've got is Neb Healy's word that the roadster was in Louis Boyer's yard the morning of the murder. He didn't see anybody around it; doesn't know who it belongs to. Besides, you'll never get him to testify in court about it."

"No," Buckner agreed. "But maybe I can use Neb to crack Albert. And if I can crack Albert, I can get to Charlotte."

"If that's what you think you ought to do."

"What does that mean?" Buckner asked.

"I mean Charlotte, by your own account, was taking revenge for her mother's death."

"I know," Buckner admitted. "But she still committed murder. And part of my job is catching murderers and putting them in jail. Courts and juries are supposed to decide if it was all right for her to take revenge for a crime a quarter-century old."

"That sounds like evading responsibility to me," said Peck, finishing his coffee with a shudder.

"Bullshit!" said Buckner. "People can't go around taking personal revenge. If that happens, then you don't have a civilization anymore."

"What civilization are you talking about?" Peck's voice had a bitter edge to it. "The civilization that gave us the Western Front? You haven't forgotten that, have you? The civilization that pays workers starvation wages and hires men to shoot them down if they ask for more? Men like you?"

"I don't shoot people down," Buckner returned angrily. "What in hell do you want me to do? The county pays me money to arrest people who break the law. Am I supposed to take the money but only arrest people when I feel like it? I signed on to do a job, and until I quit, or they fire me, I'll be doing that job as best I can."

"There are other jobs."

"Not for me, there aren't," said Buckner, practically shouting. "Don't you understand? All I've ever done is be a soldier and now a policeman." He lowered his voice. "I'm not a kid anymore, and I've got a game leg and no skills beyond wearing a uniform and carrying a weapon. If I don't have this, what do I have?"

"Jesus," Peck said wearily, getting up. "You talk like an old man. Well then, you just do your job. But don't expect any thanks from the people who hired you. As far as they're concerned, you're just about one notch above the people you put in jail. They'll bounce you out on your ass in a minute. Then you can sit in the dark and feel sorry for yourself."

Buckner sat and listened to Peck's angry footsteps retreating down the hall. He sat motionless for a long time and stared down at the disassembled pistol on his desk. Who am I doing it for? he wondered. Surely not Estes and his crowd. They obviously care more about Baxter Bushyhead's corrupt but comfortable little system than about whoever killed Louis Boyer. And Peck was right, of course: arresting Charlotte Boyer would not advance the cause of civilization, not even in this little corner of it. Maybe if he could arrest enough politicians and generals and bank presidents, maybe that would help.

His lips twisted into a bitter smile. Now he was thinking like Jeff Peck.

At the same time, he also recognized that as long as the people in his particular corner of civilization were safe from crime, they took no interest whatsoever in the people who ensured that safety. Besides, no one mourned Louis Boyer. And no one but her children, and perhaps Ibo Mary, had mourned Victoria Boyer. Certainly, no one, except perhaps her brother and sister and Serena Hastings, would mourn Charlotte Boyer. Neither civilization nor Highland County would be one jot better off for Charlotte's arrest.

Why, then, was he pursuing this?

Was his curiosity driving him to uncover the complete explanation for what went on in that squalid shack on the Jackson Road some twenty-five years ago? Buckner shook his head. That was only part of it. Partly it was to satisfy his personal sense of the correctness of things: his sense of duty to his employers, to himself.

But if he did all this to satisfy himself, how was his action morally different from revenge? In fact, wasn't it just a fancy version of a similar motive? Bluntly stated, was it simply: arrest Charlotte so James Buckner could feel content; so he wouldn't lose his precious job and his precious self-respect?

Buckner cursed loudly and stood up. He jammed his hat on his head, and walked out. On his desk, in neat, orderly rows lay the pieces of his disassembled pistol.

* * *

A few minutes later, Buckner entered the old barbershop. The aged sweeper glanced up from his work, smiled slightly, and waved him up the stairs. Does he ever rest? Buckner wondered as he climbed; did anyone ever ask for a haircut? At the top the door opened at once, and Buckner entered the wide, bright room. The grinning Buster showed him to a table.

"Mist' Elroy's not here right now, Deputy," he said.

"I don't want to see him," said Buckner.

"You want some champagne?"

"I want rye," Buckner answered, reaching into his pocket and pulling out a wad of bills, which he tossed into the middle of the table.

"I don't know as Mist' Elroy'll let me take your money, Deputy," said Buster, hesitating.

Buckner looked up, his eyes flat and hard. "I tell you what, Buster. You bring me the rye and I'll pay for it until that runs out and neither one of us will tell Mister Elroy anything."

"Our little secret?" said Buster, chuckling.

"Our little secret," said Buckner.

Buster went away, and in a minute, a waiter appeared with a bottle of rye whiskey and a glass on a silver tray. His short white jacket seemed to sparkle in the lights, and the crease in his black trousers was sharp enough to shave with. He put the tray down on the table and picked up the wad of bills. He unfolded it, extracted two dollars, smoothed and carefully folded the rest, and replaced them on the table. Then he executed a curt, almost insolent, bow, turned on his heel, and walked away.

Buckner ignored the whole performance. He was uninterested in one black waiter's distaste for the entire white race. He had other things in mind. He opened the bottle and poured the glass half full and drank it off, then poured more whiskey and put the bottle down. He sat back, put his bad leg up on a nearby chair and sipped from the glass as his eyes scanned the room.

It was early, and the place was barely half-full. A foursome all in somber black, mourning bands on their arms, sat at a corner table and drank wine. The women dabbed handkerchiefs at their eyes, the men, with their hats pushed back on their heads, grinned and puffed on fat cigars. Nearby, several couples danced slowly to the music coming from the upright against the wall. The man who played it was still under-dressed in overalls, heavy work boots, and battered straw hat. He seemed on the point of falling asleep. Looking like a bum who had wandered in and sat down to play, he played beautiful ragtime, slow and clear, each right hand note a separate gleaming piece fitted into the structure of the melody and sustained in the air by the gentle, solid alternating bass line.

A man and a woman sat at a table nearby, arguing about money over their beer. Men in work clothes stood at the bar.

Buckner relaxed into the gentle hum of music and conversation and drank his way slowly, steadily into the bottle of rye. He watched the people in the bright room talk and drink and dance, some leaving, to be replaced by others. There were a few white faces among the black, including one couple he knew from church, but no one approached him, indeed, no one had even looked at him since he sat down. He seemed to be invisible. Even the waiter who came to his table to ask if he wanted some water to go with the rye did not look directly at him.

Buckner did not want water.

He smiled to himself. Someone appeared at his shoulder. He leaned back and gazed up, struggling to focus his eyes.

"Buster says you're scaring customers away," said Elroy Dutton.

"Sit down," said Buckner, removing his leg from the chair. "Have a drink. They serve pretty good rye whiskey here. Fellow that owns this joint must have connections."

Dutton sat, and the waiter appeared with a crystal flute and chilled champagne in an ice bucket. Dutton poured and drank.

Buckner sipped his rye. "Whatever you're paying the piano player, it ain't enough," he said.

"Boston Conservatory graduate," Dutton grinned. "Always telling me he'd rather be playing Chopin, Liszt. I tell him he can leave whenever he finds a better paying job playing those fellows."

"The hillbilly clothes your idea?"

"His. I think it's his way of protesting against having to play country music."

"He plays the hell out of it, though."

"Yeah, he does."

Buckner looked at Dutton a long time without saying anything.

"Yes?" said Dutton over his champagne flute.

"If you were a woman," Buckner blurted out, "and your father killed your mother, what would you do?"

Dutton reached over and put the cork in the rye bottle. "I think you've hit your limit, Deputy," he said in a soft voice.

"What would you do?" Buckner persisted.

"I'd kill him," Dutton said casually.

"Would you wait twenty-five years to do it?"

"Well," Dutton said, thinking. "Maybe I'd have to wait a while, if he was big and I was small. But sooner or later, I'd find a way and I'd kill him."

Buckner nodded. He sat forward and reached for the rye bottle. Dutton pushed it beyond his grasp.

"I wasn't joking, Buck," he whispered. "You need to take it easy. Let me have Buster make you up a pot of coffee."

"*Deputy* Buckner to you, *Mister* Dutton," said Buckner with a sneer. "I'll drink what I paid for."

"Not in my place, Deputy," responded Dutton, his voice still quiet, but cold now, and with an edge.

Buckner was suddenly aware that the argument between the couple at the nearby table had become a shouting match. As he looked over, the man reached out and struck the woman in the face. The woman fell back onto the floor, blood spraying from her crushed nose. Elroy Dutton got up and went to the man's side, placed a placating hand on his arm, and spoke quietly in his ear. The man shook off Dutton's hand, and, when Dutton continued to speak, stood up and punched him in the side of the neck. Dutton stumbled across the floor, tripped over the woman, and sprawled on his face.

Buckner jumped up, grabbed the man's arm, and spun him around to face him. The man was big, almost Buckner's height and twenty pounds heavier, with a light tan complexion and small, bright eyes. His eyebrows and cheekbones were lined with scars. The man coiled his fist to strike as his eyes focused on Buckner. He stopped cold.

"I don't want no trouble with no white police," he said.

"Don't let that stop you, friend," said Buckner. "I'm off duty."

"All right, then" said the man with a grin, and he hit Buckner in the face, knocking him back into his chair and onto the floor.

Buckner got up. He saw that Dutton was also on his feet, and a nearby rumbling told him that Buster was on his way.

"Forget it, Buster," said Elroy Dutton, his eyes still on the man, who stood now, legs apart, fists bunched, glaring triumphantly at the entire room. Buster stopped in his tracks and watched.

Buckner stepped in, and as the man pulled a razor from his pocket, hit him with three quick rights over the heart, taking delight in the electric jolt each blow sent up his arm. The razor went flying. The man staggered back, bending over slightly, but as Buckner moved closer, he straightened up and hooked Buckner with a hard left just under the ear. Buckner shook his head but the ringing wouldn't stop. The big man was closing, hands outstretched to grapple. He was not very fast, Buckner realized, but he was incredibly strong, and a wrestling match would be no contest at all. Buckner took the full impact of the man's forward rush, shoving the heels of both hands up under the man's chin, pushing up and back, and as the man straightened and fought for his balance, Buckner brought his knee up sharply into his groin. The big man bent over with a loud whoosh, but, to Buckner's horror, he stood up, his eyes glittering, his gasping mouth open in a manic smile.

"I'm going to bust you up good for that, White Folks," he said.

As he moved in again, Buckner met him with a left that landed just under his belt buckle. He bent forward again, and Buckner quickly stepped around and stomped down hard on the side of the knee. The joint collapsed with an audible popping sound, and the man dropped to the floor. Then Buckner kicked him in the side of the head, aiming for the soft spot in the temple, and the man fell over onto his side without a sound and lay still.

Buckner stood with his legs apart, gasping, and waited for the man to get up. Elroy Dutton came over to him and tapped him on the shoulder. Buckner, startled, turned to face him, fists ready. Dutton showed him his palms.

"You win, Deputy," he said lightly. "But I think you'd better head home now." He nodded toward the room, where several men had risen to their feet. "Nate has a lot of friends."

Buckner nodded slowly and dropped his fists to his sides, letting them uncurl. He felt dizzy, and the blood was racing through him. Dutton went to his table and sat down. He took the linen cloth that wrapped his champagne bottle, soaked it in the ice bucket, and applied it to the side of his neck. Then he refilled his flute and drank.

Buster showed Buckner to the door. As he stood at the top of the stairs, Buster reached out and shook his hand.

"That was mighty pretty to see," he said, smiling. "Mighty pretty."

"Thank you, Buster," Buckner said. "And tell your boss I said I was sorry."

"All right, Deputy. Good night. You be careful getting home."

The door closed, and Buckner made his way down. He walked carefully, like a man on a wire, ignoring the stares he got, until he had crossed the tracks. Once on the white side of Corinth, he relaxed a little; there were fewer people on the street to see him stagger.

Buckner was furious with himself. He hadn't been drunk in years. He hated the way his senses were blurred. He had worked hard for a long time to master his emotions and sharpen his senses, and getting drunk represented a loss of that control. Finally, getting into a drunken brawl in a black saloon was stupid. Careless.

Jim Buckner believed in respect. If men did not respect him, they would not follow him in combat, no matter how many stripes he had on his sleeve. If the people of Highland County did not respect him, they would not obey the laws he had been hired to enforce, and his job would become impossible. That meant that he could never let down, never relax. He could have human weaknesses; he just couldn't display them in public, as he had tonight. By breakfast, the story would be all over Corinth.

He stormed through the town, raging at himself, muttering curses under his breath, turning down side streets if he saw anyone. He walked for a long time, letting the chilly night air clear his head, winding through the back streets eventually to the square, where he stopped to look at the memorial to the war dead. He read the names on the plaque at the statue's base.

"At least you fellows got a nice statue," he said, looking up at the blank bronze face. "The rest of us didn't get a damned thing." He shook his head.

The doughboy continued to stare determinedly off to the East, watching for a resurgence of the Hun.

Buckner walked on. Eventually, his course brought him to a place he had unconsciously been avoiding: the corner of Maple and Jefferson. The brown cottage with the rose bush was not hard to find. The other three houses at the intersection were big old buildings built sometime in the middle of the last century, with Italianate roofs and porches running along two sides.

Buckner looked at the little cottage. Through the roses, he could see a light in the front window.

Probably not at home, he thought. Then a shadow passed before the light.

Too late, anyway, he decided, fumbling in his pocket for his watch. Before he could find it, the clock in the town hall struck eight times.

Buckner stood for several more minutes, letting the cool air clear his head, then crossed the dark, empty street and knocked on the door. As he was turning to go, it opened. He turned back.

"Well, good evening, Deputy," Judith Lee said. "My, you look terrible. And you smell like a distillery, too." She wrinkled her nose.

"Of course," said Buckner, sweeping off his hat and giving a deep, formal bow. "I beg your pardon ma'am. I should not have presumed."

"You're not presuming," she said with a smile. "As I recall, I invited you. So you might as well come in. You must be freezing, without a coat like that." She backed up and swung wide the door.

Buckner entered and stood in the small vestibule while she closed the door and took his hat and hung it on a peg on the wall. He could feel the heat rising on the back of his neck. Then she took his arm and led him into the room with the light.

There were chairs and a sofa and a long desk with a student's lamp. A small fire burned in the fireplace. Papers and books sat in piles on the desk and on the chairs and the floor next to the desk. Some of the books were closed, but more were open, lying face down, or blocked open with other books. Judith Lee scooped up the pile on the sofa and dumped it on top of the pile that sat on the nearest chair.

Those few surfaces not covered with books and papers were coated with dust. Here and there sat crumb-covered plates and cups with dried tealeaves in the bottoms. There were cobwebs in the corners of the ceiling. Sober, Buckner would have been tempted to tidy up; under the circumstances, he merely realized, fleetingly, that his mother would be horrified.

"Sorry about the mess," she said gesturing to the sofa. "Please, sit down." Buckner sat. Judith Lee sat opposite him. Buckner noticed that she held a pair of horn-rim glasses in her hands, and that the fingers of her right hand were smudged with ink, as was the cuff of her sweater.

"I've interrupted you," he said.

"Yes," she answered. "And I am grateful. I am writing a paper for the state education journal in Columbia, and I kept falling asleep. Not a good sign."

"Paper?"

"Yes. On teaching history to fifth and sixth grade students. Discussing Tocqueville's observation that democratic peoples don't pay any attention to their history, that all they think about is the future. And if that's so, then how do we teach history in school, especially to ten-year-olds."

"I see," said Buckner.

"There you are," she said. "I can't even explain it to you without putting you to sleep. But if they'll publish it, it will increase my chances of getting promoted to principal some day."

"My sister is a writer," said Buckner.

"Yes, I know. With *Reedy's Mirror*, although now that Reedy's dead, I don't know what will happen to the magazine."

She stopped speaking and looked at Buckner, who seemed to be staring at her now. "Are you all right, Deputy? James? Can I get you some coffee? You look like you could use some coffee."

Buckner had stopped drinking over two hours before, and the blood was no longer pounding in his head. Walking in the cold night air had awakened him, but sitting in Judith Lee's warm, stuffy parlor was like another blow on the head. His neck throbbed where Nate had hit him. He felt woozy, and he had trouble focusing his eyes. Her closeness intensified it. She smelled like clean muslin, freshly washed and sun-dried. It confused him as much as the alcohol he had consumed earlier. It couldn't be her figure, shrouded as it was in a voluminous sweater and ankle-length wool skirt; and her face was very pretty, but it wasn't that either. No, her gray eyes were looking right into him, assessing exactly the kind of effect she was having on him, and that bothered him. It didn't help that she seemed vaguely amused by the process.

"Yes," he said. "Coffee would be nice."

She got to her feet; Buckner stood. "I'll go heat the water," she said, and left the room. Buckner sat back down with a sigh. He looked into the fireplace and felt the warmth spread over him; then abruptly he heard the creak of floorboards and he awoke, suddenly on his feet, hands groping.

Judith Lee, holding a tray with cups and saucers and a coffee pot, stepped back, unfrightened, watching calmly with her wide gray eyes.

"I'm sorry," she said. "I didn't mean to wake you."

"I did not mean to fall asleep," he answered. He waited until she sat down, then sat next to her. She poured and they sipped their coffee.

They talked, and Buckner drank more cups of coffee. They discussed the presidential campaign; she chatted about her work at the school. He told her about the incident at Elroy Dutton's place in a way that made her laugh.

Buckner heard the town clock strike nine, then ten, and he began to think about going home. Surely this woman must have better things to do than help him sober up.

"Are you feeling better?" she asked at one point.

"Yes," he answered. "I got no sleep at all last night." He laughed. "I used to be able to do that and never notice, but I guess it's catching up with me." And I'm getting old, he thought.

After another pause, she asked, "Whatever possessed you to become a deputy sheriff?"

"I like to eat regularly," he said with a shrug. "I needed the job."

"Was that the only job available?"

"It was the only job I felt suited for at the time. All I'd ever done before that was to be a soldier."

"Why did you decide to be a soldier in the first place, then?" she asked.

"Didn't Martha Jane tell you all this?" The conversation had taken a personal turn, something he preferred to avoid.

"She told me about what happened to your father, and that you left school to go into the army to help support the family. But she never knew why you picked the army."

"It was a bad year, 1907," Buckner said. "There weren't too many jobs available. Besides," he smiled, "I guess I'd always wanted to be in the cavalry after listening to my father's stories of the war. I wanted to try it for myself. You will not be surprised to hear that it was not what I expected."

"And now here you are," she said. "Drinking coffee in my parlor." She put down her cup and saucer and leaned toward him, resting her hand lightly on his arm. "Why are you here, exactly?" she said softly.

"I'm not sure," he said. "I didn't want to go home just yet, and I've got a problem I can't seem to solve, like an itch I can't scratch, so I'm just stalling for time until I figure out what to do."

Buckner continued to hold his empty cup and saucer. She looked down at it then up at him with her level gray eyes. She smiled and took the cup from him and leaned forward and kissed him on the mouth.

Buckner, too startled to move, found himself kissing back, devouring her mouth hungrily. After a bit, she leaned back and inhaled deeply.

"Oh, my," she said.

"I apologize," Buckner muttered.

"Stop apologizing!" she said sharply. "I kissed you, remember."

"Yes, I remember." He got to his feet.

"Where are you going?" Judith asked.

"I think I've imposed on your—hospitality—enough," Buckner answered. "I really should be going."

"Don't be ridiculous. Sit down."

He sat and poured some more coffee, promising himself that this would be his last cup.

"I don't think I've ever met anybody like you," he said.

"Really? In what way?"

Buckner smiled. Every woman he had ever known wanted to know that she, and only she, was truly unique.

"I don't think I've ever met anybody so . . ." he groped for the right word.

She helped: "Confident?"

"Yes," he said. "But 'forward' is the word that comes to mind first."

"Forward!" She laughed. "I suppose so. But perhaps you've been spending your time with the wrong kind of girl."

"I suppose," he admitted.

"Every girl I knew at Mount Holyoke absolutely refused to let herself be ruled by some man, whether it was a father or a husband, or even a lover."

"I'm not trying to . . ."

"You have no idea what a difference it can make in a girl's life, to go off to college, to learn about the wide world, about the possibilities that are out there. Possibilities for all kinds of things. I was born in a little town in Iowa, smaller than Corinth, and I grew up walking corn with my five brothers. But my father believed in education, even for women, so I went to college, and it changed my life. Some of the girls I was in school with are doctors now, or attorneys, or in the business world. And very few of them are married, too, by the way."

"Really?"

"Yes. Really." Some of them fell in love in school . . ."

"With other girls?" He remembered the way Charlotte and Serena kissed.

"Yes, sometimes," she said, looking closely at him, adding, somewhat defiantly, "And some of them are still together. Others are single, living by themselves, pursuing their careers. Just as men have done for ages."

"I guess so," Buckner said. "You sound like my sister."

"Of course I do. The world is changing, and women's role in it is changing, too. It's been changing, right along, all around you, but most men are too blind to see it. And if they do see it, they think it's the end of civilization. But think about Martha Jane, about how different her life has been from your mother's."

Buckner thought about Antonia Clay, too, working from the time she was eighteen, and Ibo Mary, who had done hard physical labor for eighty years; Angelina Robideaux, who had been simply a kept woman, first of Louis Boyer, then of Blumberg; and Victoria Boyer, who seemed to have been more her husband's slave than his wife. He certainly could not see Martha Jane, nor Judith Lee, ending up like that.

"All right," he admitted. "Things are changing."

"Of course they are!"

As she became more emphatic, Judith Lee gestured more, her eyes seemed on fire, and her whole face was lit with the glow. Suddenly she had gone from being pleasant-looking to beautiful. Buckner put a hand on her upper arm, drew her gently to himself, and kissed her.

"Wait a minute," she gasped, pulling away. "I'm not finished lecturing you yet."

"I'll remember where you left off, Assistant Principal." Buckner kissed her again. Then he got up. "But now I do have to leave."

She also stood.

"I suppose you realize that you are developing an enormous bruise on the side of your neck."

"Yes." They walked to the vestibule and he got his hat. "Drinking, brawling, stealing kisses: not exactly putting my best foot forward, so to speak."

"You did quite well, I think," Judith Lee said, and opened the door. Buckner stopped on the porch and turned to face her. Once again, he bowed.

"I thank you kindly for your hospitality, Miss Lee. Will you do me the honor of permitting me to call again?"

"Why, of course, sir," she responded. "Shall we say, Saturday evening for tea?"

"I am your servant, Miss Lee." He bowed once more, turned, put his hat on, and walked off into the darkness.

Judith Lee went inside and closed her door. She surveyed the pile of books and papers in her living room and found that she had lost what little interest she had in finishing that paper tonight.

Instead, she went upstairs and went to bed.

FRIDAY, OCTOBER 29

"MORNING," BUCKNER SAID as he walked into the police department.

"Uh, good morning."

Buckner stopped. "Is there anything wrong?" he asked.

"No," said Givens. "But . . ."

"What?"

"Well, was that you whistling when you came down the stairs?"

"I suppose it was. That all right with you?"

"Just fine, Sarge," said Givens. "Just fine."

"Uh huh. See you later." He waved and continued down the hall to his office. The pieces of his pistol still sat on the desk in clean, orderly rows. He smiled and sat without taking off his hat and quickly reassembled them. He loaded the pistol and replaced it in the drawer, then got up and left the office.

He found Peck writing out a prescription while an elderly man waited patiently in the chair by his desk.

"'Lo, Buck," the old man said.

"'Lo, Charlie."

"You sick?"

"No, just visitin'."

"That's all right, then. Don't get sick. It'll kill ya."

"I know that, Charlie."

Peck handed the old man the slip of paper. "You make sure you take these, Charlie, you hear now?"

Charlie grunted something that might have been an assent, got up, and left.

"It's killing him, that's for sure," Peck said softly as they listened to the old man's slow footsteps down the stairs.

"What is?"

"I don't know."

"What?"

"Well, I know he's dying of cancer and there's nothing I, nor anybody else, can do about it."

"But you don't know how he got it."

"No, but I've got a pretty good idea it was working in the smelter up in Taylor." Taylor was the property of the Bull Run Mining Company, the town where most of its workers lived, the men who dug the ore and processed it into lead bars. It lay several miles east of Corinth, up in the St. Francois Mountain, the south end of Missouri's so-called lead belt. It was the largest single employer in the county and one of the largest in the entire state. "Breathing that air," Peck said, "that poisoned air, that's enough to kill anybody."

"What were the pills for?"

"They'll ease his pain. Of course, it'll also addict him, but that's hardly going to matter in the little time he has left."

"Are you doing anything today?" Buckner asked after a minute.

"I might be," said the Doctor. "Has there been another murder?"

"Probably, but that's not why I'm here. I have to talk to Charlotte Tilly. I would like you to come along."

"Why do you need me there?"

"I don't think Serena Hastings will let me talk to her alone; I don't think I want to talk to her alone. But Serena is a formidable woman, and I'm pretty sure I'm going to need someone in my corner, someone with some authority."

"What makes you think I have any authority?"

"Those letters, M and D, after your name."

Peck gave Buckner a long, skeptical look.

"All right," he said finally. "I doubt if my degree will make a difference, but I'll go. But only out of vulgar curiosity." He stood up and put on his coat and a battered cloth cap. "Do I need to bring my little black bag, so the ladies will know I'm a real doctor?"

"I don't think that will be necessary."

They got to the Katy station in time to buy two round-trip tickets to Jackson just as the train pulled in. No one else got on, and they took their seats in a half-empty car.

Peck glanced briefly out the window as the train lurched forward. He began to read a medical journal he pulled from his back pocket. Buckner sat and thought about Judith Lee.

"Tickets, please," said the conductor, interrupting him. Buckner glanced up and handed over his and Peck's tickets. "Thank you," said the conductor as he punched them.

Buckner went back to his thoughts until he fell asleep.

He awoke when the train, steel screaming on steel, pulled into Jackson. They climbed down and Buckner led the way. The day was cold and damp, the sky gray and forbidding. There was a steady, chilling wind and they saw few people as they walked along Grand Street. There were no signs of life as they walked up to the house in which Serena Hastings and Charlotte Tilly lived, but when Buckner knocked, Charlotte opened the door a crack and peered out.

"Yes?" she said, wide eyes glancing from Buckner to the Doctor and back, finally showing recognition. "Oh. You were here the other day, weren't you?"

"Yes," said Buckner. "James Buckner, from Corinth. I'd like to talk to you and Serena, if I may."

"Just a minute." The door slammed shut and a lock clicked. After several minutes, it opened again. Serena Hastings was there.

"What can I do for you, Buck?" she asked. Her voice was flat and hard, and her face was expressionless.

"I need to talk to Charlotte about the murder of her father."

"You think she killed him, don't you?" Her voice betrayed her fear.

"I believe she may have been involved, but I'm not sure how. That's why I need to talk to her."

"If she's a suspect, then get a warrant, if you can, and arrest her. Otherwise, get the hell off our porch." She swung the door shut. It stopped at Buckner's foot.

"If I was here to arrest anybody, Serena, I'd already have that warrant. I'm just here to talk."

"Who's this?" she demanded, nodding in Peck's direction. "Another deputy?"

"I'm flattered, ma'am," said Peck, sweeping off his hat and bowing over it. "But I am only T. Jefferson Peck, MD."

"Oh?" she said, scrutinizing Peck. "Are you Professor Peck's son?"

"You've met my father?" Peck asked, surprised.

"Yes, in St. Louis. Before the war."

"Ah," said Peck, as if it explained everything. "Before the war."

"Yes. He was a remarkable man: knowledgeable, commanding, very dignified."

"That's him," said Peck. "But please do not let that prejudice you against me. I am none of those things."

"I can just imagine," sniffed Serena. To Buckner she said, "I won't allow him to poke and prod Charlotte. She's had her fill of doctors over the years." She peered closely at Peck. "And I won't let you psychoanalyze her, either, if that's what you've got in mind."

"I attended Doctor Freud's lectures," said Peck, "But I am not qualified to psychoanalyze anyone."

"That's not what I've got in mind, either," Buckner promised. "I just want to ask a few questions, then we'll be on our way. Doctor Peck is a friend of mine who came along only because I asked him to."

Serena Hastings stood in the door of her house and looked at Buckner for a long time with her skeptical and unyielding eyes. Buckner waited and watched, and he thought he detected a flickering there, not a softening, but a shifting. Still he waited, saying nothing.

"All right," said Serena, stepping back and opening the door. "Come in. We can sit in the parlor."

She led them into a large front room with a big window draped in heavy cloth. The fireplace was laid but not lighted, and the room was cold. Serena Hastings showed them to chairs but did not offer to take their coats nor to light the fire.

"I'll be right back," she said.

Buckner and Peck sat silently for several minutes. Finally, the two women came and sat together on the couch. Charlotte looked skittish; Serena was calmly resolute. Peck and Buckner sat back down. Charlotte's hands twisted themselves together in her lap, her fingers, with chewed, ragged nails, intertwining like restless snakes. She looked as though she had not slept since Buckner's last visit, and what little confidence she had then had vanished completely.

Serena Hastings had confidence for both of them. She challenged the two men with a look. She reached over and took one of Charlotte's hands in hers. Charlotte glanced quickly at her, then at Peck and Buckner, and then at her lap.

"Ask your questions, Buck," said Serena.

"Miss Tilly," he began slowly. "I'm sorry to bother you again in this matter. It must be very distressing to you. I realize that you had not seen your father in many years, but still, it is never easy to lose a relative, especially to murder."

Charlotte looked quickly up at him, then back down at her lap. Buckner saw, in that one flashing glance, the fear that filled Charlotte's eyes. He thought he heard her say something.

"I beg your pardon?" he said.

"I said, I did not care for my father, and so losing him has been perfectly easy." Her voice rose, but her eyes remained downcast.

"Why is that?" Buckner asked.

"What do you mean?"

"Why is it that you care so little for your father?"

Charlotte did not respond.

"Is it because you found out he killed your mother?" Buckner asked.

Charlotte jerked as though he had struck her, but she did not look up.

"You had recently received proof of that, hadn't you, Miss Tilly?" Buckner asked. "From the Corinth policeman Serena hired to find out?"

"What of it?" Serena demanded when Charlotte said nothing. "We thought it would help Charlotte if she knew for certain."

"'We?'"

"Elizabeth and I." Serena was defiant.

"You and Elizabeth?"

"Yes," Serena said. "Of course. She's is Charlotte's sister."

"I know that," Buckner said, "But why didn't you tell me what you had found out? It might have saved a lot of trouble."

"It was a long time ago," Serena said.

"There is no statute of limitations on murder in this state," Buckner pointed out. "If you had reported this to the county sheriff, I could have arrested Louis Boyer for the murder of his wife."

The two women were silent.

"But there was more to it than your mother's death, wasn't there?" Buckner asked, turning to Charlotte. "Something else from back then."

Both women remained silent, holding their breath, it seemed, waiting.

"When I went out there, after your father's body was discovered, I searched his . . . living quarters, behind the shop. Where you lived back then."

Again, nothing but silence.

Buckner took another step.

He said, "I found something under your father's bed. It's a suitcase, and it has clothing for a little girl. There was a cotton dress with daisies on it."

He thought he saw Charlotte nod slightly. He asked his next question.

"Did your father, ah—try to interfere with you when you were a child?"

Charlotte's hands were fists now, quivering, the knuckles white with tension, Serena's fingers caught in their grip.

Buckner pressed on. "Did he, Miss Tilly?"

Slowly, Charlotte raised her head until she was staring straight at Buckner. Her face was twisted with rage and her eyes flashed an anger that cut straight through him. Soon, words came tumbling out.

"He didn't *try*, Deputy," she said, her teeth clenched against them. "He *did*—interfere with me." Her tone mocked the word. "Call it whatever you like. God knows I never responded to him. I was too young at first. I couldn't have been much more than eight or nine. And it went on as I got older. Even though I told him I didn't like it; even though I began to fight him, or try to; he was always too strong. He ignored me and my feeble complaints; he laughed at my struggling. He said it was his right; he said I belonged to him and he could do anything he wanted with me. And so he did." She shuddered in disgust. "God, how I hated him."

"Did your mother . . ." Buckner began.

"My mother," Charlotte repeated sadly, shaking her head. "My poor mother. She hardly knew what was going on. She suspected, I think. I know that she tried to keep me with her whenever she could, tried to keep me from being alone with him. She took me and Albert around with her every chance she got. To gather her laundry with that old colored woman, everywhere. But she couldn't watch me night and day, all the time. He found his opportunities, and he took them. And once, I remember, when she came in and found us together, he hadn't started in on me yet, she tried to take me away, and he hit her and drove her out into the yard; locked the door. I remember lying there with his greasy, sweaty body writhing around on top of me, listening to my mother sobbing outside the door. She left—disappeared—not long after."

"What about Albert?"

"He beat Albert. He made him work in the shop with him, made him fetch and carry, even when Albert was a little boy. He shouted at him all the time, hit him with his fists, whipped him with his belt his whole life long, until Albert almost wet his pants just at the sight of him." She looked down at her hands, which were still now, and held lightly by Serena Hastings, then up again. "Albert loved me, but he couldn't protect me. No one could. I was completely at his mercy. Whenever he wanted, whatever he wanted, he did."

There was a long silence. Buckner finally broke it.

"When your mother disappeared, did you suspect anything unusual?"

She shook her head. "He told us lies, like he told everybody else. But I believed him. Everybody else did, too, because we all knew how he treated her. He made no secret of it. I suspect most people were only surprised she hadn't left him sooner."

"So now you were alone with him."

"Yes. But nothing changed. I mean, he didn't try to get at me any more than usual." She thought a minute. "It seemed to come in cycles. He always drank, of course, but if he didn't have much work, he drank more, and the less work there was, and the drunker he was, the more he seemed to have to—use—me. To make himself feel better, I suppose, because those were the times when he mistreated Albert the most, too."

"And then you ran away."

"Yes." She closed her eyes. Tears ran from the corners down her cheeks. "I ran off and left Albert and the baby with him." She paused and held a handkerchief to her eyes before looking at Buckner. Her eyes were wet and swollen. "I've never forgiven myself for that."

"You had to protect yourself, dear," Serena said, speaking for the first time.

"But not at the cost of hurting them," Charlotte said. "I was wrong to do that. It was cowardly."

"What happened last Friday when you went to the shop?" Buckner asked.

"It was horrible," Charlotte said, her calmness slipping away once again. "Nothing had changed. The place looked exactly the same, shabby and filthy and stinking of oil and grease. He was fat and slimy and smelled of drink. He leered at me and asked me if I'd come back for some more 'good times.' That's what he called what he used to do to me: 'good times.' I almost couldn't speak, he disgusted me so. I tried to stay calm; I think I was crying, I don't remember. But, anyway, I told him I knew now what had happened to my mother. I knew that he had killed her. He asked me what I was going to do about it. I may have said something about the police, I don't know. All I remember is him laughing at me, walking toward me with that kind of swagger he had. Then he reached out his filthy hands to me, and I, I really don't remember anything very well after that."

"How did you get there?"

"Albert drove me there in his racing automobile."

"Did he go in with you to speak to your father?"

"No," she smiled slightly. "Albert was still too afraid. It took all his courage just to drive me there. I asked him to come in, but he refused. I didn't press him any further."

"Your brother drove you to your father's shop; you went in to speak to him while your brother stayed with the automobile. Your father laughed at you and then . . . what? . . . reached out at you? . . . as though he were attacking you again?" Buckner looked at Charlotte for confirmation. She nodded. "And then you don't remember anything?"

"No. Not until I felt the cold wind on my face as Albert drove fast along the road." Her shoulders drooped and she seemed to collapse against Serena Hastings.

"Did Serena go with you?"

"No! Of course not. She knew I was going somewhere, but I deliberately did not tell her where or with whom."

Buckner nodded and said nothing for a moment. He looked at Serena, but she avoided his gaze now, her lips compressed into a thin hard line. What was she holding back? he wondered.

He thanked the women, finally, and they got up and left the room. Peck and Buckner sat for a moment, looking at each other, uncertain what to do next. Suddenly, Serena Hastings returned and sat down.

"I hope you got what you wanted," she said, her voice cold and restrained.

"I'm sorry," Buckner said.

"Are you going to arrest her?" Serena asked.

"I don't know. Not now. But, please don't try to run away."

"We're not going anywhere. We have been through too much, and this is our home now."

"Has she ever told anybody else about that time?"

Serena shook her head. "I doubt it. Honestly, I don't know what came over her, telling you all that. It has always been extremely difficult for her to speak of it."

Buckner nodded.

"When I first met her, it was buried so deep that she simply never spoke of it. Not ever."

"What about Albert and Elizabeth? Do they know?" Buckner asked.

"Oh, yes. In response to Charlotte's letters, Elizabeth began to work to put the family back together."

"But it had never been together for her," Peck observed.

"No," Serena agreed. "It hadn't. But perhaps that made it more important to her. In any case, she seemed convinced that bringing the three of them together again would solve everything: Albert's drinking, Charlotte's . . . fears, her own loneliness. The family would make it all better."

"Has Charlotte been receiving psychiatric care?" Peck asked.

Serena shot him a glance. "Precious little, Doctor. Your

colleagues are not particularly sympathetic to women in cases like this. They are convinced that no man could treat his daughter in that way, and that if she says he did, then she must be making it up: the fantastical ravings of adolescent girls."

Peck only nodded.

"I'm the one who finally got her to confront what had happened to her, Doctor," Serena Hastings said. "Because I cared about her, I believed her; and she in turn trusted me. But it took a long time."

"But if it's just a fantasy," said Peck, "you may have done more harm than good."

"Fantasy my eye!" said Serena Hastings, her voice just below a shout. "Did it seem to you as though she were making that up?"

"I can hardly tell," he answered.

Serena Hastings looked at Buckner.

"That will be all for today, then, Deputy. Do not come back without a warrant."

"All right, Serena."

He and Peck showed themselves out. As they crossed the porch, Buckner glanced back, and through a parting in the drapes that hung in the big front window, he could see Serena Hastings, still seated on the couch.

Buckner and Peck walked back to the center of town.

"Could we stop and get something to eat?" Peck asked.

"All right."

"Any place in particular?"

Buckner shrugged. "There's a place across from the station."

The restaurant, The Limited, was bright with fresh linen and gleaming silver. The luncheon rush was over, and the only person visible was an elderly man in overalls sipping coffee at a window table. They sat down. Buckner stared out the window. Peck examined a knife.

"Dining car," he said, holding it up for Buckner to see. The words "Katy Line" were stamped in the handle.

A man appeared at their table wearing freshly pressed black

trousers and a gleaming white jacket. He stood with his feet apart, as though to steady himself against a swaying floor.

"That's right," the man said, a pleasant smile on his light-brown face. "I was with the line for thirty years, ran the dining car on the old 'Delta Limited' by the time I was done. They gave me a complete set of silver and china when I retired." His smile widened. "Second-hand, but still worth more than I could afford."

"Got the company insignia on it," Peck said.

"Yeah," the man admitted. "The free advertising's pretty nice for them, too. I don't mind, though. Me and the company always got along real good. Still do. They send folks my way whenever they can." He took out a small pad and pencil. "You gentlemen know what you're having?"

"Coffee," said Peck, sniffing the air. "You do your own baking?"

"My son does," the man answered.

"What have you got today?"

"Bread, rolls, and cherry pie."

"Cherry pie for both of us," Peck said. "My treat." He looked over at Buckner. "I'll just bill the county later."

Buckner shrugged.

The man nodded and grinned and went away. He was back quickly with coffee in two cups. Buckner and Peck sipped in silence and asked for refills when the pie came. Peck ate slowly, savoring the sweet sharpness of the pie, the bitterness of the coffee. Buckner, surprised at how hungry he was, ate his pie and ordered more.

"Did you really hear Freud lecture?" he asked Peck.

"Yes."

"When?"

"Back when I was a promising young medical student, he gave a series of lectures at Clark University. In 1909." Peck looked out of the window. "A lifetime ago."

"Yes," Buckner agreed. "Why did you go to France anyway? You must have been exempt from the draft."

"My father insisted," Peck said. "He believed in service to the nation."

"But he couldn't force you, could he?"

"Oh, no. Nor did he try. He just made his opinion very clear. As he always did." Peck shrugged. "Besides, I believed in service, too, back then. I was actually eager to go. I thought it would be an adventure. I would save lives; be a hero."

"But you did, didn't you?" Buckner asked. "Save lives, I mean."

"What I did was spend endless hours up to my elbows inside boys who had never been ten miles from home and wanted to go adventuring, too. Instead, what they got was their bodies blasted full of hot, jagged metal. More metal than I could ever dig out in a hundred years." His voice was flat, toneless. "And I couldn't save them all. They just died."

"Not all of them," Buckner said.

"Too many," Peck said. "Too many."

They were silent for a long time.

"What are you going to do now?" Peck asked as they worked on their third round of coffee. "You going to arrest Charlotte?"

Buckner sighed and turned to the window. The day was gray and cold and people hurried past with their heads pulled down into their collars, their hands jammed into their pockets.

"I don't know," he said. "Do you believe her story?"

"About her father having sex with her?"

"Yes."

Peck thought a while before speaking.

"Hard to know, for sure," he said. "Freud is very clear on this: it is a fantasy; it's not real."

"It sounded real to me. She got pretty damned particular about the whole thing."

"That doesn't mean it's not a fantasy," Peck insisted. "Besides, even if it is a fantasy, it seems certain that Louis killed Victoria. You've got some evidence to prove that, haven't you?"

"Maybe, but whatever Louis Boyer may or may not have done, it was not his daughter's place to try and convict him, and then deal out punishment."

"Perhaps not," Peck agreed. "For a normal person. But Charlotte's not normal. Whatever happened to her as a child, she is convinced it was real, so convinced that it guides her actions to this day. You saw how enraged she became, talking about him. And frightened. It's almost as though she's still terrified of him. She's so fragile right now that the slightest touch causes her to start vibrating, like a violin string drawn too tight. I think Serena Hastings is the only thing keeping her out of the asylum."

Buckner nodded bleakly and sipped his coffee.

"Why do you suppose she told you all that in the first place?" Peck asked.

"Well, I pushed her," Buckner said.

"Sure, but she didn't have to tell you a thing. Her friend was there to protect her. Hell, I think Miss Hastings was more surprised than we were when she started talking about her father."

"Yes, I think she was."

"That story puts her on the spot. She admitted she was there on Friday morning."

"Yes."

"And she gave you chapter and verse on how much she hated her father, and why."

"Yes."

"Then she tries to back out with that stuff about not remembering anything until she was on her way down the road with reliable old Albert at the wheel." Peck snorted. "Does she expect you to believe that?"

"I don't know," Buckner admitted. "It doesn't seem to give her much leeway."

"That's for sure."

"But it still doesn't leave me a lot of room for action," he said.

"What do you mean?"

"I mean, legally. As far as evidence is concerned, she can tell me just about anything at all, and unless I can get somebody who was there as an eyewitness to support her story, it doesn't mean a thing."

"But I heard her. So did Miss Hastings."

"Sure. But that's no different from me hearing her. As far as the court is concerned, it's just a story. She could say she made it up and you'd probably support her."

"But if it's a story, why tell it?"

Buckner thought a long time. "I'm not sure," he said at last. "To protect Albert?"

"Maybe."

They finished their coffee, paid their bill, and crossed the street to the Katy waiting room, where they sat in silence until the train pulled in.

Buckner slept all the way back to Corinth while Peck read his medical journal, or looked out the window at the darkening land flashing by.

They got off the train in Corinth and stood together on the platform.

"What now?" Peck asked.

"Back to Cape Girardeau to talk to Albert," Buckner said.

"What good will that do you?"

"At least I'll know," Buckner said, and walked off.

SATURDAY, OCTOBER 30

BUCKNER GOT UP early the next morning. The weather outside his window looked gray and cold, and he could smell moisture in the air. His mother was at the stove when he walked into the kitchen.

"We're having chicken for dinner," she said. "Will you be joining us?"

"No. I'm sorry. I have to go to Cape Girardeau again."

"It can't wait?"

"I'm afraid not. I'm almost there on this Boyer murder. If I can talk to Albert Boyer today, and if I get the answers I need, it'll be done."

"Did he kill his father?" His mother seemed saddened by the idea.

"I don't know for sure," said Buckner. "But I doubt it."

"Well, then?"

"That's why I have to talk to him. To find out." He put on his coat and hat and kissed his mother on the cheek. "I don't know when I'll get back."

"Will you eat something, at least?"

"I promise." He had a late meal with Judith Lee to look forward to, but that was none of his mother's business.

The drive had not become more interesting in a week, and it was no shorter, so it was noon by the time he turned down River Street. His leg nagged at him the whole trip. As he drove, he watched the flat, dull sky and thought about the coming of winter.

He did not stop at the Sheriff's Department, but went directly to Boyer's body shop. The place looked abandoned. He parked the Ford, went to the shop door, and knocked. He wiped clean a patch of dirty window and peered in. Whatever had been under the tarp was gone now, and the tarp lay in a wad in a corner. There were no signs of life.

Buckner went back to the Sheriff's Department. Polk, looking as crisp and gray as he had the week before, greeted Buckner with a smile.

"Good day. Didn't expect to see you so soon."

"I went over to Boyer's shop. It's closed up."

"Is it?"

"Where can I find that Negro boy that works for him?"

"That is William Smith. He lives just a couple of blocks away. Why?"

"I need to ask him a couple of questions."

"Want me to send a deputy along? Strange white man in that part of town would be running a risk. You'd stand a better chance of getting your questions answered, too."

"Sure," said Buckner. "Much obliged."

"My pleasure." Polk opened his door and called, "Tell Grover I need to see him!"

"Right, Sheriff!" a voice returned.

Buckner was only mildly surprised when the door opened and a black man wearing a deputy sheriff's badge walked in.

Polk performed the introductions, and the two deputies shook hands.

"Buckner here needs to talk to William Smith, Grover."

"Colored or white?"

"Colored," said Polk.

"Which colored William Smith? There's three in town that I know of."

"The one that works for Albert Boyer."

The deputy nodded. "Lives with his aunt and uncle now. Come on," he said, and walked out without a backward glance, Buckner tagging along.

Buckner drove. They headed through town, Grover giving directions, until they crossed the invisible line that separated the white from the black neighborhoods. In this case, it was nothing as obvious as the railroad tracks in Corinth, but it existed anyway. They stopped outside a neat, small frame house with a truck garden in the front yard, beans climbing the side of the house, and a stand of corn in the back. A little girl with her hair in braids and wearing a patched denim coat over a frilly white dress was sitting in a big rocking chair on the porch. She was busily combing the blonde hair of a similarly dressed doll. As Buckner and Grover got out of the Ford, she saw them and ran into the house without a word. The two policemen halted in the yard.

It began to rain lightly in small, scattered drops that disappeared at once into the dry earth.

In a moment, a tall man came out onto the porch. The sleeves of his white shirt were rolled above his elbows and his vest was unbuttoned.

"Good day gentlemen," he said. "What can I do for you?"

"Is William here, Mister Smith?" asked Polk's deputy.

"Yes. Why?"

"I just need to ask him a couple of questions," Buckner said. "Won't take but a minute." He added, "We can do it right here."

The man on the porch looked from one deputy to the other, then nodded and disappeared inside. In a moment, the door opened and William Smith emerged. He was dressed neatly in a dark suit, but wore the same surly expression as the last time Buckner had seen him.

"Yeah?" he said.

"Come here, please, William," said Polk's deputy. "We need to talk to you for a minute."

"It's raining," said the young man, gesturing at the gray sky.

"Not hard," said Grover. "You won't get wet."

Smith reluctantly stepped down off the porch into the yard. Buckner and Grover went toward him, and they met by the brown, shrunken tomato plants.

"Go ahead," said Grover to Buckner.

"I went by the shop," Buckner said. "It was all closed up."

"So?"

"I want to know about the automobile that was under that tarp?" Buckner asked.

"What? What tarp?"

"The one on the far side of the shop. The one that had the automobile under it."

"What about it?"

"Where is that automobile?"

Smith shifted his weight to his other foot and glanced at Grover.

Grover's impassive stare offered no comfort. Smith looked back at Buckner.

"Why do you want to know?"

"I'm investigating a murder, William. Didn't your boss tell you?" he said. He waited while that sunk in. Smith's eyes grew wide and glanced quickly from Buckner to Grover and back. Buckner heard a sound and looked up to see movement in the darkened doorway.

"I didn't kill anybody!" Smith whispered frantically.

"I'm not accusing you of a crime," said Buckner, loud enough for anyone behind the door to hear. Then, more softly, he said, "I just think you might be able to answer some questions that will help me find the person that did."

"This is white folks' business, William," Grover said flatly. "The kind you don't want to get tangled up in. Tell the man what he wants to know."

"What was under the tarp, William?" Buckner asked.

"Mister Boyer's racing auto," Smith answered.

"Does he race a lot?"

"Some. He designed it himself, and the two of us built it. Split the take, fifty-fifty. If there is any."

"How fast will it go, William?"

"Oh, it'll do eighty on the flat." He grinned, comfortable on familiar ground. "We put a Stutz engine in it, but we made the body lighter and redesigned the transmission so you can . . ."

"Get you up to Corinth in no time at all," Buckner interrupted.

"I wouldn't know about that," Smith said, enthusiasm instantly draining out of him.

"Where is it now, William?"

"In the shed out back," said Smith, nodding in that direction.

"You've got it?"

"Sure. I helped build it. Mister Boyer asked me to keep it for a while, take a look at it. He said the engine's been missing, but I couldn't find anything wrong with it."

"Thank you William."

"That's all?"

"No. One last thing. Last Friday, the twenty-second, Boyer wasn't in the shop with you that day, was he?"

Smith hesitated.

"Tell him, William," Grover prompted. "Unless you want to go to jail for a white man."

"But Mister Boyer been nothing but good to me," Smith protested.

Buckner nodded. "Was he in the shop with you on Friday?"

After a pause, Smith, his eyes on the ground, shook his head.

"Where was he?"

"I don't know."

"But he took the racing car, didn't he?"

Smith nodded.

"Fine," Buckner said. "I'd like to look at the racing car."

"All right. Come on."

William led them around to the back of the house. The ten-foot square corn patch had been harvested, and the stalks had been gathered together into a rough cone.

Behind the corn patch stood a small shed. Smith pulled open the door and Buckner saw the back end of a low, bullet-shaped, dark blue automobile. He ducked his head and entered. The automobile had an open cockpit, with barely room in it for two small seats.

He saw a handle and the outline of a hatch in the back, behind the cockpit.

"This the boot?" he asked Smith.

Smith, who was standing nervously in the yard, shook his head.

Buckner turned the handle and pulled and the hatch opened into a rumble seat big enough for one person.

"William," Buckner said. "Sit in the driver's seat."

The young man glanced briefly at Grover, then got in. Buckner stepped back out into the yard. His view of Smith was blocked by the back of the rumble seat.

"Thank you," Buckner said. The young man got out, closed the hatch, and went back out into the yard.

"Let's go," Buckner said to Grover.

"That it?" Smith asked, surprised. "You through with me now?"

"Yeah. But don't wander off, William. You may have to testify in court."

Smith looked horrified as he turned and went into his home.

Grover and Buckner got into the Ford.

"Where does Albert Boyer live?" Buckner asked.

"Above his shop," said the deputy. "I thought you knew that."

Buckner shook his head. "But I should have," he said as he pulled out.

"I don't know about how they do things where you come from, Deputy," said Grover, "But down here they won't allow a colored man to testify against a white man. Especially not in a capital case."

Buckner nodded. "Depends on the judge," he said.

"Not down here it doesn't."

"Don't you have to testify in cases you've worked on?" Buckner asked.

"In cases involving my own people, yes. If I'm investigating a case against a white man, then he's arrested by a white officer, and the white officer testifies in court."

"Using evidence you've gathered."

"Yes," Grover admitted.

Buckner just nodded. The complexities of race relations in his home state struck him, as they often did, as unnecessarily convoluted.

He drove up to the door of Albert Boyer's shop and stopped the Ford. As before, there was no sign of life.

"You got a weapon?" Buckner asked.

"Yes," said Grover.

"All right. If he comes running out, you shoot him. Is that allowed?"

With a suddenness that startled Buckner, Grover reached under his jacket and a pistol instantly materialized in each hand. He held them out for examination. One was a .38 Smith & Wesson with a four-inch barrel. The other was a little nickel-plated .32 that looked like it would fall apart if it ever discharged.

"I'll just put this in his hand," Grover said, indicating the .32. He grinned. "I'm allowed to shoot if it's self-defense."

Buckner left the deputy still chuckling as he got out and walked to the door of the shop. He pulled. Nothing happened. He went to the back of the building and found another door. It too was locked. Buckner jabbed hard with the heel of his hand. The rotting wood splintered and the door swung open. Stairs led up into darkness. Buckner looked for a light switch, found none, and started upstairs.

The switch was at the top. He turned it and lights came on. He saw a small, neat apartment. The floors were swept and there was flowered wallpaper on the walls. One room was empty except for two small beds that had been carefully made up. Dust arose when Buckner patted the bright, flowered bedspreads. A second bedroom showed signs of occupation. The bedclothes were rumpled on a full-size bed. Clothing hung on hooks. But everything was neatly in place.

There was a small kitchen with an oil stove. Pots and pans

stood in ordered rows on shelves; others held cans of food. A plate, a cup, and utensils sat in a rack next to the sink.

Buckner looked into the last room. He saw a rocking chair and a low table, a small shelf with books and stacked magazines, and an imitation Oriental carpet. The two windows overlooked the yard. Buckner looked down. He could see his Ford, with Grover's elbow sticking out of the window. He looked at the yard again, missing something. He thought for a moment and remembered. A small Dodge truck that had been there earlier that morning was gone now.

He went downstairs and closed the door as securely as possible.

"Nobody around," he said as he cranked up the Ford.

"I know some other places we could look," said Grover.

Buckner shook his head. "No, thanks. He's gone to ground, and I think I know where. I doubt he'll run much farther."

He drove the deputy back to the department and the two of them went inside.

"Any luck?" asked the Sheriff.

"Some," said Buckner. "We talked to William Smith. But I need to talk to Albert Boyer, and he's gone. Can I borrow your telephone?"

"Sure." The Sheriff gestured to the telephone on his desk.

Buckner called Jackson. He didn't even bother to ask if Aubuchon was there. He simply left a description of Albert Boyer and the Dodge truck he was probably driving, and told them he was probably headed for Jackson.

"Why Jackson?" asked the Sheriff when Buckner had hung up.

"That's where his sister lives."

"They in this together?"

Buckner nodded.

"Thanks for the help, Sheriff, Deputy Grover," Buckner said.

"It's Cleveland. Grover's my first name."

"Oh. Sorry."

"Yeah. Being named after a fat white Democrat president's been nothing but trouble for me all my life," he said with a smile. They shook hands and Buckner headed back the way he had come.

He drove through the thickening darkness and growing cold. It rained the whole way.

He did not stop at home, but went straight to Judith Lee's house. Stiff, chilled, and tired, he climbed her porch steps. She answered his knock on the door with a smile.

"I am glad to see you," she said. "Come in."

She showed Buckner into her front room.

The sofa was still stacked with books and papers, but the cobwebs were gone, as well as the maverick china; and somebody had dusted the exposed surfaces.

There were two chairs flanking a low table set for tea. Buckner pulled out one of the chairs and sat. Judith Lee excused herself.

She returned at once with a steaming pot and a plate of cookies. She sat and poured and gave a cup to Buckner, then picked up her own. He sipped carefully, but burned his tongue anyway before turning to the plate of cookies.

After a long silence, during which Buckner ate all the cookies, Judith cleared her throat. Buckner looked up, startled.

"Yes?"

"You're so quiet. Is everything all right?"

He did not answer, but only looked at her.

"What is it?"

"The Boyer family," he said.

"I don't understand."

"Neither do I." He stopped, and for a long time he didn't say anything. Then he started abruptly.

"I've seen some terrible things," he said. "I will not go into detail, but I've seen what Apaches do to whites; what Villistas do to rurales. I saw what the Germans did in Belgium. Those were," he shook his head, unable to find the right word, "pretty bad, but I got to where I understood them. War, revolution, bred-in-the-bone race hatred can make people do terrible things to each other. But in the three years that I've been a deputy sheriff here, barely thirty miles from where I was born and raised, I have seen the things people do to old friends, to members of their own families . . . ." He stopped and looked at her. "I truly do not understand."

She looked at him, at the confusion and pain on his face, and could not think of anything to say. He went on anyway.

"One of the first things I learned in police work is that if there's been a killing, chances are it was a friend or a relative that did it. And often there's no motive to speak of. Or nearly so. It'll be over a bottle, a woman, a man, an argument over something meaningless that gets out of hand." He stopped again and remembered Charlotte's story, then went on. "And there's worse things than killing that people do."

"What do you mean?" And when he did not answer right away, she asked again, quietly, "What do you mean?"

"Do you believe that a man would have sex with his ten-year-old daughter?" he asked suddenly. And then, when she did not answer at once, he said, "I'm sorry. I should not have asked that."

"No. It's all right. I insisted. I'm just surprised, that's all." She frowned slightly. "Because I do believe it, know it."

"You do?"

"Yes. At school." She explained. "I act as sort of an adviser to the girls. I think that's why they hired me in the first place, to tell you the truth. They needed an assistant principal and they needed someone to counsel the female students who were beginning to attend in greater numbers, so they hired me and killed two birds with one stone."

"And is this the sort of thing you counsel them on?"

"No, of course not. Mostly I deal with discipline problems, scheduling matters, grades, questions about college, marriage, that sort of thing. But I do get a surprising number of questions about sex."

"Why you? Why don't they just ask their mothers?"

"That's usually why I get the questions," she said dryly. "Their mothers have either told them nothing at all about reproduction, or they have filled their heads with the most awful nonsense, lies, really, that are worse than total ignorance."

Buckner listened and poured more tea.

"The farm girls know, of course. You can't grow up on a farm and not know about reproduction, believe me. It's going on all around you; if you have livestock that you market, then reproduction is how you live. But the same applies, in a way, to the very poorest girls, who grow up in one-room houses, sometimes sleeping in the same beds with their parents and numerous brothers and sisters. They learn at an early age because, once again, it's all around them.

"No, strangely enough, it's the better sort of girl, from the nice home in town, who invariably knows the least. So I do find myself having to explain matters from time to time."

"But fathers?"

Judith nodded. "Two, over the years. Two who have actually spoken to me about their fathers; I suspect there are more. I've heard rumors about what goes on, but I have no real evidence."

"Did they come to you? That is, how did you . . . ?"

"I sought them out and spoke to them," said Judith.

"How did you know to talk to them?"

"Their teachers had come to me. In both cases, and these were over a year apart, the girls in question were having trouble with their school work, and they seemed upset about something. So their teachers spoke to me, suspecting some sort of boy trouble, which is what it often is. Anyway, I called the girls into my office. When I asked the first one what was wrong, she became hysterical. I was afraid she was going to have a breakdown there in my office."

"What did you do?"

"Well, my secretary and I got the poor thing calmed down, gave her a drink of water, let her catch her breath. Then, when we were alone again, she told me that her father had forced himself on her, in fact, had been doing so since she—ah—reached maturity." She looked closely at Buckner to see that he understood. He nodded. "In any event, she just blurted it out; I didn't ask. I didn't even suspect." She sighed. "This was not the sort of thing they prepared me for at college."

"What about the other one?" Buckner asked.

"Her story was even worse. First of all, I practically had to drag it out of her with a team of horses. She was a serious behavior problem in her class, short-tempered, sometimes violent, but sullen and morose the rest of the time. When I spoke with her, she kept insisting that nothing was wrong, that the other students and her teacher were picking on her. I kept pushing, gently but constantly, and then I remembered the other girl. This was about a year later. So I asked her directly, the second girl, if she was being bothered by her father."

"And she told you about it?"

"Hardly," said Judith with a short laugh. "She denied it, vehemently. So vehemently, in fact, that it made me suspicious. So I shifted to another line of questioning, then circled back to that one. Finally, I wore her down, drove her into a corner, and she confessed."

"You might have made a good cop," said Buckner. Judith Lee smiled bleakly at him.

"I don't think so," she said. "I used the word 'confessed' intentionally; because that's the way she explained it all to me. As though it were her fault. She was 'making' him do these things to her. And evidently had been for as long as she could remember."

"'Making him' do things?"

"Yes, that's the way she put it; and the way he justified it to her, I have no doubt," said Judith. "It was all her fault. Her father was totally blameless."

"How did these girls feel about their fathers?" Buckner asked. "Did this make them angry?"

Judith shook her head. "It made them afraid. The basic attitude both girls had toward their fathers was terror. Even the one who had apparently suffered almost her entire life with this, at least as far back as she could remember, the one who had been told the whole time that it was all her fault. She knew it wasn't right. But she was too frightened to do anything about it."

"What about their mothers? Did they know? Didn't they do anything?"

"Nothing. I called the mothers in, to talk to them. But they both denied that there was anything at all going on."

"Then maybe there wasn't," suggested Buckner.

"No," said Judith, shaking her head. "You didn't talk to those girls. They were utterly believable." Buckner thought about Charlotte Tilly again and realized that he had believed her. "And the way the mothers made their denials, calling their own daughters tramps and whores, going on and on about how hardworking their husbands were, how a man had the right to 'blow off a little steam.' No, talking with the mothers only confirmed my suspicions."

"Did the girls want revenge?" Buckner asked.

"They wanted to get away," Judith answered. "More than anything else in the whole world, they wanted to get away."

After a long silence, Buckner spoke again. "These are the only two?" he asked.

"The only two who spoke with me," answered Judith. "And don't forget I had to go to them; I had to ask the questions. They weren't about to come to me."

"Do you think there are others?"

Judith Lee nodded. "I expect so," she said. "But, of course, I can't prove it." She looked up from her teacup. "And by the way, these girls weren't 'that sort.' They weren't white trash or ridge runners, or anything like that. They both come from perfectly nice, respectable families. One girl's father is a deacon in his church. One owns a good-sized farm near town, but leases it out; the other father is a prosperous businessman. I have met their parents at several school events, though now I can hardly bring myself to speak to them."

They were both silent for a long time.

"What happened to the girls?"

"They have both graduated. One of them got married right away and moved to Kansas City; the other just moved away, I believe."

Buckner poured the last of the tea, dividing it between their two cups. It was cool now, and he drank his off quickly.

"Does this help you at all?" Judith asked.

"I don't know. Jeff Peck said it was just a fantasy that girls have about their fathers."

"I think he is wrong about that." She was firm. "These girls were not making this up."

Buckner nodded. He got to his feet.

"Where are you going?" she asked, rising as well.

"Home. To bed. I think I have a busy day tomorrow."

"You can stay if you like."

"Thank you," he gave her a bleak smile. "I don't think I would be very good company."

"I don't mind," she said. "We could just talk."

"I'm about talked out, Judith. Sorry."

"All right."

She showed him to the door. He looked at her closely for a moment.

"Good night," he said abruptly, and walked through the rain to the Ford, started it up, and drove away.

She stood on the darkened porch and said "Good night," and went inside.

SUNDAY, OCTOBER 31

THE NEXT MORNING, Buckner was up early and on the road again. He was in a hurry this time, and did not want to wait for the train. The weather had gotten worse during the night. A cold, hard wind stripped the trees of their few remaining leaves, and rain lashed against the side of the Ford. It did not take him long to get to Jackson.

As it was Sunday, Buckner found nobody in the sheriff's office who seemed interested in, or able to, help him. He went up to Eldon Pinch's office on the third floor of the courthouse, where the eternally smiling, eternally knitting Mrs. Shapleigh cheerfully informed him that she had come in to hold the fort during the campaign.

"They've all gone to church, Deputy. Best place to be on the Sunday before Election Day."

"What about my murder case?" Buckner demanded.

"Do you need something immediately? A warrant or something like that? I believe Judge Pierce is somewhere in the building."

"Judge Pierce? He retired the year I graduated from high school. And he was feeble minded then."

"Yes, but he agreed to come in today, to sort of keep an eye on things, you know; sign anything that needed signing." She gave him a look charged with meaning. "Judge Pierce knows the meaning of an election."

"No rush. I was going to get a warrant, but I guess I don't need it immediately," Buckner conceded.

"Well, the election is Tuesday. I honestly don't believe you're going to be able to get anybody's attention until afterwards. Can it wait until Wednesday?"

Buckner had earlier considered the possibility that Albert and his sister might try to run away and decided it was unlikely. Besides, he asked himself, where would they go?

"Yes," he said. "It can wait until Wednesday."

Mrs. Shapleigh picked up her knitting.

"Was there anything else, then, Deputy?" she inquired.

"No. Thank you Mrs. Shapleigh."

He left and returned to the street.

The town was carrying on as usual for a cold, rainy Sunday. The rain seemed to be keeping most people indoors. The few who were out went about their business as though entirely unaware that the fate of the world hung on the election returns. Some acknowledged the coming event to the extent of wearing buttons for one candidate or another, but that was as far as most would go. The frenzy had seized only those who were in office and wanted to stay there, or those who hoped to supplant them.

Buckner cranked up the Ford and drove to Serena Hastings' house. He was not surprised to see a small Dodge truck sitting around back, imperfectly concealed by an Osage orange tree. He left the Ford near the truck and got out. There was a small garden in the back yard, and someone had just finished preparing the ground for next spring's planting. The earth was freshly turned, and a shovel and rake leaned against the Osage orange.

Buckner had to hold his hat on his head with one hand as he walked through the rain around to the front door.

Serena answered his knock. She seemed surprised to see him standing there, water dripping from the rim of his hat. She backed into the room and held the door open for him. When he stood in her hallway, she closed the door.

"I don't have a warrant, but I'd like to speak with Charlotte and Albert," he said, and to his surprise, she only nodded. She looked haggard and worn, and perhaps a little frightened. She seemed to be trembling violently.

"In the parlor," was all she said, and disappeared toward the back of the house.

Albert and Charlotte sat together on the sofa in the parlor, heads together, talking softly. They turned to look as Buckner entered. They looked like twins in the dark beauty they had inherited from their father, and the surprise that washed across their faces was identical.

"There was no place else for you go, Albert," Buckner said quietly.

The three waited like that, looking at each other, until Buckner spoke again: "You'll both have to come with me. I'll have to take you both in for questioning in the murder of Louis Boyer. I'm sorry."

They continued to sit and look at him in a kind of stunned silence, as though they did not entirely understand what he had said.

"Come on," Buckner said, the irritation he was beginning to feel making his voice rough and harsh. "I'll drive you there in my Ford. I left it out back."

Finally, the two of them stood up, still together, and walked out of the room.

They preceded Buckner down the hall, through a neat, bright kitchen, and out through the rain into the backyard. A third automobile sat near the Dodge truck. Buckner recognized it and turned in time to see Elizabeth Blumberg, as she hit him on the head with the gardening shovel. The blow crushed his hat and knocked him to the ground. He tried to get up and he could hear Elizabeth's breath, harsh from the exertion, as she swung the shovel again. The pain expanded instantly to fill him and he lost consciousness.

He awoke lying on his face in the back of a jolting vehicle. For a moment, Buckner was in an ambulance being driven through every shell hole on the Western Front by a driver who seemed to be jabbering fast in words he could not understand. He tried to move and found that he could not; the effort brought waves of nausea. He fought off the nausea, afraid of what would happen if he vomited, since someone had inexplicably stuffed a rag in his mouth and tied in place with a red bandanna. Also, for some reason he could not grasp, the ambulance was open to the sky, and a cold rain fell on him.

He blacked out again, he did not know for how long, and woke up when the ambulance jerked to a halt. The doors opened, then slammed shut. He could hear more jabbering, and he listened closely. First, he realized he could understand the words. Then he realized that he was lying in the bed of Albert Boyer's truck.

"Get him out of there, Albert," he heard someone say. A firm, hard voice. It was not Charlotte he heard, but Elizabeth.

"What're we going to do?" Albert asked in a voice on the edge of panic.

"Well, we can't just drive around the county all day with a deputy sheriff tied up in the back," Elizabeth answered matter-of-factly. "We've got to get rid of him somewhere, to give us time to get away from here."

"Get rid of him?" Albert sounded confused.

Charlotte tried to explain. "Yes. So he can't follow us. Or send anyone after us."

"How?" Albert asked.

"We'll just carry him over there by the river and leave him," she said reassuringly.

"Can we do that?" Albert's voice was pinched with fear. "What if he dies?"

"He won't die." Elizabeth was scornful. "He'll get loose, or somebody will find him. But not before we're long gone from Highland County."

"All right, we'll move him," said Charlotte, sounding more frightened than convinced. "But where will we go?"

"Don't worry," commanded Elizabeth. "It will be all right. I promise. Now, Albert, get him out of the back. You'll have to get him down there. He's too big for me to move."

"What should I do?" Charlotte asked.

"You stay here." Elizabeth gave Charlotte her orders in a soft, gentle voice. "We're not that far from the road. You call us if you see anybody coming."

"All right," Charlotte answered uncertainly.

The tailgate of the truck opened with a bang. Buckner rolled over onto his back and tried to sit up. There was nothing in the back of the truck but a thin layer of dirt that had turned to mud, along with the shovel he had seen lying beside Serena Hastings's garden. It was the one Elizabeth had hit him with.

He turned to see the three of them looking down at him. Charlotte and Albert, older with their father's dark good looks, and Elizabeth, who must have resembled the mother, younger, with her blonde hair and broad features. They said nothing, just stood at the end of the truck bed and watched Buckner struggle into a sitting position. Their faces were expressionless and their eyes were wide and staring and empty. Their bodies leaned slightly into the wind. They did not seem to know it was raining.

"Go on, Albert," Elizabeth said finally. "Get him out of there."

Albert, frowning with uncertainty, reached for Buckner's bound ankles. Buckner kicked at him, but Albert easily avoided the blow and took a tight grip on the rope. He pulled sharply and Buckner slid to the wet ground, landing on his back with a force that knocked the wind out of him.

Albert picked him up under the arms and began dragging him. Buckner looked around and realized where they were: the far northwest corner of the county, where the Osage River flowed north to the Missouri. The land was rolling, dotted with prosperous farms, but this section was remote and guarded by a thick stand of oak. The main road from Jackson to Jefferson City ran several hundred yards to the north. He couldn't remember who owned this land, but he did know that nobody would happen by this secluded place in time to find him.

Then he remembered that Elizabeth had brought the shovel and realized that she did not intend for anyone to find him.

Albert dragged him to a clearing in the trees, where a high

bank overlooked the rushing water some twenty feet below. The current was powerful here, and if he fell in, his body would not turn up until it got to New Orleans, if then.

"This is far enough," Elizabeth said, and Albert laid him down.

They stood silently over Buckner. The wind whipped at them and the rain stung Buckner's face. Elizabeth's blonde hair blew in wet strings or plastered itself against her pale skin.

"You go on back to the truck," said Elizabeth. She did not look frightened at all, or wild; just determined. She had to raise her voice to be heard over the wind. She kept her eyes on Buckner as she talked, eyes that narrowed into slits.

Albert hesitated, brushing the rain from his face.

"Why?" he finally asked. He, too, was practically shouting. "What're you going to do?"

"Nothing. Just go on back. I want to explain to the Deputy here what we did and why we had to do it."

"There's nothing to explain. Just leave him and come back with me." Albert was begging.

"But I don't want him thinking we killed Louis Boyer just to get revenge. He's got to know what really happened."

"What difference does it make if we're just leaving him here?" Albert protested.

"I want to do it. Is that enough? Now get back to the truck and take care of Charlotte. She looks ready to fall apart."

"All right." Albert turned reluctantly. "But you come quick, you hear?" he said.

"Fine. All right. Just go." Elizabeth's voice was like steel.

He disappeared into the trees. Buckner turned to look up at Elizabeth, who stood over him, the shovel in her hands. "We're finally free of that monster," she said. "It took us years to put our family back together, to get back what he took from us. We killed him, but it was no crime, and I won't have you dogging us. If you put us in jail, then everything we've done will have been wasted."

Buckner tried to shout, but the rag in his mouth permitted only a muffled whine.

Elizabeth raised the shovel. "I'm sorry."

"Elizabeth! Don't!" Albert came crashing heavily through the trees and caught his sister's upraised arms. The two of them struggled for the shovel. Elizabeth bent back against her brother's height and weight; Albert fought to break her grip on the handle.

Buckner heard a loud voice booming through the trees.

"I'm Sheriff Elmer Aubuchon! Put up your hands!" The voice rose up over the wind. Buckner sat up, looked frantically around, and finally saw the Sheriff's bulky shape. He was on the high bank of the Osage River, some fifty yards downstream. He stood there like an old-fashioned duelist, his enormous body turned to the side, a long-barreled Colt revolver in his hand, pointed straight at them.

He's too far away, Buckner thought. He looked up at Albert and Elizabeth. Albert was bigger, stronger, but Elizabeth was driven by desperation and would not let go. They seemed not to have heard the Sheriff.

"Stop right there!" Aubuchon shouted again.

Albert finally managed to free the shovel from his sister's grip and swing it away from her, knocking her to the ground. He stood looking down, the shovel still high over his head.

Aubuchon fired once. Buckner saw his hand jerk slightly amidst a light puff of smoke. He heard a light popping sound carried off by the wind, and then there was a loud thump and Albert's head exploded. Blood and brains spattered Buckner's face and stained Elizabeth's coat as Albert's body toppled back onto the ground, and everything was quiet except for the wind.

Aubuchon walked toward them. He looked at the body, astonishment on his face, and put the pistol into the back pocket of his overalls.

"I was aiming for his leg," he said. "I wasn't aiming to kill him."

He turned to Buckner as though seeing him for the first time. He took the gag out of his mouth and untied him. Buckner came to his knees. Frantically, almost wildly, he rubbed his face against his sleeves, scrubbed his face with his pocket-handkerchief, felt cautiously with tentative fingertips until he was sure no more of Albert was on his skin. When he was satisfied, he stood up.

He looked down at Albert, who lay on his back in the rain, a startled expression on his face. There was a blue hole between his bulging eyes. A pool of blood spread out under his head, thick and heavy on the wet ground. Next to him sat his sister, staring, horrified, at the corpse. The shovel lay between them.

"She was the one," Buckner said, his voice hoarse.

"What do you mean?" Aubuchon asked.

"She was the one that was going to kill me," he repeated. "Albert was trying to stop her."

Aubuchon looked at the corpse again and said, "Shit," under his breath. He ran a thick hand over his wet face.

They stood like that for a long time and waited for Elizabeth to notice them. She did not take her eyes off her brother's body. Finally, they helped her to her feet and led her back to the Dodge truck. The Sheriff's new Packard sat next to it, with Charlotte sitting inside, handcuffed to the doorpost.

"When I got here, she was just staring into space, wouldn't answer when I spoke to her, acted like she didn't even know I was around," Aubuchon explained. "I was afraid she'd wander off and fall in the river."

They put Elizabeth in the back seat with her and handcuffed her to the opposite doorpost. Then they went back for Albert. The ground was rough, uneven, the grass slick with rain, the dirt turned to mud. Albert's corpse was heavy and awkward to carry. Buckner could not concentrate, kept slipping back into the confusion of the ride in the back of the truck: he knew he was carrying a corpse through rain and mud, something he had done many times; but he seemed unable to determine exactly where this was occurring. He kept telling himself it was a dream, that he could not be back in France again; but he could not identify precisely where he was, and where else did he carry corpses in the rain and mud if not in France?

Twice he slipped and sat down hard, both times his old wound exploded in pain. Both times, his fall made Aubuchon drop

Albert's feet, so they had to pick up the body and start again. Finally, they got Albert into the back of his little Dodge truck, which Buckner drove, following Sheriff Aubuchon to the county jail.

By the time they got there, Buckner's hands had stopped shaking. It was just from the cold and the wet, he kept saying to himself, over and over, not believing it. He had not been so frightened in years, so disoriented and confused, and the experience left him feeling hollowed out, like an egg sucked dry, with only a thin, fragile shell to cover his hollowness.

He got cleaned up at the county court house and borrowed some clothes from a deputy who was almost the right size. The shirt was tight across shoulders and the pants were big in the waist, but they were long enough, and dry. He persuaded the same deputy to drive him to Serena Hastings's house so he could pick up the Ford and drive it back to Corinth.

Serena Hastings greeted him at the door.

"What happened? Where's Charlotte? Is she all right?"

"She's at the courthouse . . ."

"Is she in jail? She can't stand that. You can't put her in jail." She was clutching Buckner's arm tightly. "She didn't do anything. She was in an institution once before. It nearly killed her."

"Elizabeth tried to kill me, Serena," said Buckner, gently removing his arm from her grip.

"I'm sorry, James," she said. "I couldn't stop them. It happened so fast. After they took you away, I called the sheriff's office, but there was nobody there. It wasn't Charlotte's fault. Elizabeth made her go along with them."

Buckner nodded.

"I only wanted to help Charlotte," she said. "Can you understand? She's all I ever cared about."

"Yes."

"Elizabeth said she wanted to bring the family together. She suggested I hire that man to find out what happened to their mother. I thought that would be good for Charlotte. But she was going to make Charlotte leave me. She said it wasn't right for us to be together."

"I don't know what Elizabeth was trying to do, Serena. But Charlotte's had some kind of collapse. She hasn't been arrested for anything yet, and I doubt she will be. A doctor's seeing her now."

"Oh, bring her home, James. I can take care of her better than any doctor. I've done it before."

"I don't know what the Sheriff has in mind, Serena."

"What about Albert? What about Elizabeth?"

"I have to go, Serena," he said. There was no use telling her about the other two.

She looked up at him but said nothing and he walked out to the Ford and headed for Corinth. His body sagged, exhausted, and his head ached. His thinking was still muddled, confused, and he kept falling asleep. At one point, he awoke to find himself bouncing across an empty field. He turned the Ford back onto the road and went on. It seemed like hours later when he finally stopped the Ford behind the town hall.

He stopped in at his office.

Randall Givens was not at the booking desk when he came down the stairs to the police department. He found the door to his office hanging open, and Abel Frailey inside, standing on a ladder, stringing wire along the top of the wall.

"Howdy, Buck," said the man cheerfully. "You been sleeping with the hogs?"

"Hello, Abel." Buckner ignored the remark. "What are you doing?"

"Look in that box on the floor," said Frailey, gesturing with his head.

A large box sat in the middle of the floor. It contained a telephone. Buckner lifted it out and looked at it. It was not new: the black paint was chipped and scratched, and the wire was frayed in spots. Still, it was a telephone.

"I'll have you all set up in about half an hour, Buck," Frailey was saying.

"Will I be in your way if I stay?" Buckner asked.

"Nope. I'll just work around you, shouldn't be any problem at all."

Buckner sat and put his mud-stained boots up on his desk and stared at the far wall of his office for a long time. He started in surprise when Frailey tapped him on the shoulder.

"Sorry, Buck. I just wanted to tell you you're all hooked up now."

"Thanks, Abel. Can I call Jackson?"

"Sure. Call St. Louis for all I care." The workman chuckled as he gathered up his tools and ladder and departed. The empty box remained in the middle of the floor.

Buckner called Jackson.

"Sheriff ain't here, Buck," came the voice. "He's out making the last rounds before the voting starts on Tuesday. I believe right now he's praying with the local ministers."

"What about the prisoners?" Buckner asked.

"I don't know nothing about no prisoners, Buck."

Buckner said thanks and hung up. He smiled as he looked at the new telephone, standing on the corner of the desk next to his typewriter. Welcome to the twentieth century, he thought.

Chief Bushyhead walked in, followed by Detective Harris and two of the department's largest patrolmen. Bushyhead immediately went to Buckner's guest chair and sat, his benign smile looking like it had been glued on. The two patrolmen, badges gleaming, the fabric of their uniform coats straining across their massive chests, took up positions on either side of the door. Detective Harris, with no place to sit or to stand, stood looking uncertainly around him.

"Shut that door," Bushyhead snapped. One of the patrolmen jumped to obey, but Harris stopped him with an imperious hand, and performed the task himself. Then he went to the filing cabinet, leaned against it, and smirked.

"You look like shit," he said to Buckner.

Buckner kept his eyes on the Chief.

"You have some city property," said Bushyhead. His cold little eyes glittered. "Return it at once or I will place you under arrest."

"What are you referring to?" Buckner asked.

"You know damned . . ." Harris began. He fell silent at a glance from his chief.

Buckner was too exhausted to prolong this. He pulled open his desk drawer and took out Detective Harris's badge, pistol, and blackjack. He tossed them onto the desk but left the drawer open. He leaned back and looked at Bushyhead.

"There's more," said Bushyhead.

"Is there?" Buckner asked.

"Yes. An envelope belonging to Detective Harris. It contains important official documents."

"You must mean the money he collected that night," Buckner said. He was not enjoying this and he wanted it over. "Oh yes," he continued. "And the list of people he was visiting, along with a notation next to each one recording how much he owed and how much he paid. Those official documents."

"Yes," said Bushyhead tightly.

"What if I've already sent them off to my friend in the state attorney's office?"

"Then things are going to get real unpleasant around here. But I don't think you have. You haven't called or written anybody in Jefferson City in a week. I think you've still got that envelope. And I think you should give it to me, right now."

The large officers by the door stirred in anticipation.

Slowly, covering the action with his right arm, Buckner reached into the drawer again and took out the envelope. He transferred it to his right hand and held it up like a flag for all to see.

"What took you so long in coming for this?" Buckner asked.

"Not that it's any of your business, but there was a breakdown in communications between Detective Harris and me," said Bushyhead.

"In other words, he tried to keep it a secret that he'd lost the money and the list, plus his pistol and badge," said Buckner with a grin.

Bushyhead shrugged and held out his hand. Buckner didn't move. Bushyhead snapped his fingers at Harris, who moved forward slowly.

Buckner pushed the weapons and the badge across toward him with his right hand. Otherwise, he did not move.

Harris picked up the offered items.

"You going to call off your dogs now?" Buckner asked.

"Not until you hand over that envelope." Bushyhead's face was glowing red. He turned to the officers by the door who stepped forward, then halted suddenly. Bushyhead turned back to Buckner.

Buckner had brought his left hand out of the drawer holding his .45 automatic. He pulled back the slide and let it slam home, chambering a round. The noise was abrupt and loud in the small office. Then he put the envelope on the desk and placed the pistol on top of it.

"Nice try, son," Bushyhead said, "but it won't work. It's too late to try to use that paper against us in the election. Besides, what's in there is purely local. You're just not going to be able to tie it to the election for sheriff." He chuckled and shook his head. "Nope, Stillson Foote is going to beat Elmer Aubuchon and you're going to be out of a job. Still, it was a nice try, I'll give you that."

"I don't suppose you'd understand this, Chief," Buckner said, "but I was only interested in doing my job, not saving it. It never occurred to me to use this information to try to sway the election."

Bushyhead actually laughed at that. And under the laughter, there was the sound of clicking as Harris cocked his pistol. Everybody looked at him except Buckner, who kept his eyes on Bushyhead as he reached into the drawer and brought out six bullets, which he dropped onto the blotter.

Harris broke open his pistol, then snapped it shut with a curse, but no one was paying any attention. Buckner thought one of the officers might have rolled his eyes in disgust.

"Chief," Buckner began. "I don't want trouble with you. Not about this, not about anything. You can believe what you want about my reasons, but I'm going to hang onto this envelope, maybe leave it with a friend, just to make sure you don't start anything with me."

"I don't know what you're talking about, son," replied the Chief.

"Let's just say, the word around town is that if I had a terrible accident, nobody in your office would be surprised."

Bushyhead shook his head. "I'd never try something like that on you, Buck. I know you've got too much experience in that line of work." He smiled bleakly. "Of course, you may have enemies in town that I don't know anything about. You should be careful, anyway."

Buckner nodded. "I'll do that, Chief. But if anything happens to me, including stubbing my toe on the sidewalk, then this envelope will go to the state attorney's office in Jefferson City, and your little operation here will fold up like a cheap tent show in a high wind."

Chief Bushyhead got up. Harris practically leapt to the door and threw it open with a bang. The patrolmen smiled slightly; Bushyhead ignored Harris. He looked at Buckner for a long time, a thoughtful expression on his face. "Don't get too used to that telephone, son," he finally said. "Meantime, you take care of yourself, hear?" And he left, followed by Harris and the heavy-footed patrolmen.

Buckner sighed. He glanced down at the envelope. He slid it from underneath his pistol and opened it, unfolding the piece of paper inside. It was an old letter from his sister in St. Louis. The envelope Bushyhead had wanted so badly was folded away in a book in his room. He was going to have to find a better hiding place for it.

He put on his hat and went out.

* * *

A week later, Buckner looked at Judith Lee across her kitchen table and smiled. Morning light streamed through the window by the table. Judith Lee wore a long, blue wool robe; Buckner was dressed to go out. A plate of biscuits sat between them, next to a pot of strawberry jam. Buckner spread jam on a biscuit and ate it all in three bites.

"I still don't see why Sheriff Aubuchon was out there that day." Judith said.

"He was putting up handbills," Buckner answered. In reply to her astonished look, he added, "Yes, in the wind and the rain. Anyway, he saw Albert driving by in that Dodge truck, along with his two sisters. He saw them turn off into that field and head down toward the river, and that looked funny to him."

"Funny?"

"Yes, that's what he said. Nothing he could put his finger on, just wrong, somehow. So he waited until they were out of sight, then followed along. He saw them drag a body out of the back of the truck and he suddenly had this terrible feeling it was me. But, whoever it was, they were dragging the body off into the woods and that made it county business, so he came up as quick as he could. Charlotte was supposed to be keeping an eye on things, but she never even heard him. He walked up to her and put the cuffs on her."

"She didn't cry out or try to warn them?"

"He said she seemed to have gone into some kind of trance. She was just sitting there, staring. Anyway, he took off into the woods. He didn't see exactly where they had taken the body, my body, but he figured they were going to toss it into the river. He never even saw the shovel until it looked like Albert was going to hit me over the head with it."

"So he saved your life."

"Well, yes, but not from Albert. It was Elizabeth who was going to kill me."

"Just like she killed their father."

"Not exactly," he said. "I'd say she killed the old man when he started after Charlotte. As far as she was concerned, she was acting to save her sister."

"What's going to happen to them?"

"Well, they were all involved. Charlotte was the one who worked to keep the family together all those years. She wrote to Albert, even when he didn't write back. She knew Elizabeth had gone off with Angelina to live with Blumberg. When she figured her baby sister was old enough, Charlotte began to write to her too. It's strange, really. Their father tried to destroy their family. He murdered their mother, drove Charlotte away, sent Albert away, abandoned Elizabeth."

"He truly was a horrible man, then."

"Yes. But he failed. Albert and Charlotte were close as kids, and Charlotte worked hard to maintain contact all those years they were separated. When Elizabeth was old enough, they made contact with her. She met Albert when she was going to school in Cape Girardeau, and then Albert started answering Charlotte's letters. Elizabeth became part of what held the three of them together."

"And that was?"

"Family. The one thing the three of them wanted more than anything else in the world. Their father had destroyed that for them. They believed that their mother had loved them but had abandoned them, and their father was a monster. But they would be a family in spite of that."

"The blood-tie must have been very strong."

"I think it was. Charlotte, I think, had always been suspicious about Victoria's disappearance. She must have expressed that suspicion to Serena many times. Serena was trying to help Charlotte deal with her past. At Elizabeth's suggestion, Serena hired Harris to look into Victoria's disappearance. Harris tracked it down—a good piece of detective work, actually—and told her what had happened. Serena, hoping it would help Charlotte, told them all what had happened. Then they knew that their mother had not abandoned them, had really loved them, but had been murdered by their father."

"So they wanted revenge."

"I'm not sure of that. Elizabeth says they just wanted to confront him with their knowledge. I guess they thought that would break some kind of hold he had over them all this time. Then they could start fresh. Charlotte needed to know that her family could be safe for her. Albert, despite his every effort, turned out too much like his father. His drinking drove away his own wife and children. He thought he could recapture something of what he had lost by reuniting with his sisters. Poor Elizabeth, who actually grew up among people who loved her and treated her well, had become obsessed with finding out what had happened, back then, to break up her natural family. So the confrontation with Louis was crucial for all of them. But Charlotte and Albert, when the time came, couldn't face him. Albert managed to get them all there. He drove to Jackson in that fast racer of his, got Charlotte, then came down here and got Elizabeth, who rode in the rumble seat. But when they actually got to Louis's shop, he couldn't go any farther; he couldn't look his father in the eye. He stayed in the car. Charlotte had done the work, the letter writing, keeping them all together, keeping the flame alive. But the sight of the man who had raped her so many times so long ago, a man who now really looked like what her nightmares of him had shown her, made her hysterical. Elizabeth says that he was going after Charlotte when she struck him with the pipe."

"She admits hitting him?"

"Yes. It didn't take much. I had a long conversation with her at the county jail. She didn't even want a lawyer. I told her what I knew, or had guessed, and she filled in the rest. She and Charlotte went into the shop together. Louis's teeth had all rotted away, just a few black stumps left. He was dirty and smelled bad. He made some comment about 'Angelina's brat,' but other than that, Elizabeth said, he ignored her. He concentrated on Charlotte, like a snake with a bird. He started talking about the 'good times' they'd had all those years ago, walking toward her. Charlotte froze for a minute but managed to tear herself away and run for the door. He started after her. Elizabeth picked up the first thing she saw, a piece of pipe, and hit him on the head with it. She said it knocked him to his knees, but he kept crawling toward Charlotte, who was screaming now, almost out of her mind with fear, so Elizabeth hit him again, and kept hitting him until he stopped moving. She took Charlotte out to Albert, who was sitting in his racer like a statue. She got Charlotte calmed down, Albert revived, and he drove away. In the end, it was Elizabeth who was the strong one. Probably because she had been raised by strangers who loved her, instead of by Louis."

"But why kill you? Did they all think you had to die?"

"No. Only Elizabeth and only out of necessity, as she saw it. Killing her father changed her; she realized on the drive back that she had turned some kind of corner. She had done what she had to do to put what was left of the family together. She wasn't going to let anything jeopardize it. The trouble is, I had gone up there to tell Charlotte and Albert they would be able to plead self-defense, that no jury in the county would convict them for killing Louis Boyer."

"Why didn't you?"

"Because, when I got to Charlotte's house, Elizabeth thought I had figured it all out and was there to arrest everybody. She just panicked and hit me over the head before I could explain; then, when I woke up; I had a gag in my mouth and couldn't talk at all." He shook his head and smiled weakly. "It was pretty close."

"So you were almost killed, and poor Albert was killed, because of a misunderstanding?" Judith asked incredulously.

"No," Buckner replied. "I think all that happened because twenty years ago, Louis Boyer killed his wife."

Judith didn't say anything for a long time, just looked intently at him.

"What are you going to do now?" she asked finally.

"Beats me. Aubuchon thought the headlines in the Boyer case would help him get reelected."

"Fat lot of good that did. The Republicans won in a landslide." Judith wrinkled her face in disgust. "President, vice-president, and everything else right on down to Sheriff of Highland County."

"Yes." Buckner agreed. "I tried to talk to Pinch, in the prosecutor's office, about this whole Boyer thing before the election, but everybody was too busy then. Now?" He shrugged. "There's no case to take to court. With Neb Healy's testimony, if I could get it, I could place Albert at the scene, or that fancy car of his, but nobody else; nobody saw what happened inside the shop except Elizabeth and maybe Charlotte. I have some bloodstains that I found on the coat Elizabeth was wearing. She had washed her hands, but she never even noticed the blood on her coat. Just wore it the rest of the day and hung it up that night. But all she has to do is say she cut herself and say it was her blood on her sleeve. So it's all circumstantial, nothing solid at all. The whole thing was, as far as I can tell, a spontaneous act of justifiable homicide."

"But Elizabeth confessed."

"Elizabeth confessed to trying to protect her sister from a monster; confessed to killing someone that everybody knew to be a bad man. Most of all, confessed to trying to put back together the family her father had taken away from her. Even assuming Pinch wants to spend his last days in office prosecuting a case like that, what do you think a good defense lawyer would make of it?"

"But what about the fact that you almost got killed? What about that?"

"Nobody seems to care." He shrugged. "After all, I'm alive. Albert, a lonely alcoholic who was headed down the same road as his father, is the one who is dead. Poor Charlotte seems lost, somehow; she cries all the time, can't talk to anybody, not even Serena. Nobody's going to want to take revenge on her. And after Elizabeth talked to me, to explain about her family, she got an iron-cold look on her face, folded her arms across her chest, and shut her mouth closed up tight. Angelina's been up to see her almost every day, but she won't even talk to her. Since the election, everybody in the prosecutor's office is sitting around waiting for the axe to fall. Believe me, nobody's interested in making a case against Elizabeth: not for killing Louis, and not for trying to kill me."

"What about you? As the one she tried to kill, I mean. Don't you want justice done?"

"Under the circumstances, with Aubuchon losing to Foote, I am unable to discharge the duties of my office," Buckner said. "Personally, well, if justice needs a body, it's got Albert. So it's all right with me if they go free."

"So what's going to happen to Charlotte and Elizabeth?"

Buckner shook his head.

"I guess Charlotte will go back to living with Serena; Elizabeth might go back to Angelina. What about her job?"

"I have no power over the hiring and firing of teachers. Elizabeth was a good teacher, and popular with her students, but I hardly think the board will want to keep her on after this. I'll end up having to find someone to replace her in the middle of the term." She looked over her coffee cup at him. "This whole thing has been a disaster, hasn't it?"

"Yes, it has. They got their revenge: their father killed their mother, and they killed him. But their brother is dead, too. They get to spend the rest of their lives thinking about that." Buckner paused. "I'd say justice has been done." He shuddered slightly, remembering the rain and the mud and the weight of Albert Boyer's corpse. "I know I don't envy them."

He drank coffee and went to the pot on the stove.

"You want some?"

"Not yet." Her mind seemed elsewhere.

"You're a good cook." He filled his cup, sat down, and ate another biscuit.

"My mother insisted I learn. She kept telling me it would come in handy someday. I don't think this is the sort of occasion she had in mind, but, you never know."

They were silent for a time.

"And what will you do now?" she asked finally.

"About what?"

"About the election."

"Look for work, I guess."

"When does Foote take office?"

"Oh, not till early next year, but he made it pretty clear he wants Aubuchon out right now."

"And all his deputies with him? How can he do that? The Sheriff's term doesn't end until next January."

"Oh, he's willing to wait until then to get rid of Aubuchon. And I believe he plans on keeping all the deputies, since he has no experience in law enforcement. All of them except one, that is."

Judith stared at him, her face flushed. "You're the only one he's not keeping?" Her voice rose in anger.

"Looks like it." He laughed. "It was the price of Bushyhead's support in the election. The Chief helps deliver the vote in Corinth and in return, he gets rid of a burr under his saddle. I should have known when I saw that new telephone that I wasn't going to be around much longer."

"Does Chief Bushyhead hate you enough to do all that?"

"I believe he does."

"But what will you do?"

"I'll just be another crippled veteran looking for a job." Buckner tried to smile, but the result was an unconvincing twist of his lips that was no smile.

"I can't believe you won't find something; or something will find you," she said softly, trying to reassure him. She laughed lightly. "You could become a kept man; I make good money."

"I don't think that would work out."

"Well, at least I can help you keep your mind off your troubles."

"Yeah, I expect you could. Still, I hate to get fired just about the time I was learning the job."

He spread jam on another biscuit and ate it.

Made in the USA
Middletown, DE
13 October 2015